THE VEIL

TIFFANY AARON

The Veil
ISBN # 978-1-78430-173-6
©Copyright Tiffany Aaron 2014
Cover Art by Posh Gosh ©Copyright July 2014
Interior text design by Claire Siemaszkiewicz
Totally Bound Publishing

THE VEIL

Dedication

Thanks to all my readers who have supported me through my career. You mean the world to me. Also, to Rebecca, my amazing editor. Thank you for cleaning up my mistakes.

Prologue

He stood in the shadows, the picture of refined detachment, but a glimpse into his face would destroy that illusion. His coal-black eyes burned with rage and insanity. The service was almost over — he would be alone in a few minutes. He fidgeted as his excitement grew. He would be taking the first steps to getting his revenge tonight. The man whirled then ducked behind one of the pillars in the ancient church, as the head priest made his way down the aisle. He couldn't risk being seen. No one could know what he had done until it was too late for anyone to stop him.

Soon the sanctuary was empty, with only the candle flames to see by. He went to kneel before the altar. Staring up at the crucifix, he wondered why the Son had killed himself. The rage flared inside until he couldn't contain his snarl of hatred. His eyes met the gaze of the man on the cross, and a shock of cold raced through him.

Wait a minute, a calm voice of reason shot into his mind. *He was murdered. It was your son who committed suicide.* Anguish ripped his heart apart, and he bent his head to the floor.

The coolness of the marble brought him back to his senses. His son was dead by suicide, but the man knew his son wasn't to blame. The Devil had made him do it, and the Devil was going to pay. It would only be a little longer before he could make his move.

Standing, he didn't look at the cross again. He moved down a side aisle to where a small, dark door was located in the wall. After checking to make sure no one had followed, he unlocked the door then went down into the basement of the church. Shivering in the dank cold of the cellar, he searched for the symbol on the gray bricks. Finally, in the flickering light, he found the small inverted cross and pushed it. A grating sound ricocheted through the dark as a panel moved to reveal a tunnel leading down.

He stalked along the narrow walkway. The panel closed behind him, shutting out the lantern light. Confidence filled him as he made his way far below the church and into the catacombs. Some of the most powerful and most religious of the church leaders had been buried in the underground tombs. Their latent power hung in the blackness. He didn't fear the dark any more than he feared the light. Weak mortals believed the light would help them, when they should be reaching out for the darkness. Evil lurked in both, but it was only in the dark that he would find vengeance.

The tunnel led to a small, circular room decorated with ancient carvings and an elaborate altar. It had been built with the same gray stone the catacombs had been carved from. Two thick pillars served as supports for the large, flat top of the altar. Intricate carvings of winged creatures writhed in the midst of flames. Two iron basins seemed to originate from the center of the table. Dark spots stained the stone. He wondered if other sacrifices had been committed in this chamber. He knew it had been the meeting place for the same men whose bodies lay entombed in the catacombs.

As he entered the main crypt, a gasp came from the center of the room. He allowed his gaze to settle on the girl kneeling on the dirt floor, her hands and ankles bounds, and an icy smile crossed his face. His servants had managed to come through this time. Circling around the girl, he studied her from every angle.

Once she might have been pretty, but her time on the streets had erased any resemblance of the girl she used to be. Her dark hair hung in limp strands over her filthy face. Her bruises told him that his servants hadn't been very gentle in bringing her down to the chambers. Her clothing revealed more of her anorexic body than it covered and told him how she had made her living on the streets of Ericksberg. He shook off her clutching hands as she grabbed on to his pant leg. Disgust filled him when he saw the needle tracks marring her skin. Shivers racked her body, and he backed away from her. He went to one of the crypts set into the walls of the catacombs. Pulling the cover off, he reached in to retrieve his robe.

"Please, sir. Let me go."

"Sorry. You're needed for something far more important than walking the streets." He ignored her beseeching eyes.

Her terror shined in her expression, but she seemed willing to do anything to gain her freedom. Brushing her hair back, she cupped her breasts and lifted them up to him. "I'll pleasure you. Just let me go when you're finished."

He gagged. No way would he soil his body by touching her.

He undressed and slipped the red silk robe over his head. He loved the way the cool fabric warmed as it soaked up his heat. Reaching into the coffin again, he pulled out a length of rope. The girl squealed as he grabbed her wrists and tied them together. As she struggled to get free, he grinned at her. When she discovered she couldn't break the rope, she started to swear at him.

Another sign that her soul wasn't pure, but he wasn't looking for a pure sacrifice that night. He wanted to see how strong his power was, and he needed blood for the next step. Taking her bound hands, he hung her from a hook in the middle of the low ceiling, over the altar, and began to chant.

The earth shivered and power coalesced around him. A small jolt of surprise ripped through him. So the words in the small book were true—there were spells even the Devil feared. The girl's screams reverberated off the stone and dirt of the burial chambers. Pulling the gleaming blade from his belt, he raised his voice to mix with her shrill cries. In the sounds echoing back at him, he swore he heard hundreds of others joining in. Were the monks and priests whose spirits inhabited the crypts in agreement with him?

Before his eyes, a luminescence shimmered into view. He couldn't see anything on the other side of it, but he sensed the presence of beings best unseen. There was an urgency building, telling him something wanted to come through the curtain. The legends were true. There was a Veil hiding Hell and its occupants from the mortals on Earth. For him to get into the Devil's realm, he had to sunder the barrier. The first rip was going to be a small one, to make sure he could achieve the power he needed to create a bigger tear.

His chanting and her screams reached a crescendo until her pleas disappeared abruptly. Small holes appeared in the Veil where her blood hit it. Dropping to his knees, he cried out as triumph rushed into his heart and mind, sending him to a welcomed darkness. His last thought before he lost consciousness was that it had worked, and soon the Devil would pay for what he had done to his son.

* * * *

A small, dark demon forced its way through the barrier to stand over the man. Touching his forehead with one long talon, it hissed at the madness roiling in the mortal's brain. The man's determination to tear the Veil in two would mean the end of demons everywhere, but the creature didn't have the power to stop him. It snuck out of the catacombs to search for mortal help.

Dealing with humans could be a tricky matter for a demon. The mortals' intolerance of creatures different from them made it dangerous to ask for help, but it didn't want to die, and there was only one mortal able to stop the Veil from ripping. It hoped she would be willing to stop the destruction, because her life was in danger as well.

Shock waves had raced through Heaven and Hell when the barrier had been breached. When he'd left, the horde of Hell had begun to ready themselves, as had—he was sure—the host of Heaven. A battle was looming in the distance if the balance wasn't restored.

He knew angels were racing to Earth while demons were raging to the Veil.

Chapter One

"Oh, yeah, babe. This feels great. Keep it up. I'm gonna come. I'm gonna come."

Beltaine really wished the man would shut up. Obviously going to the bar in the middle of the afternoon to find a man wasn't a good idea. It would seem only the useless ones sat around drinking at four in the afternoon. She'd have to choose better next time, since she didn't like to talk while she was screwing. Closing her eyes, she hoped she could block out his voice. She didn't know his name and didn't want to learn it, either.

"Wow, I could do this all night."

Her eyes popped open, and she found herself hoping he would be a one-minute man. Night hadn't even fallen, and there was no way she was going to let him stay any longer than it took for him to come once. She stared into the shadows over his shoulder, hoping he would finish. Maybe then he'd shut the hell up. She stiffened when her gaze met the glowing red eyes of a small demon in the corner of the room.

"Shit," she swore softly. It was a sign of terrible things to come when she saw demons in her bedroom. "Just once I'd like to see an angel and know something good was going to happen," she mumbled to herself as she pushed the guy off her. "Get dressed and get out."

"What the hell? I wasn't done," he whined.

Her cold amber gaze impaled him. "I was. I don't have time for this." After tossing his clothes at him, she gestured to the front door. "Don't let the door hit you on the way out."

"Bitch," he snarled, as he stalked toward her.

There was no fear in her eyes, even though he stood a foot taller and outweighed her by a hundred pounds. When he got close enough to touch her, she growled, revealing her fangs. "I've been called worse by scarier men than you."

"Fuck!" He scrambled out of the apartment.

She turned back to look at the demon before the man had left. She listened to the door shutting, but she kept her eyes on the demon. "What the hell are you doing here?"

It blinked in surprise, obviously shocked that she chose to talk to it. Moving toward her, it seemed intent on touching her. She traced a cross in the air and spoke a single word. The demon hissed at her, but it was bound in the corner until she could perform the ritual to get rid of it. She wrinkled her nose to show her displeasure at the sulfuric smell.

Heading into the bathroom, she turned the shower on and ignored the mirrors over the sink. The hot water steamed the glass, easing her tension. Beltaine knew seeing her reflection shouldn't bother her. When others looked at her, they saw a petite woman with curves and a chest that could bring grown men to tears. They saw long blonde curls and a slender face with high cheekbones. They would pause for a moment at the sight of her amber eyes with the slitted irises, but most managed to convince themselves she wore contacts. She never took the time to destroy their complacent beliefs.

When she looked in the mirror, she saw a child with fear and pain in her eyes. She saw the scars marring skin but in truth, there were no marks because her skin healed as quickly as it was sliced. She could still hear the singing of the belt and the anger of the voice. The stinging feel of the leather and cut of the metal had caused tears to well up in her eyes. Beltaine never forgot, so she avoided mirrors altogether.

Scrubbing the stench of sex and sweat off, she thought about the demon in her room. Where had the balance gone wrong so that such a creature could cross over? She'd have to find the weakness and fix it. She shut off the shower, then started toweling dry.

Her apartment door burst open, and she heard Roger calling her.

"Beltaine, are you here?"

She came out of the bathroom, wrapped in a towel, as he reached her room.

"What the heck?" Roger blurted as he stood in the doorway.

She didn't know if he was remarking on the demon or on the fact that she had dropped the towel and stood naked in front of her closet. Grabbing a pair of black leather pants and a bright red top, she turned to catch him staring at her.

"Roger," she warned.

"I'm a priest, Beltaine, not a saint. If you insist on parading around in front of me, I'm going to look." He didn't avert his eyes as she pulled on the pants.

Dragging her top over her shoulders, she shook her head at him. "I think we have more important things to do than you ogling me." She nodded at the creature cringing in the corner.

"It doesn't look dangerous." He moved closer to it.

Before she could warn him, the demon leaped from the corner and slashed out at him. She pulled Roger away before the creature's claws could score his flesh. She spoke a word of power, and the creature howled.

"Damn, do you have a death wish? It isn't afraid of you."

He fingered the white collar he wore. "Why not? I'm a priest—shouldn't demons be afraid of me?"

"Like you said yourself, you're not a saint. You haven't fought demons long enough to realize that, in truth, they fear no man of God because you're all sinners in your souls."

"Yet it fears you. Why is that?"

She pulled him out of the room. Snatching her keys off the table next to the door, she led him out. "It fears me because I don't pretend to be anything other than what I am—a half-breed abomination of man and demon. I treat both creatures with equal disdain. It's only when one of the demons crosses over that I deal with them."

"Are you *really* an abomination? I didn't think God would allow such a creature to live."

"I've no idea why He chose to keep me alive. It might have been better if He hadn't. Of course, He lets you live," she pointed out as they made their way downstairs and exited the building.

"Ouch! Why are you in such a bad mood?" He followed her closely as she shoved her way down the sidewalk.

"It might have to do with the fact that my afternoon sex session got interrupted by that little demon. Don't take it personally, Roger. I don't like most men, and if any of them happen to be priests, I tend to like them even less."

"Tell me again what you have against priests?" He struggled to keep up with her.

Beltaine had never mentioned to Roger that her father had been a priest before he'd got her mother pregnant. She didn't plan on sharing that particular secret with anyone. She managed to spare him a humorous glance. "Besides the fact you tend to be self-righteous pricks who condemn those things that differ from your preconceived notions of right and wrong?"

He grimaced at her. "Yes, besides that."

She shrugged. "I don't know. I find most men are arrogant and sanctimonious jerks who think with their dicks instead of their brains. I have yet to meet one who sees me and doesn't think of sex first."

"We're only human, love." Roger laughed. "It's the way God made us."

"I don't think that part has anything to do with God." She gestured for the priest to follow her.

"Wait, Beltaine." He reached out to stop her from continuing. "The bishop sent me to get you."

"I know. That's why we're heading to see him."

"This isn't the right direction."

"Yes, it is. The bishop knows I won't meet him in a church. We'll meet at the potter's field just outside of town."

"You won't go to a church, but you'll meet him in a cemetery. What's wrong with that?"

"A cemetery is full of dead people. I don't fear the dead. A church might only be a building, but it's a place where the living worship, and it's the living I don't trust. Everyone has their little quirks." Continuing to make her way toward the cemetery, she made sure Roger kept up with her.

"Why was there a demon in your apartment?"

"I always keep one chained up like a pet. Don't you think it makes a great guard dog?"

"Are you ever serious? A demon manifesting on this plane isn't good."

"Boy, Roger, you're a master of understatement. I've learned it doesn't pay to take yourself too seriously. Pride goeth before the fall and all that rot." Skidding to a stop, she stood outside the gate to the potter's field where the city buried the homeless and unknown people who had the audacity to die on the city streets. She sent a surge of power through the graves and tombstones. No one seemed to be waiting except the bishop. "Let's get in there and talk to him, Roger. I have things to do before I can find the weak spot where the creature passed through to Earth."

They crept into the graveyard. She kept her senses open because she didn't trust the bishop any further than she could throw him. The highest-ranking priest in the diocese stood next to the plain wooden cross of a freshly turned grave. She shuddered as she saw the black dirt. The musty smell of it took her back to the day she'd buried her father, and that wasn't a day she ever wanted to remember.

"I'm here, so talk. You know I don't have time to waste."

"I know, Demon, but there are things you need to know." The bishop's voice was deep and commanding.

"What could I possibly need to know? I've dealt with this type of crossover before, and I'll fix the problem."

"The Board has made other plans for you. Kalan," the bishop greeted, as his eyes skipped over her shoulder, and she knew he and his fellow members had betrayed her.

The Board was made up of the most powerful and wealthiest members of the city. They controlled all the commerce. It was the Board who had made an agreement with the lesser demons who'd managed to cross over without interference. As long as the demons didn't cause problems and paid the high fees the members imposed, they could stay on Earth. The moment their dues lapsed or they drew attention to themselves, the Board gave Beltaine the green light to send the demons back to Hell. She worked for them, but she didn't trust any of them. It was only her power that kept them from getting rid of her. She would deal with this power play they were throwing at her. Snarling, she crouched, then whirled to face the enemy.

Chapter Two

Behind Beltaine was a large man, about six-five. His blue eyes were light and shined with a pure glimmer. His irises were slits like hers, but his face was so beautiful, she felt a sob well in her throat. Strapped across his back was a scabbard holding a large silver claymore. She hissed as she recognized the bloodred diamond on the hilt of the sword. Only the best warriors in the Heavenly Host were given a sword of power.

"Christ," she swore as she tensed, ready for his attack.

His blue eyes turned to ice. "It seems a foolish risk for a being such as you to take the Lord's name in vain."

"If a being such as I am thought to be is already condemned by Him, why should I worry about respecting His name?" She glared at the angel.

"God's waiting to offer you forgiveness, demon spawn, if you ask for it," the bishop said as he reached out to her. "Kalan is here to deal with another problem, but he'll take care of you if you push too hard."

Moving away from them, she put her back against the lone oak tree standing among the graves. There was no way she was exposing her back to any of the trio. Not even Roger—whom she'd considered her friend. "Forgiveness for what?"

The angel commanded everyone's attention with his presence. "For the evil you've committed." The matter-of-fact tone of his voice grated on her nerves.

"The evil wasn't done by me, but by a man who should have protected me." She spat the words at him.

"You are your mother's offspring. We know evil begets evil."

"I'm only evil to people who annoy me. I don't go out hunting people to destroy." Beltaine threw a glare at the bishop and Roger, standing a few feet away.

"You must have done something. By your very nature, you're incapable of not sinning."

"You hypocritical bastard. How dare you stand there in judgment of me when you don't know a thing about me?" She wanted to wipe the self-righteous smirk off his face.

He shrugged. "I don't need to know you. A half-breed demon spawn has nothing good going for it. If I had my choice, I'd kill you where you stood."

"But your Commander stays your sword. I have a use here on Earth."

"Unfortunately, yes, and I've been ordered to assist you." He didn't look thrilled with his mission.

"Why the hell would I need the help of one of the Host to deal with a demon crossover?"

He cringed at her crude language. "We fear it's more than just one demon. There was a disturbance along the Veil between the planes of Earth and Hell. If our intelligence is correct, someone is trying to breach the barrier. They have already succeeded in creating a small rip, allowing a few demons at a time to cross over. We fear what will happen if a doorway is created. Imagine if the Horde is allowed to enter Earth."

"Not only creatures from Hell, but also of the Host would be unleashed from Heaven, and Earth would no longer belong to humans." Her voice cracked as she shuddered. If the Host was released from its constraints, her life wouldn't be worth shit. The Heavenly Host was as bad as the Horde. If there was something they needed or wanted, the Host took it without remorse. They destroyed lives as easily as any demon did.

She couldn't allow that. Her strength had always resided in the fact that she didn't fear death. As the offspring of a man and a demon, she was damned. She didn't have a soul to worry about. When she died, she would simply cease to exist—a violent life erased from the very fabric of time. Yet there was a very human part of her that railed against death. It made her cling tooth-and-nail to her life on Earth.

"You're telling me I have no choice but to work with you."

"The good people of this city won't talk to you for fear of contaminating their souls. I'll deal with them while you're dealing with the evil side. Together we'll find the culprit, who'll be punished."

"Fine." She pushed away from the tree and headed toward the entrance of the cemetery. The bishop and Roger moved ahead of her. They were eager to get out of the cemetery. Kalan reached out and grabbed her arm.

They froze as a shock of electricity raced between them. Her nipples hardened as desire swamped her. Staring up at him, she saw that he felt it, too. His toned chest rippled as his breathing sped up. His face was flushed, and lust burned in his eyes. Taking a peek down at his groin, she bit back a groan as the impressive bulge told her this angel was amazingly well-hung.

Never one to deny herself, she gave into temptation. Pressing her body tightly to his, she reached up to frame his face with her hands. There was no resistance as she pulled his lips to hers. A shock of recognition raced through them when they kissed. She savored the taste of his mouth while she ran her tongue along the crease of his lips. Nibbling at his bottom lip, she enticed him to open to her.

When his deep groan tore from his throat, she took advantage. With the first thrust of her tongue, she found herself crushed so tight in his embrace, she could hardly breathe. Squirming a little, she rubbed her breasts against him. His cock throbbed where it was plastered close to her stomach.

Burying her trembling fingers deep in his hair, she tilted his head for a better angle. They hummed a mutual sound of pleasure as their tongues came together in a complicated mating dance.

He bent and cupped her ass with his hands. Lifting her up, he sealed her mound to his erection and started grinding. She threw back her head and arched her back. All she could think of was getting closer. Her clothes were too confining and her skin was itching. That was a sure sign she was about to come.

Wrapping her hands around his shoulders, she felt a shock of pain when her hand touched the silver hilt of his sword. Suddenly her desire faded and left only anger. *What the hell had happened to them?* How could something feel so good when she knew it was wrong? There was no way she could get involved with a guy who thought she shouldn't even be breathing. She flung herself from him so fast, she stumbled as her feet hit the ground. He reached out to stabilize her, but she shook her head.

"Don't touch me," she warned.

He looked as confused as she was. Beltaine knew angels didn't have sex, or at least she had never heard about any of them breaking that particular rule. Angels considered their status in the world just below God, so they tended not to deal with mortals much. If the fact that he didn't even like her didn't stop this lust, then she just had to think of her father and remember she wasn't worth anyone caring about. Yet she couldn't forget about the recognition she'd felt when their lips touched. His gaze seemed to burn into her as she headed toward the gate. This time he didn't touch her but still moved to block the way.

"Get out of the way." Then she hissed at him.

"Where are you going?" He crossed his arms and a determined expression settled on his face.

"To do my job."

"I'm supposed to go with you," he politely pointed out.

She looked him over while she tried to put every ounce of scorn she could muster into the glance. "Where I'm going, they would eat you for lunch if you showed up dressed like that."

"What's wrong with how I'm dressed?" He glanced down and blushed.

She could see his hard-on hadn't subsided. "Nothing's wrong with it if you stick to the innocent side of town—go visit the church groups and the ladies' knitting club. Where I'm going, you won't be able to tell the difference between Earth and Hell, human or demon."

"I can't let you go by yourself."

"I was chosen because I fit right in with the rest of the murderers and thieves. You'll have to trust me to be able to get the information we need my own way."

He shook his head. "I can't trust you."

His statement hurt for reasons she didn't want to look at too closely. Before she could reply, a stench filled the air. She hissed, revealing her lengthening fangs. The bishop and Roger were huddled next to another newly dug grave, where they had stopped when Beltaine and the angel hadn't joined them at the gate. Kalan drew his sword, even as she dashed to where they stood and pushed them toward him.

"Get them back to the church. I'd advise all of you to stay there. It's better protection from the creatures of the Horde."

She saw in the angel's eyes that he didn't want to leave her. "There's nothing for you to gain by staying here. I can deal with this. They might be priests, but they are still part of His family, and that falls under your protection."

She didn't gag as the smell got worse. Roger's horrified gaze went to her feet.

"Go."

Not waiting to see them move away, she glanced down. The ground around her feet teemed with maggots. With a surge of power and a whispered "Fire," she cleansed the dirt. Then she waited.

The slight shifting of the earth told her something was moving in the grave. A hand broke free and clasped her ankle. As disgusted as she was at the feel of the clammy, rubbery flesh, she knew there was worse to come. Stepping back, she kept her eyes on the body emerging from the ground. This was the part she hated the most.

Even though it was only a reanimated corpse, she couldn't overcome the feeling that she was killing the person again. Her mind understood the soul had departed the body long ago, but her heart filled with guilt every time she dealt with a zombie.

She waited until it had clawed its way free. Reaching out, she clasped its hand in hers. For a moment, she was pulled into a maelstrom of chaos. There didn't seem to be a coherent thought in the crazed mind of the zombie. It was trying to satisfy a driving urge to seek flesh. She could feel a scream building inside as she fought free of the creature's brain.

"Burn." She spoke the word while she poured a burst of her power into the decomposing body.

Shrieking, it struggled to get away.

I guess even brain-dead zombies fight to stay alive, she thought as she kept her hands clamped on its wrist. The flames burnt the remaining flesh from the creature then the fire started to work on its bones. She wanted to close her eyes, but couldn't take her gaze away. She had to remain focused for her power to work best and quickest.

At last, ashes piled at her feet. Weaving with weariness, she drew a little more power to create a breeze to disperse the dust. She stumbled out of the gate. Wind caressed her ear, and she swore she heard "Thank you" on the current.

If zombies were appearing, it meant things were worse than just a few simple demons crossing over. She'd need to replenish all the power she could before she went into Dark Town. She made her way toward another cemetery on the other side of town.

* * * *

He crept down into the catacombs. An urgent need drove him to check the holes in the Veil. Since his spell had made the barrier visible, he was glad no one went down into the old burial crypts.

Stepping into the room, he held back a shout of joy. The Veil was still there, and the holes seemed larger. As he moved closer, he shivered. Evil washed over him. He had the uneasy thought that demons were escaping into the mortal world, and he knew he should be worried about that. He shook his head sharply. He didn't care what happened to the other mortals. None of them had tried to help his son when he'd needed them. So he wouldn't help them, even if the minions of Hell destroyed the whole world.

The time was coming when he would tear the Veil in two and lead his army into Hell. The Devil would pay for what he had done. No other father would ever have to worry about losing his son to the darkness.

Chapter Three

Kalan couldn't believe he had left the half-breed to deal with the danger. He was one of the Host, an angelic army capable of great destruction. Of course, this was his first solo mission. He wasn't sure if he was being shown respect or if his Commander had decided he was the most dispensable of the Host. He had never known what fear felt like, but he'd had a twinge of it when the maggots had boiled out of the ground.

Beltaine had been so calm as she'd ordered him to escort the priests back to the church. He tried to remember that his Commander had told him she was capable enough to handle almost any kind of evil. When he'd looked back before they'd left the cemetery, she'd been staring down at the gravesite full of roiling white insects. He knew from his training that maggots were the first indication a zombie was close by.

They returned to the church, and he ordered the two men to stay within its walls. A sense of awe filled his heart when his gaze rested on the large crucifix behind the altar. Kalan dropped to his knees and prayed for forgiveness. The explosive lust he had for Beltaine had shaken him. An angel should be pure of thought and deed. He should never lose himself in a pair of secretive amber eyes and lust-inducing lips. He shouldn't imagine what her skin would feel like against his. His shaft hardened again and shame rushed through him. There was no way he could work with such a creature. She was already filling him with sinful thoughts.

"Kalan."

He bowed his head at his Commander's voice. *"Yes, sir?"*

"You must keep the Veil from being destroyed."

"I'm sure I could do it on my own." He tried, but failed, to hide the doubt in his voice.

"You couldn't. Beltaine is our only hope for success, so you'll work with her."

"Yes, sir." Kalan knew better than to argue with the Commander of the Host. He climbed to his feet and squared his shoulders. He wouldn't allow his lust to overwhelm his common sense. There wasn't anything good about her, and he needed to remember that. He turned to face the bishop and the priest.

"I'm very sorry you have to work with a creature like her," the bishop apologized.

He shrugged. "We work with what we must to maintain the balance. I'll do as my Lord orders me, even if it means I have to smell the stench of brimstone."

Roger protested, "Beltaine isn't that bad. She's had a hard start to life."

The bishop rounded on the young priest. "The demon offspring has bewitched you."

"She respects me too much to bewitch me. Or my opinion could mean so little to her that she wouldn't waste the power to enslave me."

"She's already damned, Priest. With no soul, she'll cease to exist when she dies. Evil breeds evil, and her mother was the purest kind." Kalan stalked toward the door.

"I understand why she turns her back on religion and the church." Roger's voice rang out. "We judge her guilty by virtue of her birth. Where is our willingness to accept her simply because she is one of God's creatures?"

Kalan swung around to pin Roger with his gaze. "That thing isn't one of God's creatures. She should've never been born."

"God could've stopped her birth, but chose not to. That simple fact makes her His, no matter who her mother and father were. I saw how you looked at her in the cemetery, so don't tell me you're not thinking sinful thoughts. You are no better than her." Roger's conviction was clear in his words. "Don't presume to know the mind of God, either of you. For His ways pass all understanding."

Kalan spun and stormed from the church. He felt a touch of anger at the doubt the young priest had placed in his heart. Walking out, he lifted his face to the weak sunlight and felt the warm caress of the breeze. He remembered his Commander's words when he'd been sent to work with Beltaine.

"This is a test for you, Kalan. If you pass, you will have the chance for promotion."

Kalan imagined he had to find a way to work with the creature to fix the Veil and save the humans. His body reminded him how much he liked having her pressed close to his. He tried to control the lust racing through him. Having never felt such emotions before, he wasn't sure how to erase the memory of her lips on his from his mind. Embarrassment and confusion swamped him. There was no one he could talk to about it. His Commander would expect him to handle all problems by himself. He had never heard of an angel dealing with lust, and it shamed him to be tempted by a creature like her. So he would keep his own counsel and hope he didn't need help after all.

Shaking his head, he cleared his mind. He had to find the woman and see if they could start looking for the person who had torn the Veil. Focusing his thoughts, he found the essence of Beltaine and zeroed in on her. Marking the spot in his mind, he used his power to dissolve then appear inside a different cemetery from where they'd met. He shuddered at the sight of the elaborate tombstones marking the graves of the dead. Wandering down the trails, he finally found her.

Beltaine was pacing in front of a large crypt. Lounging against the tomb was a tall blonde woman with dark wings and claws. He moved closer to eavesdrop on their conversation.

"What the hell are you doing here?" Beltaine threw her hands up in the air.

"Aren't you happy to see me?"

"Oh, yeah, I'm thrilled to see you." The sneer on Beltaine's face belied the happy note in her voice.

"Now, daughter dear, I hadn't seen you in a long time, and as your mother, it's my duty to take care of you." The demon looked down at her claws and smirked.

Beltaine snarled and her fangs gleamed in the fading sunlight. "You've never taken your duty seriously before. If you had, you wouldn't have given me to Father and turned your back on me."

"Yes, well, that was a slight mistake on my part. How was I supposed to know he'd be a total psycho? I live in Hell, for the Devil's sake—I couldn't let you grow up there. It was your father's fault I got pregnant anyway. He had to deal with the mess."

"A baby isn't a mess."

Kalan could tell it was an old argument between them. He edged closer to hear better.

"I'm done discussing this with you. What bullshit excuse do you have for showing up at this moment? Your timing is awful, as usual."

"Ah, it seems there's been a slight breach in the Veil between our worlds." Beltaine's mother became agitated, and her black wings twitched.

"Tell me something I don't know. If I don't find the person who did it, the Host is going to cleanse the world of everyone who doesn't belong, and I'm one of those."

"Worse than that, if he isn't stopped, he could take over Hell." Her mother shuddered.

"And why is that a bad thing?" Beltaine asked.

"In all of life, a balance must be maintained. For every demon, there must be an angel. If the Devil is defeated, the balance will be disrupted, and life as you know it will be changed."

"Quit the dramatics, Mother. What else do you want?"

"It seems the person who did this terrible thing has something that never should have fallen into mortal hands. I need to get it back."

"What did you do?"

"Nothing."

The protest didn't seem strong enough to convince Beltaine. Kalan knew he didn't believe the demon. A skeptical quirk of her daughter's eyebrow, and she sighed.

"I trusted the wrong man again. He seemed like a perfectly marvelous man. How was I to know he was a thief and a liar?"

"Lust tends to blind you to all faults. Why don't you go and get it back?" Beltaine glared at her parent.

"He's been terminated. Unfortunately, he sold the book to someone before he died, and we have no idea who the buyer was."

Beltaine shrugged. "Why don't you just raise him from the grave and ask?"

"Oh, no, dear, when the Devil kills someone, he stays dead."

A shiver ran down Kalan's back. He saw the look of fear cross Beltaine's face. What kind of book would bring the Devil out of Hell to retrieve it? He moved away from the tree he'd been hiding behind and stalked up to the two women.

Beltaine's mother hissed at him. Her wings unfurled and she crouched, her body ready for an attack.

"You must be a joy on blind dates if you affect all the women you meet this way." Beltaine smirked at him.

"Shut up," he ordered, without looking away from her mother. "Tell me about the book. Why is the Devil leaving Hell to find the thief? And why hasn't he killed you yet?"

"You may be one of the Host, but I won't tell you anything about the book. Get it back for me, Beltaine. Your very existence depends on it." The demon turned to snarl at him once before she disappeared.

Kalan turned to find Beltaine staring at him with narrowed eyes.

"Did you really just tell me to shut up?" Her voice was deceptively quiet.

He could tell she wasn't happy to see him. Gesturing to the spot where her mother had stood, he chose to ignore her question. "Why hasn't he killed her for losing this book in the first place?"

"The Devil seems to have a special place for my mother. It's usually in his bed, so he tends to be lenient with her."

He grimaced at the thought of the Devil having sex.

"He's gorgeous, so it's no hardship for her to do it."

"He lets her have sex with mortals?"

"Mortals are lower than animals in his twisted world. They're like slaves, so he can't be bothered to worry about them." She headed out of the cemetery.

"Your mother seems to have a bit of a problem controlling herself around mortal men."

"What can I say? She's an airhead, and a demon like her can cause all sorts of problems without even trying."

"Do you know what book your mother was talking about?" he asked, as he followed her.

"No." She stopped outside the entrance.

Her arm brushed against his chest when she looked at him, and sparks shot through his body. They both took a deep breath, but before they could step away from each other, he reached out for her. The entire time he'd been away from her, he'd remembered how soft her lips had been. He was afraid he was addicted to her cinnamon taste after one kiss.

Grasping her upper arms, he pulled her to him and lowered his head to press a gentle whisper of a kiss across her mouth. As much as his body was urging him to devour her, he didn't want to rush the experience. He eased his arms around her waist and encouraged her to rest against his chest. With the tip of his tongue he begged entrance. Unwilling to take from her, he would only receive what she was offering. A soft moan left her throat, and she opened to the heat of his kiss.

He wanted to shout his triumph. He had the feeling Beltaine didn't allow men to control any aspect of her life, even something as simple as a kiss. He nibbled on her full bottom lip with tiny bites as she wound her arms around his neck. Her breasts rubbed over his chest, and he moaned as her hard nipples poked through her shirt to torture him. Sliding his tongue inside her mouth, he stroked the tip over her teeth and tested her fangs. He couldn't help but wonder what it would feel like to have her bite his skin. A shiver raced down his spine. Maybe he would be able to find out soon.

A slight tilt of her head, and their tongues were dueling. When she sucked on him, he groaned and felt a smug laugh shake her body. He moved his hands down her back to cup her butt. Lifting her a little, he fit his erection into the juncture of her thighs and they both cried out. Her hands fisted in his hair, and she leaned her head back to give him access to her throat. Rubbing himself against her, he could smell her desire rising from her heated body. He could make her come right there if he moved harder and faster.

Lowering her gently to the ground, he eased away from her. This wasn't the place or time to indulge his fantasies. He brushed her hair off her face and whispered another kiss over her swollen lips. The stunned look in her eyes made him smile.

Shit, she was in some serious trouble here. She could feel the protest building in her body as he stepped back. Growling with frustration, she reached for him. He wasn't going to leave her without giving her an orgasm. There was no way she was wandering around town this aroused.

"This isn't the right place, love."

She looked around at the tombstones and graves. As far as she was concerned, this was as good a place as any, but if he didn't want her, she wasn't going to beg. Without saying anything, she turned to head out.

"Where are you going?" he asked.

"I have to go back to my apartment."

"I'll go with you."

Beltaine knew there was no way in Hell or Heaven she was going to let Kalan come with her. She needed time away from him. "Maybe you should go and talk to the bishop. See what he has to say about the book." She sounded breathless. Damn, she didn't want him to know how he'd made her thighs clench and her pussy wet. It would give him an unfair advantage over her, and she wasn't about to give any man that kind of control again.

She wondered if he felt the same, since he didn't argue, just nodded and disappeared.

Breathing a sigh of relief, she headed back to her apartment. She needed to grab a few things before she went into Dark Town.

* * * *

The whore stared down at her customer. The greasy man was passed out on the hotel bed. His skeletal frame was covered with scars and tattoos. Tucking the money into her bra, she snuck out of the room. She shivered in the dark as she made her way out into the street.

The meth was wearing off, and she found herself thinking back on some of the things the man had said to her. She was used to her johns wanting to brag to her about the grand things they were doing. Why they thought a whore would care how important they were was beyond her. As long as they paid her, she would believe they were king of the world. Yet this customer's ramblings had drawn a cold line down her spine.

He had talked about an army and Hell, midnight mumblings of ripping a Veil and defeating the Devil. A long-buried hint of self-preservation told her that she needed to get out of the city. Bad things were going to happen, and she didn't want to be involved with them.

Shadows seemed to chase her down the alley. She would go to Dark Town. Business was good there, and she could disappear into the cesspool of wretched lives that called that place home.

Chapter Four

Beltaine unlocked her door and pushed it open.

"Shit," she muttered as the smell of sulfur hit her. She had forgotten all about the demon in the bedroom.

Standing in the doorway of her room, she stared at it. Its red eyes looked back at her, and she saw the flicker of flames in the irises. She wondered if there was hellfire burning in her gaze.

It slowly blinked, and the trance was broken. She was getting soft if she was worrying about what she looked like. She traced the scar on her neck and growled. She thought she had come to terms with her past, but obviously not.

"I'm not scared of you," she told the demon.

It made a gesture almost like a shrug. Of course, it didn't care. It was a small, minor demon. Only the medium-level and higher demons fed off fear and panic.

Making her way to the closet, Beltaine reached in to grab a black bag. She pulled it out, threw it on the bed, and dumped the contents. An assortment of knives and one gun fell out with a clank. Picking up a large, serrated blade with a plain grip, she relished its perfect balance before she slid it back into the sheath after she strapped it to her thigh.

Her hand shook as she reached out to the Glock nine millimeter handgun lying on the comforter. The deadly weapon gleamed dully in the light. She had owned the gun for years. It had saved her life, and she couldn't bring herself to get rid of it, but the memories tied up in it could give her nightmares if she let them.

She left the gun where it lay and strapped another blade between her shoulders. Dark Town was a dangerous place, and she didn't plan on going into that part of the city without weapons.

Exhaustion rode her hard. Burning the zombie had been bad enough, but having to fight to keep from jumping that annoying angel and devouring him was testing her strength and self-control. She had to find a good cemetery to meditate and recharge.

* * * *

Kalan went back to the church to talk to the bishop. The tension he was feeling lifted the second he walked into the foyer. He took a moment to soak in the peace before he searched out the man.

He found the bishop in his office. *The parish must be well-off,* Kalan thought as he took in the expensive furniture, the beautiful oil paintings and rare books spaced along the walls.

"Sir, welcome." The bishop stood and came to offer Kalan a seat.

Kalan found the man's fawning irritating. He knew being visited by an angel was proof of God's regard and would raise the bishop's status in the church. If

Kalan had a choice, he would be asking anyone beside this bishop. There was an unclean feeling about him.

"What about Roger?" a small voice whispered in his ear. It was a good choice. The young priest would be eager to help him, and he could find out more about Beltaine at the same time.

'Use all resources available' was another rule his Commander had taught him.

"How can I help you?" The bishop was an eager puppy wanting to please.

"I would like to talk to Father Roger privately."

"I could provide more assistance than Roger. He's new to the clergy and still sees good in even the most evil creature."

He knew the man was talking about Beltaine. He wondered if the bishop treated his parishioners the same way. 'Once a sinner, always a sinner' seemed to be the motto around this church.

"No, Father Roger will be more than capable of helping. Bring him to me," Kalan ordered.

"Yes." The bishop scurried away.

A few minutes later, Father Roger knocked on the door. Kalan studied the young priest as he waved him in. The man's attractiveness would bring the women to the services, but there was a haunted look in his eyes.

"How can I help you?" Father Roger asked.

Kalan leaned on the desk and crossed his arms in front of his chest. "I've got some information that I need verified."

"Why not ask the bishop?"

"Right at the moment, I prefer to keep him out of the loop. How much have you been told about why I'm here?"

Roger shrugged. "Not much. I think my friendship with certain people makes the Board feel like I can't be trusted."

"Are they right? Can I trust you?"

"Yes, you can, but don't tell me anything if you don't want to." Roger moved to sit down. Placing his elbows on his knees, he leaned forward. "Beltaine and I don't trade secrets. On good days, she barely tolerates me."

Kalan had to smile. From the little time he had spent with her, the angel knew she didn't suffer fools. "Why do you continue to be friends with her?"

"I wouldn't call us friends. She uses me for the few things she can't do herself. Also, if she has questions about the church, she asks me."

"Why doesn't she ask the bishop?"

"You've seen the way he treats her. She's managed to keep from killing him so far, but if she had to actually work with him, I don't think she'd be able to restrain herself."

Kalan shook his head. "I probably wouldn't be able to, either. How did a young priest and a demon meet?"

Roger looked down at the floor and smiled. "I used to live next to her in Dark Town."

"Really?"

"Her dad was a total bastard. Did nothing but drink and beat up on her. I felt sorry for her." Roger's laugh was harsh. "I tried to protect her, but she ended up protecting me more than I ever helped her."

"Dark Town is a rough place, huh?"

"It might be as close to Hell on Earth as you can get." Roger stood and walked to the window. He looked out into the darkening sky. "Being different and living in that place was hard. For whatever reason, Beltaine chose to stand beside me and make sure I wasn't killed before I could get out of that part of town."

"What's so different about you, besides your preoccupation with religion and God?"

"Don't you think that's enough to make me stand out in the midst of thieves, murderers and con artists? I was a throwaway. My mother left me on the doorstep of the apartment building Beltaine lived in. An old man took me in, and I spent my time begging for money. He wouldn't let me come back inside until I got enough for him to eat. There were times when I wouldn't get enough money and he'd make me sleep out on the street."

"How old were you?" Pity rose in Kalan's heart.

"I had to be around ten by the time my mother abandoned me."

"How old was Beltaine?"

"She was seven. She was small, but she had grown up fast and hard. There was no fear in her and no backing down." Roger's eyes dimmed as if he was remembering those long ago times.

"She was so young," Kalan murmured.

Roger's laugh was scornful. "Beltaine was never young. She was old from the moment she entered the world. Life in Dark Town can destroy a person, if you let it."

"How did you and Beltaine manage to survive?"

"I grabbed hold of the first thing that seemed to offer comfort. The church was a haven to me from the evil lurking in the shadows."

"And Beltaine?"

Roger turned to study Kalan. The angel knew Roger was wondering why he was asking all these questions.

"She chose the only way out she could."

"Which was?" he insisted.

Shaking his head, Roger moved toward the door. "I won't betray her secrets, especially to a man who doesn't hide the fact he doesn't like her."

"Wait. I might have been a little abrupt. I was just trying to find out what makes her tick."

The priest's gaze burned into Kalan's soul, and Kalan found himself wanting to confess all of his secret desires. That confession would be only one word — *Beltaine*. He wanted the woman with every fiber in his body, and he had a feeling — right or wrong — that he would have her before the mission was over. He shifted self-consciously. Who would have thought he could feel embarrassed?

Roger relented a little. "Survival is what makes her tick. She'll do anything and everything she must to survive."

"Would she sell you out if it came down to it?"

"I've never put her in a position where she had to choose — mostly because I might not like the answer." Roger's eyes shuttered. "Was Beltaine the only reason you wanted to talk to me?"

Kalan was shocked to realize he hadn't even mentioned the real reason he had wanted to talk to the priest. "No, she's not. Were you ever told about a Veil between Earth and Hell?"

"I vaguely remember someone mentioning it."

Kalan waved Roger back to his seat. He glanced down at the clock on the bishop's desk. It had been about a half-hour since he had left Beltaine. Good. He didn't want her on her own for too long.

"God and the Devil decided to create a barrier between Earth and Hell, like there is between Heaven and Earth. This Veil keeps mortals from blundering into Hell. It also keeps demons from rampaging over the earth."

"Okay, I'm following you so far."

"A day or two ago, it seems someone tore the Veil. There are small holes at the moment, but my Commander is worried about what might happen if the barrier is ripped in half. Demons would feast on mortal souls until evil was a living creature."

"With some of the things I've seen, are you sure demons have a monopoly on evil? Mortals are just as destructive at times."

"Your worst nightmares aren't as horrifying as what will be unleashed if the Veil falls. So I came down here to find the person who did this and stop him before he destroys it. Beltaine has been recruited to help me."

"Against her will."

Kalan smiled ruefully. "Yes, very much against her will, but she'll do it because her life is at stake as well. Now, her mother has brought us news about a book the perpetrator might have used. Neither one of us knows anything about it. We thought maybe you might know something."

"What kind of book would it be?"

"We're not sure, except that it's so important, the Devil left Hell to punish the man who stole it. Unfortunately, the thief had already sold it to the person we're looking for."

"Damn," Roger swore. Kalan knew the priest was well aware of the implications of the Devil coming to Earth to punish someone. "I haven't heard anything either, but I have a friend who is a scholar. He might know about suppressed books that would frighten even the Devil."

"Any information you and your friend can get us would be appreciated. We're working on a tight schedule. I don't think the man who did this will be patient enough to wait until we're ready to confront him."

"I'll contact my friend as soon as we're done here. Whatever information he can get me, I'll make sure you know it the minute I get it." Roger stood and held out his hand to Kalan. "I'll help you, but here's a warning. I don't care if you're an angel—you hurt Beltaine, and I'll punish you in ways that will make you wish the Devil found you instead of me."

Intrigued by Roger's transformation from mild-mannered priest to fierce protector, Kalan shook his hand and said, "I'd think she'd be able to take care of herself."

"She can, and never underestimate her, but buried deep inside is the child who never knew love. If you're not careful, you can break her heart."

Roger left, and Kalan stood thinking about what he had learned. He was having a hard time imagining the wise-cracking, smart-ass woman he'd dealt with as a frightened girl. Yet he wasn't shocked to hear she had protected Roger. He found himself wondering about the strong and strange bond the two abandoned children had formed. It was a bond resilient enough to endure Roger's entering the very establishment Beltaine had come to hate.

An urge to find her and talk to her welled up in him. He needed to look at her and hold her, even if she swore at him and kicked his butt. He focused on her and found her presence at yet another cemetery. Drawing from his well of power, he willed his body to her side.

Chapter Five

Beltaine sank down on top of the crypt and tried to empty her mind. As she drew in power to replace what she had used, she couldn't free herself from memories. Seeing her mother again had taken her back to the life she wanted to forget.

The strongest memory was the day, fourteen years ago, when she'd received her freedom. Staring down at her father, she had known her life would be her own from that moment on. Even though she had wanted to deliver punishment for what he had done, she had knelt in the pool of blood forming beneath him and had closed his eyes.

She had answered the frantic pounding on the door. She should have realized Roger would come to check on her. Somehow, she had managed to involve him in her secret. He had been the only one to stand with her the day she'd buried her father. She never visited the cemetery where her father was buried.

Pain and anger intruded on her trance. The flow of power stopped, but the void wasn't full. She needed to find something else to think of. An image of a tall, dark-haired angel came into her unwilling mind. She felt her skin flush and her nipples harden. It seemed Kalan could turn her on just by her thinking about him.

She fantasized that his hands cupped her breasts and his rough fingers pinched her nipples. She almost groaned aloud as her juices drenched her pussy. She became uncomfortable, but the power poured in. She allowed the erotic images to swamp her mind.

Kalan found her sitting on top of a crypt in the cemetery. Her legs were crossed, her palms resting on top of her knees. Her amber eyes were closed, and she was breathing deeply. Her skin was flushed, and he swore he heard her groan. He took the opportunity to study her. Her body showed no signs of her demon mother. It was petite, but curvy. Her breasts were large and firm. He had enjoyed the feel of them rubbing against his chest. Her waist was so small he could easily span it with his hands. Her legs were toned, and he felt his groin go hard thinking about them wrapped around his hips.

"If you're done staring…"

He shot his gaze up to meet hers. The irises were the first sign she wasn't fully human. They were catlike and now dilated to catch the fading sun. Smiling at him, she bared her fangs.

"Do you like what you see?" Her question was nonchalant, and he knew she didn't expect him to answer.

"Yes, I do." His honesty surprised them both. He justified his answer by telling himself that an angel wasn't supposed to lie.

She regained her feet and jumped to the ground with graceful ease. There seemed to be a shimmer in the air around her.

"What were you doing up there?" He ignored how his hands itched to grab her and his mouth longed to taste her again.

"Meditating. I needed to replenish my power. Burning zombies can use up a lot." She moved through the graveyard.

He noticed how she glided over the ground. "Can't you replenish the way other demons do?"

Stiffening, she turned to stare at him. Anger burned in her eyes. "Other demons receive power through pain and death, ripping it from their victims."

"What's different about what you do?" He moved to stand in front of her. Heat flared between them, and he felt sweat bead on his chest.

"I meditate and ask the dead to give me their power. I collect only what is willingly given. It doesn't follow that I'm a demon just because my mother is." Her voice trailed off, and he noticed her eyes focus on a bead of sweat winding its way down his skin.

He couldn't help but groan as she leaned forward. With the tip of her tongue, she followed the drop down to where it disappeared beneath his waistband. In shock, he watched her drop to her knees and unbutton his pants. He told himself he was going to stop her as he reached down for her head. Instead, he fisted his hands in her hair. He urged her forward even as she lowered his zipper and his member sprang free.

He moaned as her moist mouth slowly swallowed him. Her tongue swirled around the hard length. He looked down to see her face nestled in his groin, and his hands tightened in her curls. He caught a glimpse of a cross out of the corner of his eye. Freezing, he couldn't believe he was allowing her to give him a blow job in a cemetery. He started to pull away.

"Not here. This is holy ground," he protested.

The shake of her head rubbed her lips over the tip of his shaft. It jumped as if it was eager to be licked again. "This is a cemetery for suicides and undesirables the church refuses to acknowledge."

She sucked him in again. Her hum of appreciation shot lust through his body, and his mind went blank. He felt pleasure and desire build with each lick and pull. She bathed him with her tongue, and all he could do was plead with her.

"More, Beltaine. Please." His voice was hoarse.

She pulled back a little, and he wanted to protest, but when the tip of her tongue swiped over the slit in the head of his cock, he groaned. She released the suction on his shaft and trailed her fangs in gentle caresses along the sides of his tingling skin. She played a game of tease-and-run with the throbbing vein running down the length of his erection. Who would have thought that such a sharp-tongued woman could use that same tongue to pleasure a man?

Widening his stance, he allowed her access to his balls. She slid one hand down to play with them, to stroke and tease. He had never known they could be so sensitive. The rough pads of her fingers massaged his sac lightly. Squeezing it with a firm grip, she then released it with an apologetic little tap. Her hand returned and fondled him like precious crystal.

"Good. That feels so good." He yelled as he threw his head back.

She whispered a finger over the small patch of skin right behind his balls, and his entire body tensed. He started thrusting as fast and as far into her mouth as he could, trying to find release. Another gentle touch and he exploded.

She didn't pull away as his seed shot into her mouth. She knelt long after he finished coming. He hung his head and tried to slow his breathing and his heart rate. Her soft licks and tender sucks helped calm him. He unclenched his hands and smoothed her hair back. When she was done cleaning him, she leaned back on her heels and looked up at him. He wondered what one said at a time like this.

A strange light burned in Beltaine's amber eyes, but when he remained silent, it went out. She rose to her feet and dusted her knees off. "Hope you enjoyed that. It's the only time you'll ever see me on my knees." She took off toward the east side of the city.

"Wait," he called to her, as he stuffed himself back in and fastened his pants. When he caught up to her, he pulled her to a stop. Forcing her to look at him, he said, "I don't know what to say."

"You've never had a demon go down on you in a cemetery before?"

"No, and I can't believe you made me forget this was holy ground."

"I made you forget? That's right. Blame the demon for your own guilt." She waved to the stones. "I told you this is a cemetery for suicides and other people the church won't allow to be buried in sacred ground." She pulled away and moved off again.

His long legs made keeping up with her easy. "Why are there crosses and stone angels?"

"Suicides have families. Thieves and murderers have people who loved them. The crosses and statues are to give the living hope that their loved ones didn't go to Hell. A waste of money, if you ask me."

"Where are you heading?"

"I'm going to Dark Town."

"What's it really like there?"

"Some people call it Hell on Earth. It's where the worst of humanity congregate." She brushed her hair off her neck, and he caught a glimpse of a scar.

"What's that on your neck?"

Her hands paused a second, then she touched the mark lightly. "The only punishment of my father's to leave a scar."

She stopped under one of the flickering streetlights. Pulling her hair out of the way, she gestured for him to look at it.

He felt bile rise in his stomach. Burned into her golden skin was the perfect image of a crucifix. "Why would he do that?"

"He got enraged one day when he realized that all the cuts and other burns he had given me healed without a trace. He figured a holy object would leave a permanent mark on my flesh. He was right." She told the story as if it had happened to someone else.

"What kind of person would do that to a child? What sort of monster was your father?" He forgot his own contempt for her in his outrage that a father could do that to his child.

"He was a priest." She dropped that bombshell and walked away.

The horror flooding his heart threatened to make him ill. He couldn't deal with the sympathy he felt for her, so he fell back on scorn. "Your mother seduced a priest. There's nothing sacred to a demon."

She didn't acknowledge his scorn. "On Beltaine night, he was there as a man in priest's clothing. His faith was weak, but his flesh was more than willing."

"You place no blame on the creature that gave birth to you."

"They're equally to blame for the whole damn experience, but my mother was only acting according to her nature. My hatred for my father comes from what he did after I was born." She stopped at an intersection and looked at him. "Just because he was a priest doesn't mean he was a good man who was led astray. I've seen more Godly acts performed by men the church refuses to admit exist than miracles performed by priests."

He couldn't form an argument for that. A disgusted look came across her face. He had the feeling the truth about her father wasn't something she brought up in casual conversation. A twinge of hope rose in him. Maybe she was beginning to trust in him a little.

"Speaking of priests." Kalan wanted to change the subject, and she didn't fight him about it. "I spoke to Roger, and he knows someone who might be able to get us some information."

"Good idea. Roger has a lot of contacts. If there's mention of a book, he'll find it, but why ask him? I would think you'd talk to the bishop."

"There's something about him that makes me uneasy."

"There's something about the man that makes me want to puke." She grinned at him. "As you can tell, we don't like each other much."

"I would've never been able to tell. That's why I chose Roger. I figured we'd be able to trust what he tells us."

"We should. He hasn't let the church corrupt him yet." She was glancing down the street. He saw that night had fallen quickly in the city and the streetlights were fighting a valiant effort against the dark. In the direction they were headed, the lights had gone out and blackness reigned.

"You aren't going there in the dark, are you?" he asked.

"Murderers and thieves aren't really daytime people. The light tends to bother their eyes. You aren't coming with me dressed like that." She gestured to his white vest and pants.

"I'll change, because I certainly won't let you go alone." With a wave of his hand, he was dressed in black. "Won't I be mistaken for a fallen angel?"

Studying him, she shook her head. "You could *never* pass for one of them."

"Why not?"

"No insanity burning in your eyes. No pain etched on your face. The fallen are easy to spot." She gestured to his sword. "You need to get rid of the sword."

He didn't like the idea of giving up the sword, but unless they were going to run into high lords of Hell, he wouldn't need it for defense. With a flick of his wrist, he sent the sword away. "Are you happy?"

"Not really. My happiness would be complete if you weren't anywhere near me right now. Let me do the talking. There shouldn't be any demons around, but if there are, try to ignore them. At the moment, we want to find the person doing the damage before the Horde gains total access to Earth."

"I'll do my best."

"Not good enough, angel man. If you start a fight with a demon in Dark Town, don't expect any of the human monsters to help you. They're more likely to side with the demon." She took a deep breath. "Let's go."

"My name is Kalan."

"All right, Kalan. Remember what I said." Her voice was huskier than it had been before.

The tingle racing through him when she said his name worried him. They took the first step together and moved toward Dark Town, where Kalan was to get a small taste of what Hell might be like.

Chapter Six

Beltaine led the way down the dark street. There was no gradual decay of the surrounding area as they moved from downtown into Dark Town. One moment they stood under the street lights and the buildings were clean, painted, and in good repair. The next step, the darkness enfolded them, and the buildings took on the aspect of a bombed-out city. Broken windows stared down at them like sightless eyes. There wasn't any light to relieve the unnatural night, except for an occasional flicker of flame.

She saw Kalan shiver, but she didn't comment. Dark Town was unnerving to her as well, and she had grown up there. From the shadows, eyes followed them as she picked her way through the garbage. Breathing through her mouth, she tried to ignore the stench.

Kalan gagged. "How can you stand the smell?"

She pushed him forward. "Don't stop until we get to Hell's Hole. The stink isn't too bad tonight."

He rolled his eyes. "I can't believe anything is worse than this."

"Zombies reek tons more than this." She squeezed his arm to focus his attention on her. "Listen, when we get to the Hole, don't make eye contact with anyone. They're animals and see eye contact as aggression."

"What will *you* be doing? How are you going to find out anything if you're not looking at anyone?"

She snarled at him. "I'm alpha dog in the pack that hangs out there. They fear me because I've killed some of them before. They know I'll do it again if they provoke me. Tonight you're going to be submissive to me."

"I'm not sure that word's in my vocabulary."

Her hand shot out and gripped his throat tight. With little effort, she pinned him to a rickety wall. She bumped the back of his head against the brick and growled, "Tonight, submissive better fucking be your motto, angel. I don't plan on dying here, and if getting killed isn't on your agenda either, then you need to adjust your attitude." She banged his head once more for emphasis before letting him go and walking away.

Rubbing the lump, he caught up with her. "I can't die."

"When you came to Earth, you retained all your powers, but you became as capable of dying as any other mortal here. Unlike me, though, you'll head back to Heaven and be greeted by an angelic choir."

"That doesn't sound too bad."

"Of course, you'll no longer be an angel. You'll just be another ordinary soul hanging around Heaven."

He looked horrified. "You're making it all up. Why would they make me mortal?"

She shook her head. "You're mortal so you'll think twice before you start a fight. If you're in danger of dying, then you'll think of other ways to solve conflicts. What was your Commander thinking? I've never seen him send one of you out so unprepared for Earth."

"Have you met the Commander?" He seemed surprised to hear that she might actually know the head of the Host.

"Yeah, I've met him. A long time ago I had the pleasure of seeing him face-to-face. I don't ever want to repeat that experience." She shuddered.

"He's not that bad."

"Maybe not to you, but to a child raised on the horror of the church, I was shaking in my boots. I had heard all my life how God hated me because of what I was. Then comes this warrior angel, and I thought for sure my days were over. Finally God was sending someone to correct the mistake He had made by allowing me to live."

Kalan was silent for a moment. "Obviously he didn't hurt you."

"No, but he did issue a warning. I'm walking a thin line. At any moment, my life can be recalled if I tread just an inch to the other side." She sighed. "Do you know the temptation to do just that? To finally put an end to the anticipation?" Staring at him for a second, she said, "No, I don't think you understand how I feel at all."

He wanted to apologize for not understanding how it felt to want to die.

Holding up her hand, she stopped him from saying anything. "I've also met his counterpart in the Horde. I'll tell you, no matter how scary the Master of the Horde is, I'd rather deal with him a hundred times a day than talk to your Commander for five minutes."

"He can be intimidating."

"That isn't it. It's the fact that with a wave of his hand, he can have me destroyed. I'm lucky I haven't pissed him off enough for him to decide to do that yet."

"Scarier than the Master of the Horde? That's not possible."

"Have you ever met the Master? He isn't that bad, just a normal demon."

"A normal demon? I don't think those exist."

She ignored his sarcasm and kept moving. They were only a few blocks away from the Hole. Beltaine didn't want to encounter any of the beings haunting the streets. As unsafe as the bar was, there were still walls to protect them and exits only she knew about. She didn't fear the human monsters they would meet in the Hole. The uneasiness racing down her spine was because of the angel beside her. There was no way Kalan would be able to ignore the strange things that went on in Dark Town. She hoped she could find the whore she was looking for before the angel started a fight. She stopped outside the dilapidated building housing the bar. Turning, she forced Kalan to look at her.

"Remember. No eye contact and stay behind me. It's bad enough I have to go in there—I don't want to have to save your ass."

Before he could protest about her 'saving his ass' comment, she opened the door and they were bombarded by music and smoke. Throwing her shoulders back, she headed into the Hole. All eyes came to rest on them. As she stared directly at each person in the bar, the odor of fear mixed in with the scent of lust and evil hanging in the air, she knew they were afraid of her. There was no way she was going to drink anything—not only didn't she trust the glasses to be clean, but she also wouldn't put it past the bartenders to doctor the alcohol.

The singing of a whip slashing through the air brought their attention to one corner of the room. Beltaine hissed as the leather cut into the pale skin of a woman tied to a post. The woman cried out, and the men gathered around her laughed. Kalan took a step toward them, and Beltaine stuck her arm out to stop him. Glaring at her, he protested with a soft growl. She shook her head then pointed to a table on the opposite side of the room. Pushing him into the chair, she leaned over to breathe into his ear.

"He might be hurting her, but she's more than willing to let it happen. Don't make the mistake of trying to save her, angel boy. Not all humans want to be saved."

Heading for the bar, she flagged down the female bartender. The woman glared at her until she saw Beltaine's slit irises. The woman's gaze immediately dropped.

"What can I get for you?"

"I need to know where Betsy is." Beltaine slid a hundred-dollar bill across the bar.

With a flick of her head, the woman indicated Betsy was out back. "She's entertaining a customer at the moment."

"When she comes back, let her know I'm looking for her. I'll pay for her time."

The bartender grunted and palmed the bill as she moved down the bar. Beltaine joined Kalan at the table. She stared the waitress off when the black-dressed woman would have come to take their order. The tension rolling off the angel grew with each snap of the whip and each cry the bound woman made.

"Is the man holding the whip a demon?" Kalan asked.

She didn't let her eyes pause as she scanned the room. "He could be. There's so much evil in the room that any demon blends in with the others."

He asked her, "Are any of my fallen brethren here?"

"Are you kidding? They might be crazy, but none of them have a death wish. It's open season in Dark Town on fallen angels. I think some of the humans have even put out bounties." She saw an emaciated blonde come in from the back. The bartender pointed in Beltaine's direction, and the whore nodded. "I have to go talk to someone. Don't move from this spot." Even as she said it, she knew she would be pulling them out of an ass-kicking that night. She joined the woman at the end of the bar.

Betsy was staring at Kalan. "Where'd you find him?"

"On a street corner, where I find all my guys."

The whore shook her head. "There ain't no way you found that on a street corner. He looks like an angel, and those kind of guys don't come cheap." Betsy seemed rather taken with Kalan.

"He *is* an angel," Beltaine said, then groaned as he stood up and stalked across the floor. "Get a good look at him now, because I don't think he'll be looking that good in a few minutes."

Kalan rocketed across the room toward the large creature whipping the woman. He'd had enough of listening to her scream in pain and hearing the men laugh as the whip cut deeper into her. There was no way he was going to believe she wanted to be treated like a slave. Striking out, his fist hit the side of the man's head. The man dropped the whip and whirled with a howl. It was then that Kalan saw the glow of the demon's red eyes.

Kalan had fought his fair share of demons. He could gauge how they would attack, and where, by studying the type of demon it was. The creature standing in front of him was a medium-level demon. Whispering a silent prayer of thanks that it wasn't one of the high lords, he circled the creature, looking for weaknesses. Unfortunately, it didn't look like there were any. He heard Beltaine yell from across the room.

"Get your back against a wall, you idiot."

That was when he noticed he was surrounded by four or five humans and remembered her warning about the humans being as likely to attack him as any creature from Hell would. The attackers tensed at the sound of Beltaine's voice, but relaxed when they realized she wasn't getting involved at the moment. He gauged the distance between him and the closest wall. With his back covered, he would be able to defend himself better. He leaped and made it to the wall as the pack descended on him. He got a glimpse of the demon standing behind the other men. It was obviously waiting for the humans to wear him out before it attacked.

Hesitation would get him killed, so he blanked his mind and started defending himself. He wasn't sure if Beltaine would come to his aid or let him get the crap beat out of him. Since either outcome was a possibility, he decided to fight like she wasn't going to save him. There was no point in getting his hopes up.

Betsy winced at the first crack of flesh hitting flesh. "Shouldn't you go and help your friend?"

"I'm not really sure he's my friend, and I need to get some information from you." Beltaine turned her back on the fight to look at the whore. "What can you tell me about a possible rip in the Veil and the person who is causing it?"

Betsy was reluctant to say anything. Beltaine knew how harsh the streets were for a person accused of snitching. Sliding another twenty-dollar bill toward the whore, she said, "I really need to know what you've heard."

The blonde's hand snatched up the bill, and she looked around. "Okay. You need to go to Ericksberg."

"That's all?" Beltaine asked.

Another twenty appeared, and just as quickly disappeared into Betsy's pocket.

"All right. Rumors are flying on the streets. Some guy up in Ericksberg wants to take over Hell, so he's raising an army to attack. He's working on ripping the Veil enough to get his forces over on the other side."

"The man must be insane. Does he have any idea what the Horde would do to him? And if the Horde didn't get him, the Host certainly would." Beltaine checked over her shoulder. Kalan's face had several cuts and bruises, but he was holding his own. Two of the humans were down. She had a little time. "Do you have a name? Is there any place in Ericksberg I should be looking?"

Betsy cringed as a shrill scream came from the opposite side of the room. Her eyes widened as she looked over Beltaine's shoulder, but Beltaine wasn't about to turn. She needed to get the information before Betsy fried her brain on meth and forgot it. "Betsy?"

"I don't have a name. No one I've talked to has ever seen the man, but they say if you have any questions, you should stop at St Benedict's Cathedral in Ericksberg."

"St Benedict, the patron saint of war," Beltaine said with a bitter laugh. "An appropriate guide for this insane adventure. Why am I not surprised that a church would be at the center of the problem?" She pushed another bill to Betsy. "Thanks for your time and information. Find a corner to hide in." Turning, she headed toward the melee.

The demon was about to enter the fray. She heard Kalan try to shout a warning as she strolled up behind the creature. Light flashed off the blade of a knife, and Kalan cried out in pain as the edge sliced into his thigh. Beltaine shook her head. *He doesn't have any self-preservation. He's fighting like he's still invincible.*

One of the humans came rushing at her before anyone could warn him who she was. Without wasting a movement, she grasped his wrist and, using the man's own momentum, threw him over her shoulder into the brick wall behind her. She made sure it hurt and tossed a surge of her power out after him to bind him to the wall. The man's eyes widened when he realized whom he was fighting. The others backed off. She knew there was no way they would risk getting her angry. She could see Kalan was pulling his punches with the humans. She couldn't believe he would kill them, no matter what they did to him. She wasn't inclined to play nice and would kill anyone there if she felt like it.

The demon found itself alone, facing Beltaine and Kalan. It hissed and chortled. "So, the half-human spawn has decided to help her friend. I didn't know you had such softness in you, Beltaine."

"Maybe I'm turning over a new leaf, Fathi." She glanced at the woman tied to the post. "Someone get her down from there." Without seeing if anyone obeyed her, she looked back at the demon. "I told you not to do that shit here."

"Are you turning into a prude? I thought you were the wild child who believed in everyone's right to do whatever they wanted." Fathi tried to sneak closer.

She shot a small ball of flame at his feet, causing him to jump back. "I don't give a damn about you or that freak you were working over. One day the police are going to get the nerve to raid this place. I don't want it shut down, because this is the only place I can find all you rejects without having to search for you." She felt Kalan standing behind her and she took a step toward Fathi.

The demon held his hands up and stepped back. "You've been lenient so far, and I'll respect that. Why not ignore my little indiscretion and allow me to take the woman?"

"You're not taking her anywhere, you vile creature." Kalan snarled over her shoulder.

She elbowed him hard in the stomach. A warm wetness trickled down her arm and she knew he had a wound somewhere on his chest. Damn, they had to get out of there before the vultures really started circling. She didn't think her reputation would hold them back for long if they realized Kalan was wounded. Focusing her power, she felt her fangs lengthen and her fingernails sprout as claws. Snarling at Fathi, she hoped the demon would back down. They had never confronted each other before. Both preferred to believe they would win the fight, but neither wanted to test out that theory.

Fathi spat at her. "If your mother knew what you were doing, she'd be furious."

"Nice try, but I gave up worrying about dear Mother around the time she dumped me on my sadistic father.

Don't push me. I'm willing to walk away and let you live to beat another slave." Taking another step, she thought they just might make it out of the bar without the demon attacking, but she had forgotten about Kalan.

The angel leaped in front of her and went for the creature. She tried to grab hold of his vest, but her claws shredded the leather. Shit, she had forgotten about those. She loosened the flow of energy so her claws disappeared and her fangs shortened. She scanned the crowd, making sure none of them thought about trying to join in the fun.

"Kalan, stop it. Get the hell out of here," she ordered, anger swelling in her mind.

He ignored her. The demon and the angel circled each other, looking for an opening to slip in and score a blow. Kalan scored the first hit and smirked at her, taking his attention off the demon for a second. Fathi took advantage of his distraction to slide the tip of a claw down the middle of Kalan's chest. The angel fell back and touched his hand to the blood seeping from the scratch.

"Both of you stop it right now. I don't have time to deal with little children quarrelling." Her anger caused the air around her to shimmer with heat waves. The humans backed off. In the fourteen years since her father's death, she had learned the hard lesson of keeping her temper under control, but she was in danger of losing it now. She felt beads of sweat roll down her cheeks and drip from her nose.

Neither of the combatants looked at her. They were focused on each other, to the exclusion of perceiving the real danger they were in. Kalan had gotten a knife—Beltaine didn't know from where, and he waved it before Fathi's face with a cocky grin. The demon dove for him, and Kalan sliced a deep cut across the creature's arm, earning a howl. Seeing the blood dripping from the demon, Kalan laughed with arrogant pride. He turned toward Beltaine and she didn't have time to warn him as Fathi lunged forward and drove his claws deep into Kalan's side. The pain burning across his face finally drove her over the edge. The angel might be a pain in the ass for her, but from the moment they had met, there had been something driving them together. She didn't want to lose a chance of getting to know him better.

Her hands shot out and gripped Kalan's arm. She pulled him away from the demon and pushed him to the door. "Get out of here and head for downtown."

Protesting, he pressed his hands to his side, but his blood oozed from between his fingers.

"For the love of God, if you don't go, I'll kill you myself. I'll catch up with you. Now go."

Betsy risked getting close enough to Beltaine to pull Kalan toward the door. Beltaine didn't watch them leave, keeping her gaze fastened on the demon. "I've had enough. I would have let you go, but you've gone too far now, Fathi." She waved her hand at the retreating back of the angel. "You fought an angel and might have even killed him. Here in Dark Town, killing an angel might be a badge of honor, but in Hell, the Master of the Horde looks down on renegades like you."

"There's never been any trouble about killing those freaks." Fathi sneered.

"Things have changed, and the new rules say killing an angel is punished by death. I think it's time you go back on the other side of the Veil to see the Master. He might have a different view than you do."

Fathi scuttled back from her. "You can't do that. We made a pact. I would stay in Dark Town, and you wouldn't send me back. What happened to honoring that?"

She gripped his wrists and pulled him closer to impale him on the blade she had pulled from the sheath on her thigh. The strength of her thrust forced him to his knees, and the wave of heat rising from her skin made his eyes water. Her eyes blazed with anger and power as she stared down at him. "You should never trust a demon, Fathi, especially a half-demon spawn of a priest. We have no honor. Go back to Hell and face the Master." With a thought, she thrust her power into him, using the steel blade to conduct it and causing his back to arch in pain.

Throwing back his head, he screamed as light shot from his eyes and he began to disintegrate. When there was nothing but a pile of ashes before her, she raised her gaze and looked at each individual in the bar.

"Remember...I have no honor. If any of you choose to risk pissing me off again, your fate will be worse than his." A wave of her hand broke all the glass in the building.

She smiled viciously to herself as she left. Hurrying to catch up to Betsy and Kalan, she knew she had to get the angel back to her apartment and treat those wounds. When she reached them, she wrapped her arm around his waist, and between the two women, they got him to the edge of Dark Town. Thanking Betsy, she warned the whore not to go back to Hell's Hole. They stepped from the dark into the streetlights of downtown. They both took a deep breath of clean air, and Beltaine felt the residue of anger wash away with the gentle breeze.

"We have to get you home." She moved them down the street toward her apartment.

Chapter Seven

Beltaine carried Kalan over her shoulder up the last few steps to her apartment. She was happy her half-demon blood gave her the strength to be able to get him home safe without asking for help. She didn't think the Board would be thrilled to find out she had managed to get him injured. Using a surge of power, she unlocked the door without having to put him down then went into her bedroom before laying him on her bed. The demon in the corner hissed at the sight of the angel.

"Oh, shut up," Beltaine ordered.

It blinked, and she knew it was surprised that she'd spoken that way to it. Most people would have treated it with more respect, but she had never been like most people. She heard the scratch of claws against her hardwood floor.

"Great. I'm going to need to have the floors redone." She sighed and set about stripping what was left of Kalan's clothes from him while she talked to him.

"I told you to ignore any demon we saw. What do you do but attack the first one we come across."

"He was hurting that woman." His voice was low and filled with pain.

"I think someone better give the soldiers of the Host a more in-depth education. He wasn't hurting her." At his skeptical glance, she amended her statement. "Okay, yes, he was hurting her, but she wanted it."

He still looked like he didn't believe her. "She didn't look like she was enjoying it."

"Trust me, she was. Some people get off on pain. It doesn't do anything for me. I have a low threshold for pain."

The demon snorted. She grinned at it maliciously. "Unless I'm sending demons back to Hell. Then I tend to really enjoy causing them as much pain as possible."

The demon turned its back on her and pouted in the corner. She couldn't help but laugh. Her smile disappeared when she looked back at Kalan and his wounds. She ran her fingers lightly over a couple of scratches on his chest. He groaned with pain at her touch. There were a few knife wounds, as well, but those would heal fast. It was the three claw punctures in his side she was most worried about. She got up and went into the bathroom to grab her first-aid kit.

"I'm not sure what to use on the claw marks. If we don't clean them out, the sulfur and brimstone will make them fester, and you could get really sick." Opening the kit, she pulled out some gauze pads and a bottle of alcohol. "How's the pain?"

"I can deal with it. Holy water will help clean the demon's marks."

"Well, I'll have to call Roger and have him bring some over. Surprisingly, I don't have any on hand." She poured some alcohol on the pad and started cleaning the knife wounds. "You're lucky there weren't more people in that bar. They could have done some real damage."

"Why didn't you try to help me?"

"As long as Fathi stayed out of it, I knew you could take care of the problem, and I had to talk to Betsy." She studied the cuts closely. "None of them needs stitches. By the morning, you should be healed."

"Who's Betsy—and was she able to help you?"

"Betsy's one of the whores who works the corners in Dark Town. She usually knows everything going on down there. If she doesn't know, she knows who I can go talk to. Don't move. I'm going to call Roger." She headed out of the room to make the phone call.

When she came back, Kalan and the demon were staring at each other. There wasn't any anger or hate coming from either of them. It was as if they were studying each other.

"Roger's on his way." She finished binding the knife wounds. "I'm glad to see you two can exist without trying to kill each other. Of course, it's bound to the corner and you're wounded at the moment."

"Did you learn anything about the person who might have done this?" Kalan tried to sit up.

She leaned down to help him, and her skin tingled where her breast brushed against his arm. Stuffing pillows behind him, she tried to ignore the feeling. There was no way she was getting involved with an angel. She was still trying to get over the fact that she had actually given him a blow job. Where was her sense of self-preservation? It wasn't like Kalan was some guy she'd picked up at a bar and could get rid of in the morning. He was a member of the Host, and she considered them her bitterest enemies. She moved to a chair beside the bed and vowed to keep her hands off the luscious angel.

"Yes. Betsy told me she's been hearing rumors of a man in Ericksberg wanting to take over Hell and trying to destroy the Veil to bring his army across."

"Is he insane?"

"Well, he's found a way to rip the Veil, so we have to go on the assumption that taking over Hell is a real possibility and that, yes, he is insane."

"Ericksberg? Where's that?"

"It's about four hours north of here. I'll head up there tomorrow and check it out."

"You're not going by yourself. I'll be fine by the morning, and I'll go with you."

"I can't trust you not to attack another demon. If he's ripped the Veil like you think, Ericksberg will be infested with them. They congregate where the power is."

The demon made a choking sound. They glanced at it and saw that it was trying to say something. Her binding spell stopped it from speaking, so she lifted the ties a little. The demon moved farther into the bedroom and tried to speak again.

"It *is* Ericksberg where you will find the man who has ripped the Veil." Its voice hissed through burnt vocal cords.

Narrowing her eyes, she moved closer to it. "Why should we believe you? Do you think I'll let you go if you act like you're helping us?"

The creature shrugged its shoulders and managed to look guilty. "I know it must seem strange for a demon to help angels or humans, even if that human is demon spawn. You don't have the most cooperative reputation, but I believe you'll be reasonable and accept help from anyone who is willing to give it. The truth is, if the Veil is pierced and the Horde crosses over, then the Host shall be released. The Host does not discriminate between the demons who are feasting on human souls and those who are testing a different path. They shall destroy us all, and I don't want that. I like my life the way it is, and I don't want to die."

Kalan started to protest the statement about the Host, but Beltaine stopped him. "Don't try to make us think you'd separate us into good and bad demons, Kalan. We know the truth. A demon is a demon to you, and the only good demon is a dead one. I've seen members of the Host in action, and they're just as savage as demons when they cleanse." She turned to the creature. "Do you know the name of the man we search for?"

It shook its head. "No. I am only a minor imp. I crossed over as the first holes were made in the Veil. The man was unconscious on the floor. When I touched his mind, there was too much madness. I couldn't grasp what he planned to do after the Veil is torn. I know the town you mentioned is the one where my brethren are going. You must be prepared. Many have already crossed over, but are in hiding until the Horde can cross. The town is a sewer of anger, pain and blood."

Beltaine heard her door crash open. Roger raced into the bedroom a moment later and stopped in shock at seeing Kalan, Beltaine and the demon conversing calmly. She stood up to give the chair to the priest.

"I can't touch holy water, so you're going to have to help him, Roger. I'm going to take a shower while you're doing it." She headed to the bathroom.

Kalan watched in trepidation as Roger sat down while keeping a wary eye on the creature crouched on the floor. Uncorking the bottle, the priest said a prayer as he poured a little of the water on each claw mark.

Kalan hissed as smoke drifted up, and the smell of sulfur and brimstone assaulted his nose. The holy water was burning the contamination of Hell from his flesh. Praying, the priest took more gauze and wiped the wounds down with alcohol.

Kalan met the gaze of the demon. "You said the Host doesn't discriminate between those demons that have chosen a different way. What do you mean by that?"

The demon nodded toward the bathroom door. "Beltaine is only the daughter of a demon. Gathering her power by asking—not demanding—she isn't tainted by blood or pain. A few of my brethren have figured out how to gather power her way. We aren't as strong as other demons, but we aren't as prone to violence or death, either. We don't need blood and pain to survive."

"I've never heard of that. You're a demon. You can't change your nature," Kalan pointed out, wincing as Roger bandaged the wounds.

The demon nodded. "How do you know I'm not able to change my nature? Do you truly understand the nature of a demon?"

"No."

"Then don't tell me I can't change. I thought angels and men of the church believed everyone could stop their sinning, if given a chance." It sent an inquiring glance at him.

"Yes, but..."

"Ah, I see. Everyone but demons can change." It smirked.

Kalan grimaced when he realized the demon had tripped him up. "You're created to be evil, but I guess you might be able to change." His doubt showed on his face and in his voice.

"Angels and priests are the most rigid creatures. You are so unwilling to bend or change your own minds. Now you might have an inkling as to why she doesn't like religious men. She has no reason to like demons, either, given who her mother is." An emotion suspiciously like aversion crossed the demon's face.

"You fear her," Kalan stated.

"Yes."

"Why do you fear her, if she is one of your kind?"

"There are those of your kind that you respect more than others, aren't there?"

Nodding, Kalan thought about his Commander.

"For some strange reason, she is more powerful than most of us. Her ability has been growing since she was a child. I wouldn't be surprised if it would be only the high lords of Hell she'd have trouble dealing with now."

"You would think with her being half-human, she would be weaker than the purebreds."

The demon shrugged. "I don't understand it, but I know her power is such that we fear her. She has no respect for anyone."

"That's for sure."

Beltaine walked out of the bathroom, and the sudden silence told her the men had been talking about her. Roger coughed, and she caught his wide-eyed gaze with a wink. Looking at them all, she smiled and walked to the dresser to grab another set of clothes. It didn't bother her that she was naked and they were all staring.

"You should really learn to wear more clothes." Standing up, Roger moved toward the front of the apartment.

"Why? I'm comfortable in my skin. It isn't my problem that you're uncomfortable about seeing it." She snickered as he raced out of her place.

"That wasn't very nice of you. Temptation isn't something you should put before the priest. He's young and his faith isn't strong enough to resist you." Kalan's voice held disapproval.

Pulling on a cropped T-shirt then a pair of men's boxers, she shrugged. "Roger has been trying to convince himself that he's in love with me, but he's done a fine job resisting me so far. And to tell you the truth, I'm not tempting him."

"You parade around in front of him like a piece of meat being waved before a starving dog. How can that not be termed temptation?"

"A piece of meat? What an interesting analogy. I'm not really tempting him, though, because he's gay. He just hasn't figured it out yet." She sketched a symbol in the air and lifted the binding on the demon. She stared at it for a moment. "I can't trust you, so I don't want you in the same room as I am while I sleep. I'm moving you into the living room. There's a corner there that doesn't get any sunlight. You should be safe from burning until I can figure out exactly what to do with you."

The demon nodded and followed her. After she had bound it to the corner, she turned to study her couch. There was no way Kalan was going to fit on it. She barely managed to squeeze onto it. His feet would hang over the edge. She shivered at the thought of sharing a bed with him.

"He is rather fine, for an angel," the demon murmured.

She glared at it. "Mind your own business."

"There's something going on between the two of you. I can feel it, but I see you're fighting it. Why?"

"Why should I tell you anything about my personal life?" Beltaine asked.

The demon shrugged. "There is no one else here for you to talk to, and I would try to lift your confusion if possible."

"How does my confusion end up being your problem?" She paced to the window and back.

"If you are confused, you won't be as dedicated to solving the mission you've been hired for. Distraction can cause mistakes. If talking to me helps with the distraction, then do it. I'm a captive audience, and I have no interest in telling anyone your secrets." The demon settled into the corner while watching Beltaine with a steady gaze.

She wasn't really sure why she was about to tell the demon her problems, but she knew it told the truth. She needed to talk about her thoughts, and it wasn't going anywhere. "The reasons are endless, but let me give you the most important one—he's an angel, and I'm a half-breed demon. We're not supposed to like each other."

"Yet I sense you do like him."

"Kalan? He's an arrogant jerk who thinks he's perfect because he's an angel. He's narrow-minded and overbearing."

"Yes, but he's also the best-looking thing you've seen in a very long time." The demon chuckled. "Why not take advantage of the fact that you can't keep your hands off of each other?"

"I don't want to seduce him, demon. That would make me live down to his expectations."

"I don't think he has any expectations about you. Maybe you can change his mind about you."

"By making him forget where and what he is? By seducing him into having sex with me? That's the way to convince him I'm not a totally amoral person just looking out for herself."

The demon looked puzzled. "But you *are* looking out for yourself. I don't see why that should be a problem. No one on Earth is taking an interest in your life."

"You're being awful pushy for a demon who isn't interested in my life. What should I call you?"

The demon shrugged and rolled its eyes. "Why are humans obsessed with names? You can call me Azubah."

"Forsaken—it's a fitting name. Okay, Azubah, tell me why my love life is so interesting to you."

"It might be that while you're busy with the angel, I'll be figuring out a way to free myself and wreak havoc among the humans."

"I wouldn't put it past any demon to do that."

"It could also be because I see you're in need of someone to hold you close. You're in need of a warm body to share your bed. Don't put the angel on the couch. Keep him in your bed for as long as you can—or at least until the morning comes."

Staring out at the dark street below her, she wondered at the motives of the demon. Could she be as much of a hypocrite as she had accused others of being? Was Azubah trying to prove that demons could change their ways? Then she thought about lying down next to Kalan's warm body. It was odd that she was even considering it, because she didn't share her bed with anyone. Any lover she had ever taken got sent home long before she fell asleep. Shaking her head, she turned to look at the demon. "Sorry, friend. You'll get to look at him all night because I'm not sharing my bed with him."

"That's too bad. I happen to know he'd like to share more than your bed."

She laughed. "I'm not crazy enough to believe a demon. Good night."

Moving back into the bedroom, she saw that Kalan had maneuvered his body so he was lying down on top of the covers. His face was drawn, and she found she didn't have the nerve to wake him up and make him move again. *He really needs to stay still so his wounds will heal,* she told herself as she shut off the lights and slid under the covers.

Even through the sheets and blankets, Kalan radiated heat. She wanted to snuggle up to him, but her head kept warning her about getting involved with an angel. She knew nothing but heartache and pain could come of it. Determined to ignore the pleading of her body, she rolled onto her side and shut her eyes. She needed all the sleep she could get if they were going to Ericksberg in the morning.

Chapter Eight

Beltaine was having a wonderful dream. She was encased in something warm and silky. Arching her back, she rubbed herself against the silk and found that it was rough in the areas that caressed her nipples. Warm moisture bathed her right nipple as she moaned. The sound of a matching moan woke her up.

Her eyes popped open to see Kalan leaning over her. It was his hand and mouth she had felt on her breast. She pushed him away and rolled off the bed. Standing, she tugged the T-shirt down over her bare breasts and glared at him.

"What the hell do you think you're doing?" she demanded, as heat flared up her body from his wandering gaze.

"I was enjoying the tasty treat I found in bed with me." He held out his hand. "Come back to bed, Beltaine. I'm sure there's much we can enjoy together."

"Oh, no, I'm not getting caught in that. You think you want me now, but it's just the wet dreams and the darkness talking. When morning comes, you'll be furious, and I'm sure you'd find some way to blame me for it."

"That's possible, but I'm willing to take a chance on that happening to get a taste of you again."

"Well, you know what? I'm not. I don't need you to sneer and jeer at me when guilt hits you in the morning."

Kalan slid across the bed so he was closer to her. "I don't think that will happen. There's something between us, Beltaine. I don't know what, but I'm not going to let it die."

"I think the demon got to you." She stared into his blue eyes worriedly. There was no way he would talk to her like that unless he was bewitched. His eyes were clear except for the lust burning in them. She sent out a touch of her power. If the demon had bewitched him, she would be able to feel it and take it away from him.

There was a spell on him, but it didn't have any of the taint of the demon. The spell didn't feel like any magic she had felt before. While she studied him, he had moved off the bed to stand in front of her. She dropped her eyes and stared at his chest. No hair marred the golden perfection of his skin. His nipples were dusky, and they hardened while she stared at them. Her mouth began to water as the urge to lean forward and lick him grew. She tried to back up. There was no way she was going to take that risk. She knew if she touched him, they would both go up in flames and she would say to hell with the consequences.

Reaching out and grasping her shoulders, he stopped her retreat. Lust burst into flame, and she stared up at him with need burning through her.

"This is crazy," she whispered, as his lips came nearer.

"I know, but let's enjoy the insanity for a while." His breath brushed over her lips right before he kissed her.

The press of Kalan's mouth on hers swallowed up any protest she might have made. Reaching up, she wrapped her arms around his neck and crushed herself tight to him. They kissed while his hands slid down her back and under the waistband of the boxers she wore. She purred as his hot hands cupped her ass and lifted her up closer to his cock. Beltaine's mind tried to whisper a hint of resistance to her, but she wasn't listening. Tomorrow morning would be soon enough to deal with the embarrassment, guilt and anger they would more than likely feel. Tonight she was going to take him into her body and enjoy every moment of it.

His cock was engorged, and she couldn't help but groan as the hard length of it met her pussy. She was annoyed that the fabric of her shorts came between them. With a single wave of her hand, she ripped all her clothes off and cried out as he ground his hips into hers. The head of his shaft hit her clit repeatedly as he thrust against her. She licked her tongue over his nipple then blew on it. His hips jerked and he almost stumbled.

His mouth was moving down her cheek, and she leaned her head to give him access to her neck. He nibbled his way down her skin to the crook where her neck joined her shoulder. She felt the cool smoothness of her bedroom wall on her back.

"Take me now," Beltaine groaned out as he stroked her again and again with his entire cock.

"We should take it slow and enjoy it more." He barely got the sentence out. His breath was coming in pants.

"Fuck slow. We've got all night to take it slow. I want it hard and fast right now." She bit his nipple hard. At his growl, she apologized by teasing it tenderly with the tip of her tongue.

Kalan widened his stance, spreading her legs wide as well. His weight held her braced to the wall while one hand squeezed her ass and the other slid down between them. She held her breath as he whispered a light touch of his finger over her throbbing clit.

"Quit teasing me, damn it." She pushed her hips onto his hand, trying to bring her body to orgasm.

She could feel him smile against her neck as he pressed down on her firmly and she cried out. Soon he was tweaking and pinching her clit. Her hips bucked with each movement he made. A hot and hard thrust of his finger inside her, and she almost broke his hold on her when her back bowed. Her inner muscles clenched tight around him as he pulled his finger out. She protested, but then moaned as he pushed two back inside. The tips scraped the sensitive tissue in her pussy and her desire built. Moving in and out while pressing his palm against her clit, he pleasured her in a way no man had ever done. As Beltaine whimpered, her orgasm began to break free of her control.

"No," she pleaded. "I don't want to come without you inside me."

"This time is for you, love. You'll get me soon enough."

Lifting her hips, Beltaine allowed Kalan a better angle to insert his fingers into her. He latched his mouth to her nipple as he let her ride him. Her juices drenched his hand and the awareness of it doubled her pleasure. A particularly hard thrust and a bite of her nipple pushed her over the edge. She threw back her head and cried out as lust ripped through her in waves.

He soothed her with nibbles and strokes as her hips stopped moving. Easing away from the wall, he carried her to the bed and pulled the blankets off before he laid her down. He started at her toes and with infuriating slowness, moved up her ankles. Tasting and massaging, he touched every inch of her body. She moaned as his warm breath caused the tender skin behind her knees to tingle. He made his way up to her inner thighs, and she spread her legs to encourage him to put his lips on her.

Disappointment raced through her as he skipped her pussy and tickled her belly button with his tongue. She couldn't help but giggle. Kalan lifted his head and smiled at her. There was a twinge in her chest when his eyes met hers. Reaching down, Beltaine rubbed the skin over her heart and wondered what the warm sensation she was feeling meant. He dipped his head to kiss her breasts, and she forgot to worry.

He worshiped her breasts with wet kisses and hard sucks. She fisted her hands in his hair and held him to her chest. He didn't fight and showed his compliance with his teeth, tongue and hands. She could feel the pleasure building, but this time she wasn't willing to come by herself. Letting go of his head, she reached down and grabbed his shoulders. With a shove, she pushed him over on his back and climbed on top of him.

"It's time for the best part," she growled, as she looked down at him.

"I was enjoying the first part, though."

"So was I, but I think you'll really like this."

She stroked his cock with her hand, and he groaned. Straddling Kalan, she leaned down to kiss him as she lowered herself. They both cried out as she impaled her body on his shaft. Bracing her hands on his shoulders, she raised her hips then slid him back into her slowly. Snarling, he grasped her waist to lift her again. This time he rammed into her with a quick, rough motion.

"If you're going to ride me, ride me hard," he demanded.

She was more than happy to obey. Soon the room filled with groans and the sounds of bodies meeting in rapid thrusts. The heat in the room rose as the passion built to the detonation point. Rolling her over onto her back, he held her tightly. Tilting them, he rammed into her again and hit just the right spot. She screamed as it felt like the top of her head was exploding. Dimly, she heard him join her. His hot seed flooded her passage, and she welcomed it.

Several minutes later, his hips stopped jerking when her inner muscles stopped clenching. She spiraled down from the exquisite plateau where her orgasm had sent her. Flopping to his side, he snuggled her up against his chest. She couldn't believe how tired she was. Usually sex didn't wear her out. Instead, it tended to energize her. Relaxing into his body, she closed her eyes.

Beltaine didn't want to think about what they would find in Ericksberg the next day. The thought of a rip in the Veil scared her. The Horde wasn't a group of demons she wanted to deal with, not even with an angel on her side. They had to find the person who had made the rip and stop him from making it worse. Sighing, she knew Kalan would leave after that and she would be stuck having to clean up the town. For the first time, she found herself wishing a man would stick around.

Kalan looked down at Beltaine as she lay in his arms. Her cheeks were still flushed with pleasure, and a sleepy smile graced her face. He felt a twinge of guilt for what they had done, but he wasn't willing to think about it until the morning. There had never been a woman he'd thought about leaving everything for, yet something about her tugged at his heart, even if she was the offspring of a demon. In the short time he'd spent with her, she had shown him that she wasn't all bad, and maybe his preconceived beliefs had been wrong from the beginning.

Brushing her hair back, his fingers touched the scar on her neck. He leaned down and kissed it. The hitch in her breathing told him she was awake. She didn't stiffen, but he could tell she wasn't comfortable with his tenderness.

"Is your father still alive?" He couldn't help asking.

She didn't answer right away. He knew she was fighting the urge to ignore the question and turn away from him. After a few minutes, she shook her head.

"When did he die?"

"Why do you need to know this?" She started to pull away from him.

Wrapping his arms tighter around her, he kept her close. "I'm trying to understand you."

Laughing harshly, she glanced up at him. "You fucked me, and now you want to be my friend."

He wasn't going to let her words change his mind. She was hiding something about her father, and he wanted to know what it was. "Maybe I'm just curious."

"He died when I was fourteen."

"How did he die?"

"He was killed." Her answer was abrupt.

"Who killed him?"

Rolling her eyes, she grimaced. "It was a person who was as much a monster as he was."

"Who?" he persisted.

"When I was fourteen, I wanted him dead so he wouldn't beat me anymore. One night, a miracle occurred and he was killed. That's all you need to know."

"Do you know who did it?"

"Sure I do."

"Why won't you tell me?"

"It isn't any of your business who chose to end my suffering."

"Beltaine, trust me. Who killed your father?"

She turned her amber eyes on him and swore. He knew she had seen the determination in his eyes to get to the truth. "I killed him. I'm the monster who ended his reign of terror. Now can we go to sleep?"

Before he recovered from his shock, she turned her back on him and slipped into a deep sleep. He wasn't sure how he should react to her announcement, but he did know they had to travel to Ericksberg tomorrow. How could a murderer and an angel fix the Veil? As his mind whirled, he knew he wouldn't be getting any sleep that night.

* * * *

He was waiting for a sign to let him know the best time for the next ritual. He had sent his followers out to find the right sacrifice. This time, it had to be pure and innocent. There had been no change in the Veil since the last time he'd checked.

Urgency was driving him. He knew the Devil was searching for the book and time was running out. It wouldn't be long before Heaven and Hell caught up with him. He had to take his revenge before that, or all of these machinations would be for nothing, and his son's death would truly have been in vain.

He stared down at the man groveling at his feet. Why had he chosen a strung-out druggie for his right-hand man? An addict who would never pay attention to what he babbled to anyone when he was high.

"What did you tell the whore?" His voice was cold as he reached down to haul Johnson up onto his feet.

The greasy tattooed guy shrugged. "I don't remember, boss."

"Well, find her and take care of her. I can't allow her to tell anyone about our plans." He drove his fist into Johnson's stomach. As the man doubled over, he said, "Next time you decide to fuck a whore, don't do meth. It makes your tongue too loose." His hand connected with Johnson's nose, and blood spurted everywhere. Stalking away, he left him groaning on the floor. *Maybe he learned his lesson,* he thought.

He resented that he had to deal with the mistakes of others, especially when he longed to boast about the holes he had put in the Veil. But he realized the importance of being silent. There was no way he wanted anyone to know about his progress. Someone would try to stop him, and that couldn't happen. Without glancing toward the shimmering border between Hell and Earth, he made his way out of the catacombs.

The door to the tunnel slid shut as the head priest called out, "Mr Starrer?"

Stiffening, he knew there wasn't any way he could ignore the cleric, no matter how much he didn't want to talk to him. "Yes, Father?" His jovial tone was forced.

"It's so good to see you back at St Benedict's, Richard. I thought you might never return to us."

"My son's death was a terrible blow, but I've learned to trust that it was God's will." He tried not to gag on the bile caught in his throat.

"Good. I'm glad to hear that. It was a terrible event, but no one is to blame for your son's death. Not even your son."

Another parishioner called the priest away.

Richard made his way to the exit of the church. He wondered if anyone could see how angry he was. "No one is to blame," the priest had said. *Wrong,* his heart cried out. There was one being to blame for the premature death of his son. The Devil would pay for it by losing the one thing he held dear—Hell.

Chapter Nine

What in Heaven's name had he done, Kalan asked himself as he stared down at the woman in his arms. Her luscious body was pressed tight to his, and though his mind wasn't happy to see her, his body was thrilled beyond measure. The full curve of her bottom nestled against his groin.

He slid his hands up to cup and squeeze her breasts. All the while, he was having an attack of conscience. How could he climb out of bed without her knowing he felt guilty? Especially since she had warned him the night before about this very thing. Could he slink out like the dog he was and not reinforce her opinion of men and angels?

"You're thinking too hard way too early in the morning." Beltaine's voice was rough from sleep. "Get your hands off my tits and your ass out of my bed."

He jumped from the bed. He found he was hoping she didn't realize he was regretting last night. She was sitting up in the bed, with the covers pooled at her waist. He couldn't keep his eyes off her pink-tipped breasts.

"For Heaven's sake, go take a cold shower. I'm too fucking tired to deal with you." She flopped back on the bed and pulled the blankets over her head. She rolled so her back was to the room.

He waited to see if she was going to say anything else. When nothing was forthcoming, he headed for the bathroom. The cold water poured over him, and he shivered. Hanging his head, he looked down at the drain. Any good intention he might have had had been swept away last night. He had lost himself and his purpose between her thighs. How was he going to look his Commander in the face? He couldn't help feeling he had crashed and burned, just like his fallen brethren.

Forcing himself out of the shower, he dried off then dressed. He entered the room with a hesitant step. She was standing in front of the window without a stitch of clothing on. He studied her straight back. The flare of her hips and the gentle slope of her butt called for him to touch her. He groaned and clenched his fists.

Shaking her head, she turned to look at him. The shadows hid any emotion she might have in her eyes. "Go to church, Kalan. Fall to your knees and pray for forgiveness." Wrapping her arms around her waist, she snarled. "If it makes you feel better, blame me for your transgression."

"I can't blame you. I chose to sleep with you."

"You'd be the first man I ever met who didn't blame the woman." She gestured toward the front of the apartment. "Get out of here. I've got things to do before I leave for Ericksberg."

"Beltaine, I'm..."

She didn't let him finish. "Don't apologize. Men don't seem to realize it only makes things worse."

He knew he had disappointed her, but he didn't know how or why. He ignored the disapproving glare from Azubah as he left her apartment with hunched shoulders and a desperate feeling in his heart.

* * * *

"Stupid. Stupid. Stupid," Beltaine mumbled as she gathered clothes. "You knew he was going to regret it, but you let him talk you into his arms anyway."

After slamming the closet door shut, she marched into the bathroom then almost ripped the handle off the shower. A drop of water traced a track down her cheek. She brushed it away with a swift swipe. There was no way she was going to let that man make her cry. She hadn't shed a tear for a man since she'd first realized her father hated her.

Stepping into the shower, she grabbed a bar of soap. She was going to wash his smell and seed from her body. Sighing, she knew deep inside she'd never be able to get rid of the memories. His rough hands and smooth skin had glided over her body. His mouth sucking on her nipples had caused her to groan, and his cock thrusting into her pussy had made her come.

Her skin was scarlet by the time she shut off the water and stepped out onto the bath mat. Catching a glimpse of her reflection in the mirror, she was horrified to see sadness in her eyes.

"Hell no," she muttered. "You won't let that angel know he hurt you. You're stronger than that."

She forced a look of indifference onto her face and a touch of coldness into her eyes. Maybe she would go to Ericksberg without him. It would serve the sanctimonious prick right if she up and left him. After she dressed, she went into the living room, where Azubah sat in the corner, away from the morning sun.

"He's an idiot," the demon stated.

"I guess I shouldn't be surprised, huh?" Beltaine moved to the kitchen and grabbed a soda from the refrigerator.

The demon twisted its face into a facsimile of a smile. "He is rather a delicious specimen, but angels can be an unpredictable lot."

She grimaced at Azubah. "Now you tell me. Weren't you encouraging me last night to jump him?"

It shrugged. "I might have made a slight miscalculation."

Roger came bursting into the apartment before she could say anything. She frowned at him. "Don't you ever knock?"

"When have we ever knocked on each other's door?" He nodded at the demon.

"I might have been naked," she grumbled.

Roger looked surprised for a second, and then he burst out laughing. Tears were rolling down his cheeks by the time he made it to her couch. "You've got to be kidding. You've never cared before if I saw you naked."

"Yeah, well, what if I was with someone?"

She saw his eyes light up with interest. "If that someone happened to be our friendly angel, I might pay to see that."

They stared at each other in shocked silence. Beltaine had known about Roger's sexual preference, but he had always denied it to her face—and to himself, as well. She wondered why he was suddenly talking like a regular guy instead of a priest.

"He does have a nice ass," Azubah inserted in the deepening silence.

"He's mine, Roger, just remember…I slept with him first." She set her soda on the coffee table then threw herself on the couch next to Roger. "Not that he seems to want to repeat it anytime soon."

Her friend watched her with narrowed eyes. "He slept with you?"

"Sure he did, after he fucked me cross-eyed."

A slight blush tinted the young priest's cheeks. "I'm surprised."

"Why? Don't you think I'm fuckable?" She gave him an evil grin. She loved tormenting him.

"That has nothing to do with anything." He dodged her question.

"Come on. You're a priest. You should always be honest."

"I guess for a regular guy, you would be very attractive. I just don't look at you that way." Roger waved aside her comments. "We've been friends too long for me to consider you someone I'd want to sleep with, even if I weren't a priest."

She wrapped her arms around his waist and leaned her head against his shoulder. He stiffened, and she knew it was because she rarely reached out to anyone.

"We're quite the pair, aren't we?" she whispered in his ear.

"Yes, we are. Do you suppose that's why we're still friends?" There was a smile in his voice.

"I think it's because you were too stubborn to walk away all those times I pushed you."

"You've always said I was too hardheaded for my own good." Roger pulled away and turned to look at her. "When I said I was surprised, it wasn't because of you, necessarily."

"I know what you meant." She jumped to her feet and started to pace. "I tried talking him out of it. I knew he would regret it, but there was something driving him."

"It was lust, dear." Roger laughed softly.

She snarled at him. "I know, you idiot. He didn't listen to me. It was the best fuck of my life."

A flash of envy raced through Roger's eyes. "How's this going to affect your job?"

"It's not going to. I'm ignoring the fact that I can't seem to stay away from him."

A knock sounded on the door before she could make a bigger fool of herself. Stalking over, she whipped open the door just as Betsy was getting ready to knock again. The whore cringed at the angry look on Beltaine's face. Beltaine reached out and pulled her in.

"What the hell are you doing here? I didn't think you got out of bed before sunset."

"With the money you gave me, I didn't have to work again last night. So I got a hotel room and got the first full night's sleep I've had in a long time."

Roger stood and gestured for Betsy to take his seat. The blonde woman screamed when her eyes landed on the demon.

"Shut up. It's not going to hurt you. Azubah can't move from the corner." Beltaine studied the woman. "Why are you here?"

Betsy looked around nervously before she met Beltaine's eyes. "I remembered more about the man who wanted to invade Hell."

"Tell us," Beltaine ordered.

"My last john before I left Ericksberg...he bragged about helping his master with building an army and ripping the Veil," Betsy stuttered. "He's the one I heard those rumors I told you about from."

"And you're just now remembering this?" Beltaine clenched her fist to keep from grabbing and shaking the shit out of the prostitute. Roger put his hand on her arm to calm her.

"The meth clouds my mind. Anyway, he was a skinny younger man with a lot of tattoos and scars."

"What kind of tattoos?" Beltaine asked as Roger went to fetch Betsy some water.

"They weren't well done. Mostly prison tattoos."

"Prison? What's different about them?" Roger asked as he returned.

"They're a poorer quality and usually all black," Beltaine said. "Prisoners give them to each other because there's nothing else to do." She started to pace. "What were they of?"

"One was of the Devil, I'm sure, and various demons, but the most distinctive one was of an angel wrapped in flames." Betsy shuddered. "I can't tell you how scary he was."

"Did he tell you his name? Maybe you can find him, Beltaine." Roger shot Beltaine a glance.

Betsy shook her head. "He never told me his name. I'm sorry I couldn't help you more."

"You've helped more than enough." Beltaine handed the woman some money. "Take this and disappear for a while. Once the man's 'master' figures out your john might have spilled secrets, he'll be looking for you, and you won't want to deal with him."

"Thank you," Betsy said as she walked out.

As soon as the door closed behind her, Beltaine and Azubah looked at each other and nodded.

"She'll be dead within a couple of days," Beltaine announced.

Roger's face paled. "How do you know that?"

"She's a meth addict. She'll never be able to stay off the street because she has to feed the sickness. The bad guys will find and kill her."

"Poor soul," Roger murmured. "I know we can't do anything else for her, but it seems wrong to let her go. She did risk her life to talk to us."

"I know, but there's nothing else I can do to protect her. Her addiction will be what kills her in the end." Beltaine glanced at the clock. "I'll take you to the church. I'm heading to Ericksberg after I make a stop."

"What about me?" Azubah asked.

With a wave of her hand, she lifted the binding spell and released the demon. "You can go now. Do whatever you want, as long as I don't hear about it and it doesn't break any of the Board's laws." She turned to Roger. "Come on."

Chapter Ten

Kalan was kneeling in front of the altar, but all he really wanted to do was bang his head on the floor. He was a complete idiot. Sleeping with Beltaine had gotten him nothing except a black mark against his name. *Not true,* his body shouted. *It was the best sex you ever had.* He shook his head. Yep, a complete idiot, because it was the only sex he had ever had. It wasn't as if the Host of Heaven went running around sleeping with every woman they saw. That certainly wasn't angelic behavior.

There was no way he could talk to his Commander about this, but he couldn't lie to the angel, either. Would the Commander understand why he'd done it? Laughing at himself, he realized how stupid that sounded. How could the Commander understand when even Kalan himself didn't know why?

Maybe these feelings were meant to be. Maybe he and Beltaine were supposed to be lovers. He dropped his forehead to the steps in front of him. What a fool. Now he was trying to make excuses for screwing up.

"What is your problem, child?" A peaceful voice came from the pews behind him.

Child, he thought as he rose to his feet. No one would mistake him for any mortal, especially a child. Turning, he peered into the early morning shadows.

"Don't assume anything until you know everything." The voice moved closer, and out of the dawn sunlight stepped an elderly priest. His gnarled hands clutched a cane, as he shuffled his way toward Kalan.

A pair of lively green eyes pinned him. He reached out and helped the priest sit on the front pew. "Why do you call me child?" Kalan was intrigued by the endearment.

The priest leaned forward and patted Kalan's hand. "As an angel, you are thousands of years old, but you're a child when it comes to living on this earth."

Kalan nodded. "You're right, Father. I thought I understood what I was meant to do here, but from the moment I arrived, I've been confused."

"I'm Father Angelo, and confession is good for the soul. Tell me what's troubling you." Angelo settled in, as if knowing Kalan's confession would be interesting.

"Forgive me, Father, for I have sinned," Kalan started, only to be interrupted by the priest.

"Skip that stuff. I'm not getting younger, and if I'm to help you, you must get to the important things."

"I had sex with Beltaine," he blurted.

There wasn't any emotion on the priest's face besides a slight smile. "Really?"

"Yes." Kalan began to pace in front of the altar. "Aren't you shocked or disgusted?"

"I'm surprised."

"I know. I can't believe I did it, either."

Angelo shook his head. "I'm not surprised you slept with her. I'm surprised you had the good taste to choose Beltaine."

Kalan's mouth dropped open. "What are you saying?" If he weren't an angel, he'd be swearing by now.

"Sit down, child. You're wearing me out." Angelo gestured to the pew next to him.

Kalan dropped down and leaned forward with his elbows on his knees. He groaned. "What am I supposed to do now?"

Angelo laughed. "What do you *want* to do?"

"I don't know. Part of me wants to complete my mission and get back to Heaven."

"The other part?"

"That part wants to grab Beltaine and hide her away, just for me."

Shaking his head, Angelo grinned. "You've learned nothing about Beltaine. She'd never allow you to keep her. Her heart is wild."

"'Wild' is a good word for her."

"Yes, but she's one of the most honest people you'll meet."

"Honest?" Kalan couldn't believe a priest would be calling a demon-spawned woman honest.

"Beltaine is nothing more than what she shows you. You can trust her in all things."

"Even if she's in danger?" He remembered what Roger had said about Beltaine doing anything to survive.

"Should I trust you if your life were in danger?"

"Yes. I'm a member of the Host. My life is expendable."

"Very admirable, child, but not even you can tell me what you would do. I've known angels who have committed sins. Why should we expect more from you than we do of ourselves?"

"Maybe because I'm an angel." A surge of annoyance raced through him.

"So being an angel makes you superior to us? Be careful with that way of thinking, child. That's what got Lucifer in trouble."

Kalan stared at the elderly priest. He didn't know what to say. No self-respecting angel wanted to be compared to Lucifer.

"You delight in leaving them speechless, don't you, Father Angelo?" Roger entered the sanctuary. His blue eyes were laughing at Kalan, even while his face was set in a somber expression.

"Sometimes it's the only enjoyment I get in my old age." Angelo chuckled. "We were talking about your friend."

"Ah, discussing the fact that you two slept together last night?" Roger's grin bordered on smug.

"She told you?" Kalan's voice rose.

Roger shrugged. "She told her best friend, not her priest. She isn't given to confessing her sins to me, or any other priest, for that matter."

"It's true. Beltaine doesn't have a high opinion of the clergy or the church," Father Angelo agreed.

"Yet she believes in God. I find that hard to believe." Kalan was puzzled.

"She believes in the Devil, as well," Roger pointed out.

"Why?"

"She believes because she has met both of them. Each has shown her far more respect than any of their minions — mortal or otherwise." Father Angelo sighed. "Demons and angels tend to be more intolerant of her than God or the Devil ever could be."

"I tolerate her. If I didn't, I wouldn't be working with her."

"If you did, you wouldn't be here now, beating yourself up over sleeping with her."

Roger's logical comment made Kalan pause. Could the young priest be right? How much of his angst came from his disgust for what Beltaine was rather than his feelings of failure?

"Why are you here, Roger?" Father Angelo asked, taking his understanding gaze off Kalan.

"I need to talk to Father John. I've got a few important questions to ask him."

Angelo shook his head. "I'm sorry, but John isn't up to having visitors today."

"Did he have another episode?" Worry tinged Roger's voice.

"Yes, he did. He's resting now. Maybe later tonight, or even tomorrow, would be better." Father Angelo struggled to his feet. He held out an arthritic hand to Kalan. "Remember, warrior of the Host, don't judge unless you're willing to be judged."

Kalan kissed the old man's ring then stood with Roger to watch Angelo leave.

"He's a wise man," he commented with quiet reverence.

"He and Father John have been my mentors since I entered the priesthood."

"How do they feel about your friendship with Beltaine?"

Roger smiled. "I think you can tell by Father Angelo's comments how much he likes her." Roger turned to look at Kalan. "Not all the priests are like the bishop. There are some who see Beltaine's usefulness, not as a weapon or tool, but as a person."

Kalan grunted. He wasn't sure he could be included in that small group yet. At the moment, she was a tool to slake his lust.

"Where is Beltaine now?" he asked as he made his way down the aisle.

"I don't know. She had the taxi drop me off here and said she had some things to take care of before she left for Ericksberg. You might want to catch her before she deserts you," Roger called.

"I can find her whenever I want to."

"You might not want to tell her that," Roger suggested with a chuckle as Kalan stepped from the church.

Kalan wasn't going to mention that little tidbit to Beltaine anytime soon. He could imagine the choice words she would have to say about that particular power of his. He sent out his power to find her. She was on the west side of the city. He wasn't in a hurry to join her.

With a thought, his sword reappeared in its scabbard on his back. He would never leave it behind again—not even if Beltaine ordered him to. A snide voice in his mind asked him if he really thought he could have defeated that demon with his sword. He realized that he had gotten in deeper than he could handle the night before by forcing the issue with Fathi. He was lucky Beltaine had decided to step in and help him out.

She could've allowed Fathi to kill him. That way, she wouldn't have had a partner anymore, and she wouldn't have been given the blame for his death. Yet no matter how much she didn't like him, she had still saved him. He might have to rethink his opinion of her.

Chapter Eleven

"Beltaine, you know I can't sell that stuff to you. If the Board found out, I'd have my license revoked," the short man whined up at her.

She really hated arguing with people who were right.

"If you don't sell it to me, I'll send your ass back behind the Veil." Hell, that was as empty a threat as she had ever heard, much less uttered.

Abbrevio was an imp. The border between Hell and Earth meant nothing to him. If she sent him back, within two seconds he'd be standing in front of her again.

"I've never done anything to you. Why would you be mean to me now?" He glanced at the bottle she wanted to buy. "Angel's bane. You're not plagued by a Heavenly spirit, are you?"

She leaned over and snarled at him. "It doesn't matter why I want it. Just sell me the damn vial."

Shaking his head, he crossed his arms. If he was afraid of her, he didn't show it.

"No can do. Not without knowing why you want it. You can do bad shit to angels with that stuff, and I don't want the Board or the Host coming down on me because I sold it to you."

When she took a deep breath to argue again, she gagged on the taste and smell of sulfur coming from behind her. Whoever was there was scary enough for Abbrevio to drop to the floor and curl up in a little ball.

"I suggest you allow her to buy it, Abbrevio. Beltaine's reputation is such that you should know she would never use it to harm an angel — much to my disappointment." The voice swarming over her shoulder held brimstone and fire.

The imp didn't uncurl. He waved a limp hand at her to take the bottle. It wasn't until she stood outside that she turned to face the creature following her.

Dressed in a black Armani suit with a blue silk shirt and a bright yellow tie, the Master of the Horde looked like every other successful executive. Well, almost like any other man, she amended. His blood red eyes, visible fangs and the small horns sprouting from his head were dead giveaways that he was more than mortal.

He glanced at the bottle in her hand, his gaze like a burn.

"Angel's bane isn't to be used lightly, Beltaine." The slight rebuke in his voice slapped her hard across the face.

Narrowing her eyes, she tried to show she wasn't afraid of him. Even though, in truth, he and the Commander of the Host were the only two beings she feared. "I don't plan on harming any of the creatures. I want one particular one to leave me alone." She tried not to flinch when he leaned closer and sniffed.

"Is it the same one I smell on your skin?"

Damn. Of all the creatures she didn't want to run into, the Master was at the head of the list. Actually, he was third behind the Commander and her mother on her Never Want To See Again list.

"You're spending time with an interesting crowd. Maybe you're more like your mother than we thought."

She almost went for him, but her thin streak of self-preservation stopped her. "I'm *nothing* like her."

His fangs gleamed in the sunlight. "You hate her more than I do. I would have killed her long ago if it didn't suit me better to have her live." He shrugged. "Maybe you fucking an angel is part of an elaborate joke the universe is planning. It'll be interesting to watch it play out."

In an instant, he was gone, but his voice singed her ears. *"Watch your back, Beltaine. There are many who would enjoy seeing you fail."*

"You're one of them, I'm sure," she muttered as she opened the vial of angel's bane. Dabbing a drop on each wrist and one on her neck, she hoped it worked. Scientists had discovered the mixture several years ago. Given in large doses, the chemical could cause paralysis or even death to angels. Used in small amounts, it acted like a repellent to keep the Heavenly creatures away. That was all she wanted. As much as he had hurt her—and she was willing to admit to the hurt—she didn't want to see him dead. She only wanted him gone.

"Hey, Beltaine, my main demon killer." An oily voice slipped over her ear.

She turned to see Elaphe slithering toward her. He was one of the lesser demons the Board allowed to live and work in the city. She never dealt with them unless they broke the laws. Then, they had to go back to Hell.

"What do you want?" It was strange to have one of them approach her. Usually they were afraid of her.

"Word on the street says you got a new partner."

"Why is my having a partner so important people are talking about it?"

"Everyone knows you're a solo operation." Standing still, Elaphe still gave the impression of movement, with his tongue flicking out to lick his lips and his gaze darting about.

"Maybe I got tired of kicking your asses by myself. Maybe I thought I'd let someone else join in the fun." She hated that people were talking about her.

"I don't think that's it. You'd never get bored with punishing us. Rumor says something's going down in Ericksberg."

She whirled and grabbed his collar. She twisted it, so her knuckle pressed against his throat, and yanked him up on his toes. "Tell me what you know about Ericksberg and the rumor."

Elaphe didn't struggle. He had been through Beltaine's interrogation process and knew how far she'd go for an answer. "The only thing I know is, something big is happening. It has all the higher demons nervous. It has to be important for the Master of the Horde to come and harass you."

Shaking him, she demanded, "Is that all?"

"I've been told to stay out of Ericksberg. Evil's been unleashed there, and it isn't the demons causing trouble this time."

She dropped him and he staggered. She believed him. Every instinct in her body had warned her that demons weren't behind the ripping of the Veil. Damn, things were really starting to look bad if the lesser demons were feeling the tension.

Her pager beeped. Checking the message, she grimaced. The Board was summoning her. She had wanted to be on her way to Ericksberg before dark.

"The dog must report to its master, I see." Elaphe's voice held a hint of disdain.

Snarling, she lunged for the demon. She allowed her anger to flare in her eyes. He screeched and ran in the opposite direction. Any comment about her working for the Board wouldn't be tolerated, especially by weasely little demons whose entire lives rested in her hands.

Another page beeped through, and she ignored it. Flagging down a taxi, she decided she wasn't going to waste her power to appear at the whim of the council. She'd get there as fast as modern technology allowed. Sitting back in the seat, she sighed. It had been a long day, and it wasn't half over yet.

* * * *

Kalan appeared at Beltaine's side as she stepped from the taxi. Ignoring her annoyed glare, he gestured toward the Board Building.

"I believe you've been summoned." He didn't try to hide his smile as she grumbled and went inside.

She didn't meet his gaze, and he figured she'd dismiss him all day if he didn't repair some of the damage he'd caused.

"I met Father Angelo this morning."

She grunted. He couldn't see any softening in her face.

"He seems like a nice man, for a priest."

"Father Angelo *is* a nice man." Her voice was an almost visible wall between them. She wasn't going to make it easy for him.

"He has a high opinion of you."

"Shocking, isn't it?" She shot him a burning look.

"Oh, for Heaven's sake, are you going to be this way the entire time we're together?" He moved closer to her and wrinkled his nose at the odd odor coming from her.

"What way? And why would it matter to you if I chose not to talk to you ever again?"

He gritted his teeth as they made their way through the lobby. There was no way he was going to make a scene. Stepping onto the elevator, he waited until the doors shut before he backed her against the wall. He stared down at her and noticed flares of red in her amber eyes. A wave of desire swelled in him as her ripe curves pressed against his chest.

Leaning in, he saw a hint of fear on her face. He crushed his lips to hers, and all the reasons he shouldn't be touching her shot out of his head. He nibbled his way over her mouth to entice her to open and let him in. A hard nip, and she gasped. Sliding his tongue in, he stroked it along hers with a teasing touch.

Pinning her between his body and the elevator wall, he continued feasting on her mouth. There wasn't any hesitation in the way she threw her arms around his neck and encircled his waist with her legs. He cupped her butt and lifted her so her mound rubbed against his erection. They both groaned. His shaft was reminding him that it had been denied her that morning.

"Your clothes," he moaned.

He didn't need to say anything else. In a second, she was naked and so was he. His eyes closed and his soul sighed when he slid into her. He had the rather unsettling feeling of coming home. Her pussy fit his shaft as if she were made for him. Then her inner muscles tightened around him, and he lifted her so he could slide out.

"No, don't go," Beltaine protested when he pulled out entirely.

He gripped her hips and slammed her down on him.

Throwing her head back, she screamed, "Again."

The passion had built so fast that Kalan knew one more thrust would send them both over the edge. He wasn't interested in it being slow. It had to be quick, or he would never survive. After pulling out, he rammed into her the last time then came.

Pouring his seed into her, he cried, "Beltaine!" He repeated it with each jerk of his hips. He managed to support her while he recovered his strength.

Awareness of his surroundings returned with the simultaneous events of the elevator jerking to a stop and Beltaine swearing. With a thought, he clothed himself, and by the time her feet touched the floor, she was dressed as well.

"The little prick gave me the wrong fucking stuff."

He overheard her muttering to herself. He bent and whispered, "Why do you smell?"

"Shit, you can smell that and you still fucked me? Angel's bane isn't worth the money I paid for it." She stalked toward the Board's office.

Grabbing her arm, he yanked her to a stop. "You bought Angel's bane to keep me away from you? Why?"

Hissing at him, she said, "The way you ran out this morning, I figured you'd be thrilled I was trying to keep us from making the same mistake." She poked him in the chest. "This morning you barely looked me in the eye. This afternoon you're fucking me in a freaking elevator. What the hell's wrong with you?"

"I don't know. Running to the church, I was committed to flogging myself over that sin. Then someone made me think my sin wasn't having sex with you. My sin was not being more tolerant of what you are." That was the wrong thing to say, judging by the way her eyes narrowed and her lips curled.

"What I am? You can't tolerate what I am. Let me tell you something, angel boy—my tolerance level for self-righteous pricks is reaching an all-time low. It's going to be nonexistent after I'm done with the Board." She pushed him away and flung open the door.

Beltaine wanted to swear long and loud, but she wouldn't show an ounce of emotion in front of the bastards who ran the Board. Taking a deep breath, she cleared her mind and got her anger under control.

The members of the Board sat at a horseshoe-shaped table. She had only been in the office once, when she'd agreed to work for them. Since then, the Board had contacted her through Roger. She nodded at the bishop, but her gaze went to the icy woman at the apex of the table.

Misha St Largent was the head of the wealthiest family in the city. It happened to be the largest crime syndicate, as well. Misha had come to power through lying, cheating and killing. Beltaine didn't trust her, but she respected the woman. When they met, it was like two alphas circling each other. They managed to deal with each other because they never crossed into the other's territory.

"It's nice of you to finally join us, Beltaine." Misha's voice was cold.

She shrugged. "I got here as fast as I wanted to."

She saw Misha's gaze widen. Kalan must have come in, but she wasn't willing to look behind her and check. She saw a gleam of interest flare in the other woman's eyes. *Uh-oh*, she thought. *Kalan might want to run. He'll think I'm the best thing he's ever seen if she gets her claws into him.* She wasn't inclined to warn him, though.

"What's so important you had to drag me away from my regularly scheduled business?" She didn't try to hide her annoyance.

"What have you found out about the ripping of the Veil?" the bishop asked, his gaze dismissing her and settling on Kalan.

The angel took a breath, and she stepped on his foot. There were times when she wished her powers worked on angels, because she would have sent him far away from this place.

"I'm looking into a few leads. I'm leaving town tonight. I'll be happy to check in when I get back." She grinned at them all.

"Don't lie to us. You won't like the consequences," Misha warned.

"I don't like working for you now. What sort of consequences would change my attitude? Killing me might put you out of your misery, but it's no punishment for me. I'll cease to exist, and you'll be dealing with the demons on your own," she pointed out.

"What about your friend, Father Roger? He might have something different to say."

She managed not to tense or change her expression. "Go ahead—kill him if you want to."

She jabbed an elbow into Kalan's stomach to stop his protest.

"It's not a wise thing to do, Beltaine. Your soul is close to being lost to the darkness." The bishop sneered at her.

"Then telling you to kill Roger doesn't put any more black marks on my soul. His death would be on *your* hands. It would be *your* sin, not mine."

She knew it sounded cold, but it could cost her everything if they knew how much she truly did care what happened to Roger. The Board would know they had a hold over her to make her their slave.

"Don't bother me again. I'll report in when I know something." Whirling around, she grabbed Kalan's arm and whispered, "Don't say anything until we're outside."

His fists clenched and unclenched, portraying just how angry he was. They hit the exit door at a brisk walk. They got halfway down the block before he exploded.

"How the hell could you offer Roger up to them as a sacrificial lamb?"

Eyeing him, she crossed her arms. "What did you want me to do?"

"Maybe say no or put up some sort of protest." He threw up his hands and walked a few steps away from her.

"Then he would be used as a threat every time I didn't do something they wanted. He would never be safe."

"So telling them to go ahead and kill him keeps him safe." The skepticism in his voice told her he didn't believe her.

She resumed walking down the sidewalk. "Yes, because it makes them think they gain nothing except

God's anger. They have no bargaining chip against me."

"What if they don't believe you? What if they kill him?" His questions were soft.

"Then they die." Her voice was equally soft, but it held menace and promise. His wince told her he believed her. She was glad he did because she didn't make that promise lightly. Killing had never been the easiest solution for her. Yes, she had killed before and she'd kill again, but the pain and guilt weren't things she ever got used to.

"Let's go." She gestured for him to follow her.

"Where are we going?"

"To my apartment to pick up some clothes and then to the train station for tickets. Unless you don't want to go?" At the shake of his head, she sighed. "I didn't think I'd get that lucky."

"You got *really* lucky in the elevator." He leered at her.

"No," she said. "You got lucky. I got screwed." She didn't keep the sarcasm out of her voice because at the moment, she didn't feel lucky. She felt like fate had it in for her.

Chapter Twelve

"I'd like to introduce our keynote speaker, Richard Starrer." The master of ceremonies presented Richard.

He plastered a smile on his face and made his way to the podium. He hated the ceremonies where he pretended to have gotten over the anger and shock of his son's death. It suited his plan to pull the wool over everyone's eyes. Let them believe he had come to terms with it. He snarled to himself. *Who the hell could accept the fact their child had chosen to kill himself rather than live?*

He got to the stage and stood staring out over the audience. A swell of triumph boiled inside him. In a few days, his plan would be fulfilled and he would rule Hell. The Devil would be no more, and no more children would be lost.

"Good afternoon, gentlemen. I'm here today to talk about the death of my son and how I overcame my grief with the help of the church."

* * * *

Kalan sighed as he and Beltaine settled into their seats. "Why are we taking the train?"

He knew she didn't want to talk to him. It was obvious by the way she sat with her arms crossed and her head turned away. Her silence drove him crazy. Having sex with her in the elevator had been wrong. His mind understood that and tried without success to convince his body of it. On the other hand, his heart screamed that it wanted this woman, and it wouldn't listen to anyone else.

"I asked you a question." He poked her shoulder.

She shot him a glance. "Your power might be unlimited, but mine isn't. Since I have to replenish what I use, I don't see the point in wasting it. Also, there are only a few cemeteries I can go to in Ericksberg, and I don't want to overtax those." She turned away.

"So what's our plan of attack?" He wasn't going to let her shut him out.

"I'm working with you because I have to. That doesn't mean I have to entertain you. Find something else to do while we're on the train."

He grabbed her chin and forced her to look at him. "You aren't going to ignore me. I know you enjoyed our times together as much as I did."

Jerking her chin out of his hand, she turned to face him. The way her shoulders were thrown back and her eyes narrowed, Kalan knew she was pissed.

"I'm willing to admit I enjoyed our little fuck sessions. I would even be willing to go so far as to say I'd love to do it again."

He couldn't help the grin that broke on his face, but it died a quick death when she continued.

"But we won't be having a repeat performance, because I know when I'm in over my head. When that happens, I retreat to a place where I'm not in danger of drowning."

He frowned. "You're in danger of drowning?"

Beltaine grimaced, and he knew she was having a battle with her inner self.

"I'm going to say this once and only once. If you tell anyone I said it, I'll deny it the entire time I'm roasting your balls over a fire. Do you understand?"

He winced and nodded.

She ran her hand through her long curls then looked out of the window while gripping her hands together. Her reluctance to say anything made him think she wasn't going to tell him after all.

"Beltaine?" he asked softly.

"Love is a strange and frightening emotion, don't you think?" Her voice came out in a rush.

A tingle went through his chest. Why was she talking about love?

"I suppose so, even though I have no experience with it."

"You've never been in love? There's no one you've ever loved?" Surprise laced her inquiry.

"I love God."

"That's a given, but there's never been anyone else?"

"Angels aren't supposed to feel love. In all honesty, I'm not sure I'd know what that particular emotion was." Frowning, he searched his memories for any moment that could be termed loving. He couldn't find any, except for the times he'd slept with Beltaine.

"Then how do you know if what you're feeling is lust or love?"

He shrugged. "I don't, because I've never felt lust before you, either."

"I know, and I—"

"Quiet," a deep voice interrupted before she could finish her sentence.

Damn, he thought.

"She has corrupted you already, Kalan. Swearing, even silently, isn't proper behavior for one of the Host." The Commander stood beside them in the aisle of the train.

"You've got to be fucking kidding me," Beltaine snarled as she stared up at the imposing angel.

If Kalan had been standing, the Commander would still have towered over him. His blue eyes were so fierce, sinners wept for mercy after one glance from them. The Commander was the ultimate Heavenly warrior. His sword had a large, gleaming blue diamond inserted in the pommel.

"I've warned you about your language, Beltaine. Watch how you talk around me." The Commander scowled at her.

"Or what? You'll fucking *kill* me?" She threw her arms wide. "Take your best shot because I'm getting really tired of all of you." Her gesture included Kalan.

"Maybe I should get rid of you."

She saw the deliberation in his eyes, and she knew he was giving her death serious thought. Searching her mind, she figured out that she didn't care. She was losing the small amount of patience she had, and all she wanted was to be left alone.

"Sir, you told me only Beltaine could help me catch the culprit," Kalan spoke up.

"Don't try to defend me or help me, Kalan. Don't get into the middle of something you don't understand." She continued to stare at Kalan's superior.

"She's right. Don't let me know your loyalty has changed." The Commander closed his bottomless blue eyes and sighed. "He's right. No one else but you can help him. So you are spared once more."

"Is there a reason why you're here, or did you not get your quota of fuck-with-Beltaine this week?" The minute the words came out of her mouth, she thought she had gone too far.

An angry growl came from the Commander's throat, and he reached for her. She wasn't going to cower in front of him. He might be the Commander of the Host, but that didn't mean he automatically got her respect. She wouldn't beg for her life, because in reality, what sort of life did she have?

"Stop." A presence entered their train car.

Time stopped, and Beltaine knew they were in trouble. The angels, even archangels, could only make it appear as if time had stopped. There was only one being who could stop it completely. She fell to her knees, for that being was one of the few she respected. Kalan and the Commander followed suit.

"It does you no honor, Commander, to give way to your anger and disgust for her. More is expected of you." The voice was as infinite as the universe and as small as a single drop of rain.

The Commander dropped his head. "I'm sorry."

She shivered as a light breeze brushed over her hair.

"From the moment of your birth, you have fought— not just me, but everyone who has held out a hand in love toward you. I admit to being puzzled by you, but you must stop antagonizing my angels. You try even their nearly unlimited patience." The voice held a slight tone of amused exasperation.

"Yes, Sir. I'll try."

"That's all I can ask. Now finish your mission, Commander, and remember she is off-limits to your judgment." The presence disappeared and time resumed.

The Commander glared at her as they all climbed to their feet. "I don't appreciate being played with."

"Amazingly, neither do I. Say what you have to say then do me the favor of leaving." She held his gaze.

"You need to find the book and return it to the Devil. Worse things than the Veil ripping could happen if the wrong person gets a hold of it."

"Worse than the Veil disappearing?" Her eyebrows shot up. Shaking her head, she laughed. "I think the wrong person already has it. We'll return it to him, along with saving the world from rampaging angels and marauding demons."

"Do that." The Commander glanced over at Kalan, who had pressed up against the window, trying to become invisible. "Don't forget what your mission is."

"I won't, sir." Kalan nodded.

After the Commander disappeared, Beltaine dropped to her seat and groaned. "All I need is my mother to show up, and this would qualify as the worst day of my entire adult life."

"What the hell were you thinking?" Kalan flopped down next to her.

"Remember what he said about your language." She shook her finger at him.

"Screw my language. Do you have a death wish?"

"At the beginning of the week, I would have told you no, but it must have been buried somewhere deep inside." She winced as he clamped his hands around her biceps then shook her.

"There's no way in hell I'm going to let you get yourself killed. Do you hear me?" he demanded.

"I think everyone on the entire train can hear you, since you're shouting at the top of your lungs." She pried his fingers off her before putting a few inches of space between them. "Why are you suddenly concerned whether I live or die? Just yesterday you were telling me you'd kill me yourself if your Commander hadn't ordered you not to."

He rubbed his palms on his pants. "I don't know what changed. Now when I think of you not being around, there's this dark sadness in my heart."

She wasn't sure if she should be happy to hear his confession or if she should run screaming. She hated feeling confused, so she chose to ignore his comment.

Leaning back in her seat, she closed her eyes. "I'm taking a nap. Dealing with Heavenly creatures tires me out."

"What were you going to tell me before the Commander came?" He was circling back to their other conversation.

"Sorry, you had your chance. Due to divine intervention, you'll not be able to hear me make a total ass of myself." Turning her back on him, she hid her smile at his grumbling.

"I wish he'd never dropped in," Kalan muttered.

"You and me both. Now, try to get some sleep. Ericksberg will get here before we know it, and we have to be ready for it." She emptied her mind and relaxed.

Chapter Thirteen

So the Board was sending someone to investigate the Veil. Richard grinned and rubbed his hands together. The Board's lackey was spoken of in hushed tones. No one would tell him anything. He moved to stare out of his office window toward St Benedict's. The time wasn't right for the final ritual.

A knock sounded on his door, and he whirled around as it opened. His secretary stood in the doorway with an annoyed look on her face.

"He said he was a friend of your son's, Mr Starrer. I told him you were busy, but he wouldn't go away."

Richard's anger flared as Johnson slinked into his inner office. His servant leered at his secretary.

"It's okay, Miss Robinson. I have a few minutes free." He waited until the door shut before he stalked over to Johnson.

The ex-con's cocky grin faded as he caught sight of Richard's anger. His head dropped and he whimpered. Grabbing Johnson's arm, Richard twisted it up behind the man's back and drove a soft cry from his lips. The pain forced his servant to his knees.

Richard leaned over and growled, "Tell me why I shouldn't kill you here?" Another gasp came as he jerked the man's arm higher between his shoulder blades. "I recall telling you I *never* wanted to see you outside of the catacombs. Disobeying my orders carries a stiff penalty."

"I know, master, but I've got news," Johnson sniveled.

"This news was so important you couldn't call me with it?" He shoved the man away from him. Marching to his desk, Richard pulled some Kleenex out and wiped his hands.

"I got a lead on that whore you wanted me to look for." Johnson stared up at him with puppy-like intensity.

"So?"

"Well, she's in the city, and I don't have train fare to get there."

Richard yanked open a desk drawer and pulled out a small steel box. Fishing a key from his pocket, he unlocked it. He grabbed a fistful of bills and threw them at Johnson. The man scrambled around the floor, picking them up.

"Take it and get out. Find the whore, but don't kill her. Bring her to the catacombs. I'll find out if she told anyone then I'll use her to build my power." He knew he had to build up his strength because tearing the Veil would take everything he had.

"I thought you wanted a virgin, master." Johnson look confused.

"For the final ritual, I do need virgin blood, but the whore's blood will work for now." Richard paced toward his servant. Johnson scuttled back. "Get the hell out of here, and don't *ever* come here again."

"Yes, sir. I'll contact you when I get back." Johnson jumped to his feet and raced from the office.

Richard sighed and returned to his desk. He pulled a small, leather-bound book from the box. Its cracked cover and fragile pages spoke of its age. Stroking it, he smiled. This book would ensure all his plans went right.

* * * *

"What do we do now?" Kalan asked Beltaine when they stepped from the train into the station.

"We get settled, and then we look around." She hoisted her bag over her shoulder and headed toward the exit door.

"Shouldn't we go straight to St Benedict's and ask some questions?" Since he wouldn't leave his sword behind, he needed to disguise it. He wove his power into the spell and settled the illusion over his body. When most people looked at him, they would see a large man with a guitar strapped to his back.

It had only taken a moment, but when he finished and opened his eyes, Beltaine was standing by the exit, tapping her toe impatiently. "The nap must have done you some good." He smiled at her.

She grunted and ushered him out. He gawked in amazement. The city they'd departed was a big, bustling urban world. His ears had been assaulted at all hours of the day and night by car horns, music, and people. As he stood outside the train station, he felt he had traveled back in time. Ericksberg had an old-world charm. The buildings were brick and wood. There were flowers planted along the streets. Auto traffic was minimal, with most people either walking or riding bikes.

"Is this place real?" he asked.

"It's real. Come on. I have an apartment near St Benedict's. We'll drop our stuff and grab supper." She led the way down to the corner.

"Why do you have an apartment here?" He kept pace with her.

"You never know when you'll need a bolt-hole. I have a couple different ones in the city, as well."

"Does anyone else know about them?" He found his gaze pulled from the quaint shops around them to her firm butt in front of him.

"The only one who knows is Roger, and he only knows about this one. I've let him use it when he comes to visit some of the parishes in town."

"It's nice to know you're willing to share." He hoped she'd be inclined to share her body later on.

"How do you know it isn't our secret love nest, where we meet to get out from under the all-seeing eye of the church?"

Her tone was teasing, but he noticed her gaze never seemed to stop. She searched each face and every alley. He moved closer to her and asked quietly, "Are we being followed?"

Shaking her head, she answered, "Not yet. But something is wrong in this town, Kalan. Can't you feel it?"

He burrowed below the idyllic tranquility the town seemed to exude and found an undercurrent of nervousness and fear. There were bright smiles on the people's faces, but they wouldn't meet his eyes. "I see what you mean."

"Betsy and Azubah were right. Our problem originates here."

"So it would seem. Now that we know they didn't steer us wrong, what do we do about it?" He hurried to catch up with her.

"At the moment, we don't rock the boat. If the man who did finds out we're looking for him, he'll go underground and we'll never find him before it's too late." She turned in to one of the alleys.

"I thought you wanted this whole thing taken care of as soon as possible." Kalan kept his eyes moving. There was a sinister feel to the area they were in now.

"I did—I do—but not at the risk of making a mistake and letting the guy go free."

"So you'll tolerate my presence?"

She paused a moment to glare at him. "Is that your favorite word or something? I would say I'll *suffer* your presence, and not quietly, either." She walked a few more steps and stopped in front of a bright red door. "Here's our place."

Beltaine pulled a key out of her pocket and opened the door. She went in first, flicking on lights as she climbed the stairs. He entered the studio apartment as she was tossing her bag on the couch. Glancing around, he realized the studio was as barren as her apartment back in the city. There was one couch and a chair in the living room. The bed was hidden behind a blanket that hung from the ceiling. The small kitchen held a refrigerator, a sink and a few cabinets, but no stove.

"You don't spend much time here, do you?" It really wasn't a question.

She glanced around as if looking at it for the first time. She shrugged. "It serves my needs. I'm not looking for comforts or things to make me feel at home. It's a place to sleep, that's all."

"There's only one bed." He couldn't help but bring up that fact.

"Oh, my God, you're right. I must have forgotten about that." She grinned at him. "I guess you'll be sleeping on the couch."

He grimaced and tried to imagine squeezing his body onto the couch. He shouldn't have assumed she'd allow him to share her bed, especially since it didn't seem she had forgiven him for the way he'd left that morning. "So what's for supper?"

"Whatever restaurant I feel like eating at." She stuck her key in her pocket and walked out of the door.

"Don't you feel like cooking?" He scrambled down the stairs behind her.

"I *never* feel like cooking. Why waste my time and energy on something I can have someone else do for me?" She hit the sidewalk and turned toward the other entrance to the alley.

She had a point, he thought. Also, he assumed she didn't have the patience to cook anything. "Where are we going?"

"A little Chinese place where I might be able to get some information with my fortune cookie."

Chapter Fourteen

Beltaine cracked open her fortune cookie and growled.

Kalan glanced up from his to inquire, "What's wrong?"

"I hate it when they are ambiguous."

"What does it say?"

She crumbled the paper in her hand. "'You must dig deep to find what you seek.'" She noticed that he folded his and stuck it in his pocket. "What did yours say?"

"Nothing important. Now what?" After standing, he threw some money down on the table.

"We go clubbing." She allowed him to lead the way from the building. She wanted to be able to stare at his tight ass without him thinking she was doing it on purpose.

"Armageddon is fast approaching, and you want to go dancing." He shook his head.

Pouting, she ran her finger down his chest to where his waistband was. "A girl needs a little fun once in a while. Dancing relaxes me and if I'm not stressed, I probably won't cause problems when we go to St Benedict's." With an evil grin, she trailed her finger down the growing bulge in his pants.

"Don't tease if you don't plan on doing anything about it," he warned.

She purred. "Maybe you'll get lucky tonight, angel boy."

"What brought about this sudden change?" His puzzled frown marred his gorgeous face.

"I did some thinking on the train. If I'm already going to be hung for a lamb, I might as well be hung for a sheep. You and I are going to enjoy this strange attraction we have." She smiled at him. *And when you leave, it'll hurt, but not as much as it would if I hadn't taken advantage of it.* She wouldn't tell him that. It gave him more power over her than she was willing to admit.

Beltaine had Kalan follow her into Playground, her favorite club on the seedier side of Ericksberg. She'd told the truth when she said she liked to dance, but she had another reason for coming to the club.

"Betsy stopped by this morning after you left," she told him. "The last john she was with before she hightailed it to the city was a greasy, slender man with several prison tattoos. The most recognizable one was an angel surrounded by flames. He mumbled stuff about amassing an army and invading Hell."

Kalan's face brightened. "We'll be able to find him, then. Did she give you his name? Do you think he's the one who ripped the Veil?"

"They didn't exchange names. Professional courtesy doesn't allow for them to know each other's name. Hell, if you were the john, would you want some prostitute knowing your real name? What if you were walking down the street with your significant other and this sleazy chick started calling out your name? How would you explain that?" She laughed.

As he turned to face her, she saw disappointment race across his face. "So we don't know where to find him."

"He isn't the one who ripped the Veil anyway. I don't think anyone who would pay Betsy for sex is smart enough to figure out how to invade Hell. The way we find the man is by stopping into clubs like this and asking for him." They had stopped at the edge of the dance floor. "We'll ask after we dance."

She flowed into him and wrapped her arms around his neck. His sharp intake of breath rubbed his chest against her sensitive nipples. Oh, that was what she was looking for. Pulling his head down, she ground her hips into his and swallowed his moan.

"Beltaine," he groaned.

"Hush, love. Nothing's going to happen that either of us will regret," she whispered into his lips.

Her tongue dove into his mouth, like a bee looking for nectar. She stroked it along the ridges of his teeth. She caressed the roof of his mouth, and his body twitched. Anchoring her hands in his hair, she entwined her tongue with his and pulled it into her mouth. He groaned again as she sucked on him.

"Beltaine, we shouldn't do this here." His voice was harsh as he pulled away from her an inch or so.

"The room is dark. No one is looking at us. Dance with me, Kalan." She hated the fact that her voice sounded so needy, but she really did want to dance with him and feel his body touching hers.

"There's no music playing. We're not dancing. You're fucking my mouth." His eyes closed, and he bit his lip as she rolled her hips against his cock.

"Love, that's all part of dancing." She pulled his head back to hers and kissed him hard. She demanded he let her in, and the thrust of her tongue was accompanied by the twitch of her hips.

She hummed her approval as Kalan reached down and grabbed her ass. He raised her just enough so her pussy was moving over his cock. She wrapped her leg tight around his thigh and stroked her body against his. She made sure she kept the same rhythm with her tongue. The pleasure was building, and her pussy was drenched. Her leather pants were sliding across her clit, and with his erection, it created the right friction. His breathing sped up, and his hips were thrusting. He took one hand off her ass and reached up to palm her breast. When he pinched her nipple between his fingers and rolled it, she threw her head back and managed to apply just the right pressure to her clit to come. Her orgasm tore through her with lightning speed, causing a moan to burst from her throat.

Kalan leaned down and bit her neck as he thrust fast and hard. She longed to have his cock in her pussy when he came, but that wasn't going to happen at the club. She continued to grind herself into him as she held on, and she couldn't help a smile of triumph when he groaned long and low. His hips jerked several times, and she knew he was slowly coming down off his climax high.

Dropping her leg, she stood on her own two feet again and brushed a lock of hair off his forehead. His blue eyes were hazy with satisfaction, and his smile was pure male happiness.

"Can you hear the music now?" She laughed.

"I always hear music when I'm with you."

Shaking her head, she grabbed his hand and led him toward the bar. "Let's get a drink and ask some questions."

"Now you want to play detective." He squeezed her hand and chuckled.

Chapter Fifteen

They had been in Playground for an hour, and Kalan was beginning to doubt they would ever learn anything about Betsy's john. He was certain he was learning the meaning of frustration. Since their first time on the dance floor, where Beltaine had managed to drive him wild enough to come in his pants, she hadn't danced with him. She kissed him and rubbed that gorgeous body all over him, but she wouldn't let him wrap his arms around her.

"Come on, just one more dance," he pleaded.

Shaking her head, she said, "We're working now. I can't be distracted by that big, hard cock of yours. I need to keep my mind on what we're doing here."

Big, hard cock? Well that wasn't too bad a compliment, he guessed. He moved up behind her and pinned her against the high table they were standing by. She didn't struggle, just sighed and leaned back on his body. Sliding his hands over her stomach, he burrowed his hands under her tank top and cupped her breasts. He grazed her nipples with his fingertips, and a shudder moved her body.

"You like that, baby?" he leaned over and whispered in her ear.

"I like that very much, but don't call me 'baby' again," she told him in a low, aroused voice.

He pinched her nipples between his fingers and tugged. She pushed her hips and plastered her butt over his erection. He proceeded to torment her like she had done to him with her tongue and her hips. He tugged on her nipples while thrusting his groin against her ass. One of his hands crept from her breast down to her mound. He managed to keep her distracted enough that she didn't protest when he unbuttoned her pants and slid the zipper down. Beltaine jerked when his fingers slid between her legs. He teased and stroked her, running the tips of his fingers through her juices and caressing her warm skin, but never touching her clit. Her hips surged with each gentle touch.

She growled. "Kalan."

He knew she was warning him. "Am I not doing something right? Do you want me to do something different?"

She turned her face into his neck and bit him.

"Ow!" He jerked and got the hint.

He pushed his foot between her feet and spread them farther apart. Pressing the heel of his palm on her clit, he thrust two of his fingers into her dripping pussy.

"Ride my fingers," he ordered.

She moaned and rocked her hips in time to the rhythm he established. Each thrust caused his hand to rub against her clit, and he felt the pressure build in her. Her inner muscles tightened to a painful degree around his fingers, and he groaned. He went in deep, and as he ground his hand on her throbbing clit, he scraped them against her sweet spot.

He leaned over and kissed her as her orgasm ripped a scream from her. Her juices coated his hand. He continued to stroke her, trying to gently soothe her body. When her last quiver ended, he drew his hand from between her thighs. She turned to glare at him as she buttoned her pants.

"I'll get you for that, angel boy. Remember, I'm very good at revenge."

Her threat didn't worry him since he could see the pleasure burning in her eyes.

"Let's go talk to the bartender." She headed in the direction of the bar.

"Ok," he murmured, licking her juices from his hand.

Beltaine didn't wait to see if Kalan followed her. At the moment, she hoped he'd stay on the other side of the club. Her mind was trying to get her to rethink her decision regarding sex with Kalan. She had never been so distracted on a mission. All she could think about was Kalan's arms around her and the solid length of his cock teasing her ass as she rode his fingers. This was why she worked alone. They had been lucky so far tonight, but they would need to keep their minds out of bed and focused on getting information.

Kalan joined her as she caught the attention of the bartender. He was tall and very thin, but a flare of red in his eyes and a flash of fang told her he was a demon.

"I've no trouble with you. I only want some answers." She put her hands on the bar as a demonstration of peaceful intent.

The demon's eyes narrowed and darted to Kalan. "What about him?"

"He'll keep his mouth shut and not cause problems."

Kalan opened his mouth, and she kicked him in the shin. He glared at her, and she smiled at him.

"What do you want?" The demon picked up a glass and started to polish it.

"I'm looking for a man. He's greasy and slender. Dark hair and dark eyes. He's got a lot of tattoos. Most memorable is an angel wreathed in flames. He's probably an addict, as well." She was watching closely enough to see the flare of recognition in the demon's eyes.

"I'm not sure if I know him. Why are you looking for him?"

"We're looking for someone he knows." She was willing to give out a small piece of information.

"You looking for someone he knows doesn't mean anything to me." The demon set the glass down and started to walk away.

"It should. Your life might depend on it," Beltaine snarled.

The bartender shrugged. "The Board's influence doesn't reach this far. I know who you are, and you don't scare me. Not even with an angel backing you up." The demon leaned forward to frown at her.

She allowed her anger to flood her. Baring her teeth, her fangs lengthened. Lunging over the counter, she grabbed the demon's shirt to drag the creature toward her.

"I want to clear up some things for you. I don't need anyone backing me up. I'm perfectly capable of killing you all on my own. And it is a matter of life and death, demon. If I don't find the man that greaseball works for, then all Hell is going to break loose." She pointed to Kalan standing beside her. "This angel happens to be one of the Host. If I don't find the man, then the Host will be unleashed and we'll all be dead. When I kill, I don't usually make anyone suffer, but the Host isn't as nice about the whole death thing."

She saw understanding blossom in the demon's widening eyes. She pushed him away from her hard enough he slammed back into the liquor counter. "Tell me what I want to know."

"I only know his name is Johnson. He's been in a few times bragging about this new boss he has. He's a rich guy, according to Johnson." The demon shrugged. "Whether that's true or not, I don't know. Johnson has been flashing a lot of money lately."

"Where can I find this Johnson?" Leaning on the counter, she snarled at the bartender.

"I've heard he's gone up to the city. That's all I know." The demon sounded sincere enough, so Beltaine was willing to believe him.

She shoved several bills across the counter and grabbed Kalan's arm. "Let's go."

When they were outside, Kalan whirled on her and demanded, "Why didn't you let me speak?"

"There's no point in it. A demon isn't going to trust any word an angel tells it." She wanted to skip down the street. "Now we have a name to work with. I'm not happy to know he went to the city, though. That might mean he knows where Betsy is, but I've done all I can to help her."

"You trust me," Kalan pointed out.

"Not because I want to, but because I have to." She shrugged and glanced at him. He had a frown on his face. "Listen, I'll admit that you aren't that bad. I trust you as much as you trust me."

She knew he couldn't argue with that. Stopping, she turned and wrapped her arms around his neck. She pulled his head down and crushed her mouth to his. "To hell with trust, love—let's get back to bed."

Her mouth muffled his agreement. She laughed and dragged him down the street.

Chapter Sixteen

A crash woke Beltaine up from the best night's sleep she'd had in a long time. Roger's voice called from the other side of the blanket she used as a divider in the apartment.

"Doesn't he ever knock?" Kalan grumbled.

"Not usually." She chuckled.

"What the —?" Roger's voice cut off suddenly

She looked up to find Roger holding the blanket back. His eyes were wide at the sight of her and Kalan in bed together. Kalan clothed himself with a wave and climbed out of bed. She fell back and pulled the blankets over her head.

"Do I really have to deal with both of you this early in the morning?" She groaned.

"No, you will only have to deal with me, child." A deep, serene voice entered the room.

Beltaine shot out of the bed, maintaining enough sense to take the blankets with her. She stared in astonishment at the middle-aged man who joined Roger in peeking around the blanket.

"Father Simon, what are you doing here?"

"Get dressed, child. We'll be out in the living room." With a glance, the priest gathered Kalan and Roger and led them out into the other living area.

"Shit," she whispered. What had possessed Roger to bring Father Simon here?

She waved her hand to dress herself without worrying about leaving the room. Kalan seemed perplexed by her choice of clothing. She wore a pair of tight, faded jeans. Her T-shirt was perfectly respectable. Her hair was in a braid down her back. She knew she didn't look like her normal kick-ass self, but she wouldn't dress that way around Father Simon.

She went to where the man was standing, staring out of the window.

"Father Simon." She knelt in front of the priest and kissed the hand he held out to her. She felt Kalan's amazement pouring off him.

"No, child. There is no need to kneel before me. The guilt I bear toward you overrules any respect you should have for me."

She climbed to her feet and gestured to the couch. "I'm sorry it isn't nicer, Father. If Roger had warned me he was bringing you, I would've cleaned up." She glared at Roger and grabbed the torn tank top off the floor, where it had landed last night while she and Kalan had stripped, eager to have each other again.

Her friend still had a stunned look on his face. She grabbed his hand and dragged him to the far side of the studio, where the kitchen stood. "We'll make tea for everyone."

As soon as they got far enough away, she whirled on him. "What the hell were you thinking?" she whispered.

Roger shrugged. "He insisted I bring him here. How could I argue with him? I figured it wouldn't matter.

How was I to know you two would be in bed? Especially after you told me you wouldn't be touching him again." He glared at her.

She took four mugs down and pulled out the tea canister. "I don't want to discuss it at the moment. Besides, I've never harassed you about anyone you slept with."

"Considering there weren't that many, you didn't have time to before I went into the priesthood. But an angel, Beltaine? What were you thinking?" Roger clasped her shoulder and turned her to look at him.

She glanced into the eyes of her only friend and shrugged. "I'm tired of thinking and worrying about what will happen if I sleep with him. I can't stay away from him, and I've never been good at denying myself anything I want. So I'm going to have him, and I'll deal with the consequences later. When it comes to that rather irritating angel, I'm not thinking with my head." She filled the teakettle and heated the water. "Can we skip over all the reasons why I shouldn't be having sex with him? Why is Father Simon in Ericksberg?"

"Last night, I asked him about the book you and Kalan are looking for. He ordered me to bring him to you. We drove all night to get here."

The kettle whistled, and she poured the water over the tea leaves. Picking up two of the mugs, she gestured to Roger to grab the other two. Kalan and Father Simon were sitting on the couch. She handed out the mugs and sat on the floor at the priest's feet.

Father Simon cupped the mug in his gloved hands. "Thank you, child. I'm sorry to wake you, but when Roger came to me with your question, I knew I had to talk to you personally."

"Why? What's so important about the book?" Kalan asked.

Father Simon studied the angel, and Kalan shifted uncomfortably. Beltaine imagined his gaze felt a lot like the Commander's to Kalan.

"First, I must ask you where you heard about it?"

Beltaine wasn't thrilled about telling the priest where the information came from.

"Child, I know your history. Nothing you tell me will change my opinion of you." Father Simon reached out to touch the top of Beltaine's head.

A sigh issued from her, and she nodded. "My mother came and told me that a mortal she had been sleeping with had stolen a book the Devil wants back."

"What happened to the mortal?"

"The Devil killed him," Kalan informed the man. "It must have been after he was killed that the Devil figured out the man had sold it."

"He always goes off without getting all the information first." Father Simon shook his head.

"You speak as if you know the Devil well, Father." Kalan's casual tone didn't hide his curiosity.

The priest smiled. "I've met him on several occasions. There are times we've had to deal with each other." Father Simon's eyes drifted over to Beltaine.

"I'd think a man like you would shun that creature." Kalan's scorn dripped in his words.

Beltaine wanted to slap the superior look off Kalan's face. How dare he judge Father Simon? Ready to jump to her feet, she relaxed slightly when the priest nodded. Roger squeezed her shoulder, asking her for restraint.

"I am a man, Kalan, nothing more and nothing less. In my younger days, I made mistakes before I found my path. Judging someone without knowing their whole story doesn't become an angel of the Host." Simon rebuked the angel in a gentle voice.

"He's the Devil. He gave up Heaven for his own selfish reasons," Kalan protested.

Beltaine couldn't stop from saying, "What do you know about him?"

"Our stories are full of the Devil and his fall from grace," Kalan said.

"Stories and legends." Her contempt was plain as she curled her lip. "Each legend has a grain of truth, but those of the Devil have really been blown out of proportion."

"That's true. As much as you might despise and hate him, you must realize he has a purpose in this world like the rest of us. How do we know for sure his fall wasn't part of a larger plan?" Simon sounded so calm and assured that Beltaine found herself almost agreeing with him.

She pulled herself up short. *Don't get sucked in, Beltaine, old girl,* her cynical inner voice warned her. *Father Simon's a good man and one you've always respected, but it doesn't mean he's right. It doesn't mean that your life is anything other than a mistake.*

"This is very exciting, but can we get back to the book?" She steered the conversation where she wanted it to go.

"Okay. Do we know anything about the book, besides the fact that the Devil will come to collect it himself?" Kalan inquired.

Beltaine shrugged. "I don't care about the book. My mother let it get stolen—she can be the one to fix it. I want to find the man who's ripping the Veil and stop him before he invades Hell."

"The book is the reason why the Veil was ripped," Simon stated.

"You mean, the man we're looking for is likely to have the book in his possession?"

"Isn't that what the Commander told us on the train? He ordered us to find the book and return it to the Devil," Kalan reminded her.

"Damn, why can't I ignore all of this and find some nice spot to hide?" She groaned.

"You can't ignore this, child. It's your calling." Father Simon studied his tea as he spoke to her.

"What would happen if I stopped answering that particular call?" Beltaine dropped her head into her hands.

"I don't know, but I don't want to take a chance on finding out." Father Simon reached out to touch her hair. "We haven't found your true purpose for being here. You must have patience."

"Sorry, Father, that's one of the many virtues I didn't get." Her rueful smile brought grins to all the male faces in the room.

"I know, child. You've always been so impatient. You live your life like you only have a short time on this earth."

"Maybe my soul is trying to tell me something."

Roger's stomach grumbled, and they all laughed.

"My stomach is telling me I'm hungry. Beltaine, why don't you and I go down to the restaurant on the corner and get some breakfast for us all?" Roger suggested, as he stood from the chair.

She smiled at him and held out her hand to let him help her stand up. "Good idea. We'll bring some food back."

"We could all go." Simon started to stand as well.

"No, Father. You're still recovering from your latest episode. You shouldn't exert yourself any more than necessary." Roger stopped the priest with a gentle hand. "Beltaine and I are quite capable of getting the food ourselves."

Chapter Seventeen

Kalan and the priest watched Roger and Beltaine walk out of the door. Kalan couldn't help but smile when he heard Beltaine's husky laugh drift back to them. He turned to meet the gaze of Father Simon and was reminded again of his Commander.

"It is nice to hear her laugh." Simon's voice was reflective. "She hasn't had much opportunity to do that."

"Not unless she's laughing at me." Kalan stood to move toward the windows.

"It is often only with Roger that she allows her walls to drop enough to laugh. Her life isn't sunshine and roses. She finds no joy in the world." Simon rubbed his face and sighed. "I'm afraid that is my fault."

Kalan turned to stare at him. "How could it be your fault? You aren't her father."

The priest leaned forward and rested his elbows on his knees. Staring down at the carpet under his feet, he sighed. "I knew her father. His heart wasn't committed to the church. He became a priest because he saw the power and wealth some of the fathers have. He wanted it for himself. I was his mentor, and I tried to teach him the truth of serving God, but he couldn't learn. I believe his mind snapped when he was defrocked and excommunicated from the church."

Kalan didn't move. Father Simon's memories were a part of Beltaine he would never learn from her. Her life before her father's death was locked tight inside her heart, and sharing it with him wasn't on her list of things to do.

The priest rubbed the palm of his right hand with the fingers of his left. "The night before Beltaine arrived, I had my first episode. Maybe it was God's warning that something was coming to change my life completely."

"What kind of episode?" Kalan couldn't help but ask. He had heard Father Angelo mention it, as well as Roger.

Simon slowly eased the leather gloves off his hands and held his palms up for Kalan to look at them. Kalan gasped as he stared down at the holes in the priest's hands. No blood seemed to be leaking from them. His eyes shot up to meet Simon's gaze. The priest lifted the bangs on his forehead, and Kalan saw a series of round wounds piercing the man's skin.

"If I were to take off my clothes, you would see wounds on my side and feet, and lash marks across my back and chest." Simon dropped the bangs back down before sliding the gloves on.

"The stigmata? I thought only saints got it." Kalan bit his lip. That was a crass thing to say. "I mean..."

"I know what you mean, child, and you're right. It is usually those who end up saints who get it. I have yet to decide if this is an honor from God or a punishment. Only time and God will be able to tell me." Simon gave a soft laugh. "The ecstasy starts on Friday and lasts until Sunday. The day of Christ's death to the day of his rising. I'm in a trance and know nothing during those three days. It used to be when I came out of it, it was like nothing had ever happened. Now, the wounds are still visible and I spend several days in my room, recovering."

"You were recovering when we stopped by yesterday." Kalan thought about it. "Do you serve a parish, Father?"

"No." Simon took a sip of the tea he had set on the floor. "No parish would want a priest who wasn't able to serve them whenever they need him. I'm the archivist for the church."

"You were Beltaine's father's mentor?"

"Yes, and every day I regret that I didn't convince him to leave the priesthood before she was born."

"How are you to blame for her? There was no way you could have known God would allow such an abomination to live."

Simon stared at him with a shuttered expression. "You share her body, and yet you still call her an abomination. That seems strange to me."

Kalan shrugged. "It was a slip of the tongue, Father. I'm trying to see her as more than what my eyes tell me she is."

"Then you are learning." The priest closed his eyes. "It wasn't Beltaine's birth I regret. She is a true joy and has a loyal heart, if you can get around her prickly outside. Maybe if I had managed to get her father to leave, her mother would have picked a different priest to seduce that night. Maybe Beltaine wouldn't have grown up being punished for something she couldn't help being. Her father never believed in God, so he couldn't understand that she might have been a gift instead of a punishment."

"But why would God punish you for what happened to her?" Kalan still didn't understand.

"I knew what was happening to her. Roger started coming to confession at the age of ten, and he would tell me about the abuse she suffered. Roger doesn't know that Beltaine's father was a priest. He only knows he wasn't much of a father to her. Has she told you how he died?" Simon glanced up at him.

He nodded. His mind hadn't worked its way around that yet. It didn't seem right to him that a young girl had to kill her own father to protect herself.

"After it happened, Roger came to me and confessed. He helped Beltaine make it look like her father had committed suicide. It was then that I went to the child and offered my help. At the graveside of her father, she looked at me with those cold amber eyes and said—"

"'God turned his back on me the minute I was born. I'll take no hand-outs from another of his church.'" Beltaine's voice was cold.

Kalan looked up to see her and Roger standing in the doorway. He had been so caught up in Father Simon's story he hadn't heard the door open. He saw her anger in the flare of red in her eyes. She stalked to the kitchen, where she pulled containers of food out of the bags she and Roger carried. Roger helped her, and an uncomfortable silence descended over them all.

"I'm sorry. I asked Father Simon why he felt guilty." Kalan's gaze darted around the room, trying not to meet her eyes while he explained.

Beltaine fought her way through the anger. She couldn't believe Father Simon would betray her secrets like that. "It wasn't his story to tell." She filled a plate with food and took it to the priest.

"The parts I told him were mine to tell, Beltaine. I told him nothing of your life before I came into it. I can't tell what I don't know or what I am bound by the law of God not to tell." Simon took the plate and smiled at her. He grabbed her wrist and stared at her until she nodded.

"What about *my* plate?" Kalan asked from where he stood at the window.

"I don't see any broken arms or legs, so you can get it yourself." She moved back to help Roger with his plate.

"Shouldn't you be the good hostess and serve all your guests breakfast?" His grin had a cocky tilt to it, and she knew he was goading her on purpose.

Her hand tightened on a glass. Roger grabbed it out of her possession before she could throw it at the smirking angel. "You aren't a guest. You are a rash on my ass."

All three men looked at her with puzzled expressions. She laughed. "He's irritating and something I want to get rid of as quickly as possible."

"Last night you said you wanted to keep me." His eyes were darkening with desire.

Heat raced through her and pooled in her pussy. Damn, but the angel was hot, and he knew she wanted him. Well, she wasn't going to give him the satisfaction of knowing he was turning her on. "That was last night, and a woman has the right to change her mind." She turned her back on him and gathered some food for herself.

When she settled down on the floor across from Father Simon, Roger was handing Kalan his breakfast.

After they took the edge off their hunger, she brought the book up again.

"What is this book that everyone is freaking out about?"

"When the Devil was sent to Hell, he and God made a deal. The Devil would stay in Hell and not bother the mortals on Earth. Note he didn't make any such promises for the demons residing in Hell with him. God was fine with that, but He wanted a barrier to keep the higher lords from leaving Hell and a way to keep mortals from wandering into the Devil's domain. They created the Veil, using the powers of both Heaven and Hell. There were members of the Heavenly Host who weren't happy with the punishment the Devil received. They felt he should have died for his rebellion." Simon looked over at Kalan. "Your Commander is one of them."

"I would have never guessed." Beltaine's voice held sarcasm.

"Hush, child. It does no good to mock him," Simon admonished her.

"I know. He doesn't have much of a sense of humor." She couldn't help the shiver running down her spine as she remembered the Commander's anger toward her.

"No, he doesn't. So he and some of the other angels wrote down spells that would—if done properly—destroy the Devil and Hell," Father Simon told them.

"You're kidding. I would have thought the Devil or God would have destroyed the book." She took her plate out to the kitchen and looked back at the men.

"I don't pretend to understand why God allows those books to exist."

"Did you say books?"

"Yes, books. Two books were written. The Devil managed to get a hold of one copy, but the other was sent into hiding." Simon fidgeted with his gloves.

"Where is the other book, Father?" Beltaine had a feeling she didn't want to know, but even though ignorance might be bliss, it could end up getting her killed.

"The second copy is in the church archives." Simon leaned back on the couch and looked at her.

"Why am I not surprised?" She sat back down on the floor in front of him. "Have you read it?"

Simon shook his head. "I'm not going to get involved in a battle between Heaven and Hell."

"You're not, but it seems to me that I am. I wonder who suggested I should go after the man who was ripping the Veil. Why couldn't the Commander come down and punish the idiot?" She held up her hand, stopping whatever Kalan was about to say. "I know why he didn't. First of all, the Host isn't supposed to involve themselves in the activities of mortals. Second of all, he obviously doesn't care what happens to me. If I'm killed, that's all for the better and an event he won't be blamed for. So he wouldn't be breaking any promises he made to God. Last, if I fail, the Devil is destroyed and the Host is released to destroy demons and mortals alike. That would leave only God's most perfect creations, the angels, to rule." She snorted.

"Hey, most angels are perfect," Kalan protested.

"Honey, the only thing perfect about you is your body." She leaned over then patted his knee.

"And you're so perfect yourself," he huffed and sat back with a frown.

She joined in the laughter as Roger and Father Simon doubled over. "Oh, darling, I never said I was perfect. I'm about as far from perfect as you are from being a fallen angel."

"Whatever. Let's get back on target here." Kalan didn't look happy.

After standing, she went to sit on his lap. He wrapped his arms around her, and she snuggled close to him. Leaning over, she kissed his cheek and whispered, "I like you the way you are—an angel with a little bit of devil inside." She felt another pain in her chest when he smiled at her and kissed her back. Rubbing her chest, she turned to see Roger and Father Simon watching them. "What are you two staring at?"

"Nothing. The Devil doesn't realize there are two books. He thinks he's safe with the one, and usually it's in his possession. Now our worse fear has been realized. The book is out among mortals, and someone wants to invade Hell. You have to find out who it is and stop them, Beltaine. The world won't survive the arrival of both the Horde and the Host."

"I know. You can stay here for now, Father. Kalan and I are heading for St Benedict's. Maybe we'll get some information there." She stood up. "I have to change, and then we'll head out."

Chapter Eighteen

Trying not to be noticed, Richard was making his way down the side aisle of St Benedict's. He had been down to the catacombs, and he was brimming with power and triumph. The holes in the Veil were getting bigger without any more blood. The spell he had woven was working. A sudden chill crawling down his spine made him freeze like a rabbit in the gaze of a fox. He slowly glanced around and frowned.

A woman stood at the front of the church. She was dressed in a barely-there red tank top and painted-on black leather pants. Her blonde hair was loose and tumbled in curls down her back. She was beautiful in a cold and deadly way. He couldn't see the color of her eyes, but he knew she was staring at him.

He wondered if she could feel the power in him. There was no way he was getting any closer. Nodding politely, he turned and made his way out of the church. He would find out later who the woman was.

* * * *

Kalan chatted with the head priest while Beltaine wandered around the sanctuary. They'd figured the priest would talk to him without her presence.

"I was wondering if you've noticed anything strange going on around your church lately, Father?" Kalan asked Father Paul.

The priest's eyes followed Beltaine as she strolled around the altar and looked into the baptism fount. "Strange in what way, sir?"

"I don't know. People coming and going at odd hours or strange noises in the middle of the night? People who wouldn't normally come to services?" Kalan wasn't sure what he was supposed to be asking the priest, but he had seen the way the man's eyes had widened when Beltaine had shaken his hand. Father Paul wasn't ready to run her out, but he wasn't quite sure about accepting her with open arms.

"No, I can't think of anything." Paul's gaze didn't stray from Beltaine.

"She won't burn down the church, Father," Kalan said with exasperation.

"What?" The priest blinked and finally looked at Kalan. A blush stained his cheeks. "I know. Father Simon trusts her, and I'm willing to take his word, but I have never met one like her. So forgive me if I'm nervous."

"It's okay, Father. I take some getting used to. If you notice anything strange going on, please contact us." Beltaine appeared at Kalan's side.

"Certainly Miss... Er..." Father Paul looked confused.

"Beltaine is fine, Father. May we sit in a pew for a few minutes? We won't bother the others." She gestured to the people praying in the pews.

"Of course. St Benedict's is open to all." The priest nodded before scurrying away.

Kalan followed Beltaine to a pew in one of the alcoves off the main sanctuary. He sat down and sighed.

"Father Paul wasn't much help. I think he was more worried about you than what I was asking."

She shook her head. "He doesn't know much, I'll admit that, but it isn't his fault. His upbringing and the church have sheltered him much of his life."

"Upbringing?" He reached out and took her hand to pull her down on the pew beside him.

"He's from a privileged background. You can tell by the lack of an accent in his voice. Rich kids rarely see the bad side of life." She ran her finger over the palm of his hand and he found it hard to concentrate.

"His calling to the church came early in his life, so he went from the shelter of money to the protection of the church, and evil is a concept to him, not a reality." She leaned back and closed her eyes.

An energy wave rolled through him, and his muscles twitched as if he'd been shocked. He tightened his grip on her hand and continued the conversation.

"No wonder you don't respect him."

She rolled her head to look at him through half-open eyes. "Who said I didn't respect him?"

"Well, he is a priest and a man. I know your opinion on both those topics." He mustered a grin, but his breath caught in his throat, and a heavy pressure was weighing on his lungs as another wave rolled through him.

"I'm willing to admit I don't have a good opinion of priests or men, and I tend to be quick to judge. That doesn't mean I hate every single one I come across."

She nodded toward the priests' office. "He's young and naïve. He's part of a rich parish, so he's never been asked to deal with tough issues. That doesn't mean he isn't a good priest. It just means that at the moment, he's an ineffective one."

The energy grew oppressive, and he gasped. "Can you feel that?"

She didn't complain about the tight grip he had on her hand. "Yes. I think what we're looking for is somewhere in the church."

"The waves feel distorted, as if they have to travel a distance to reach us." It was getting hard to talk. Kalan stood and pulled her to her feet. "I need to get out of here."

He didn't give her a chance to argue with him. Tugging her down the aisle, he raced out of the church. He inhaled a huge breath, and the weight on his chest dissipated.

Beltaine stroked a hand over Kalan's shoulder as he gasped. The pulsing energy in the church had rejuvenated her, but he obviously hadn't experienced the same thing.

"Are you okay?" Worrying about someone other than Roger was strange.

"I'm starting to be. Didn't you feel as if you were choking?" He stared at her.

Shaking her head, she slid her arm around his waist, and they made their way down the steps. "I feel energized. It's the same way I feel after I've recharged in a cemetery."

"Why did it affect us differently?" He snuggled her closer to him. "If I feel like I'm choking and I'm not even close to the Veil, then how can I be in the same room with it?"

"We'll have to think on that and ask Father Simon when we see him. Let's get you back to the apartment. Maybe taking your mind off the problem will help you come up with a solution faster." She ran her free hand over his stomach and down to cup his cock through his pants.

He groaned. "I don't think I have enough energy to do anything with you, Beltaine."

"Don't worry, love. I'll do all the work." She laughed and kissed him.

They stumbled into her apartment when Beltaine opened the door twenty minutes later. She wrapped her arms around Kalan's neck and crushed her body against his while she devoured his lips. He made a half-hearted protest as she pushed him down on the couch.

"Wait. What if Father Simon and Roger are still here? There's no reason to hurry." He chuckled.

"No one's here, and yes, there is. I need you inside me soon, or I just might not make it." She pushed his hands down by his sides. She attacked the button and zipper on his pants with fierce concentration. "I told you I'd do all the work, so sit back and enjoy the ride, love."

He wasn't about to argue with her about it. "Just let me take my sword off."

"I forget that you're carrying that. At least, until I manage to touch it." She allowed him to lean forward and unbuckle the scabbard.

He slid it off and rested it on the floor next to the couch. He didn't want to be far from it, but he didn't want to risk her accidentally touching it, either. He knew the steel and the jewel were poisonous to her. He stretched his arms out on the top of the couch and smiled at her.

"I'm all yours."

She licked her lips as she looked at him. "Yes, you are."

His shaft hardened as she continued to stare at him. He sucked his stomach in as her fingers traced the waistband of his pants and stopped at the button. She popped it open and teased him by slowly lowering his zipper.

"Why are you taking so long? Just use your magic and get us both naked," he growled at her.

She smiled. "You've got to learn patience, love. There's no point wasting power when doing it the mortal way is more fun."

He drew in a deep breath when her fingers spread his pants open and his cock sprang out. He chuckled as she caressed his hips, sliding her hands around his waist to push his pants down.

"Lift your hips, angel boy," she demanded.

As he did what she ordered, he found his gaze caught by the expressions racing across Beltaine's face. He saw lust and passion there. Those emotions were to be expected, considering they couldn't keep their hands off each other. Surprise coursed through him when a fleeting moment of doubt seemed to make her hands hesitate to touch him. When a devilish gleam came into her eyes, he figured he'd imagined the doubt. Then any other thought fled his mind when she bent forward and surrounded his head with her hot mouth.

"Oh," was all he could manage.

Her laugh vibrated against his cock and pleasure shot through his body. Reaching out, he tangled his hands in her hair and cradled the back of her head. He leaned his head back against the cushions of the couch and closed his eyes. Sensations poured into him. The quick swirl of her tongue over the tip of his cock made his hips surge up toward her. She licked his shaft's slit, which leaked pre-cum. His blood raced to his groin in a frantic rush. One of her hands cupped his balls and applied light pressure to them.

"Beltaine," he moaned.

She fondled him with a firmer grip, and he moaned again. Drawing him deep into her mouth, she slid him far enough down her throat for her lips to rest at the base of his cock. Beltaine's other hand encircled him at the same spot, and as she drew her mouth off him, she pumped him slowly. Pleasure flooded him, and he felt his balls tighten. He was going to come soon. The combination of her hands and mouth drove him to the brink. Then she stopped and stood to move away from him.

"No, please, don't stop." There was no pride in him. His cock ruled his body, and it wanted more of her.

"Don't worry. I'll finish you." She grinned and stripped with ease.

He placed his hands at her waist as she straddled him. She gripped him then gave it a hard pump. He cried out as she impaled herself on him. Her wet sheath milked him with pulsing contractions. Kalan clung to her as she rode him, leisurely at first then with increasing speed. Soon he was almost pulling out of her then slamming her back down on his cock.

"Kalan," she screamed, and her pussy clenched so tight around him, he wasn't sure she'd let him go.

Her orgasm ripped through her in quick waves. He didn't fight it, and let his climax overwhelm him. He poured his seed into her. He couldn't seem to quit coming. It was like she was absorbing his soul into her body.

At last, he was drained dry, and exhaustion swelled. Every part of his body was limp. When she moved, he wanted to protest, but couldn't gather enough energy. He let her pull his vest off and help him lie down on the couch.

"We don't have time for a nap," he argued, as she tucked a blanket over him.

"Hush. Sure we do." Her smile wasn't the brittle one he had gotten used to seeing.

"I thought you said I'd never get you on your knees again," he murmured as his eyes drifted shut.

"I guess you shouldn't believe everything I say," she said quietly.

Chapter Nineteen

Maybe deciding to have a no-strings affair with Kalan wasn't the best idea she'd ever had. Beltaine stared over her shoulder at the angel sleeping on her couch. Without his piercing blue eyes staring into her soul, she relaxed and thought about the situation. She had never had this problem before. In the past when she saw an angel coming, she ran in the other direction. She had no use for them, and they had made it plain she was less than nothing in their eyes. Yet there was something different about Kalan. From the moment they had met, there was an irresistible force pulling them together, no matter how hard either of them fought it. Finally, she had decided to give up and roll with the pleasure he could invoke in her.

It didn't matter if Kalan liked her or not. She was used to men hating her. Her first experience of hatred had been from her father, and she'd become immune to it over the years. Taking another quick glance at the angel, she laughed quietly. She was just deluding herself. Even though she had told Kalan she was willing to take what he would give her, she wanted more. His intolerance of her demon heritage had waned a bit since they'd arrived in Ericksberg, but she knew it was still hidden deep inside him. She admitted to herself that it hurt to know he didn't like her but for some reason couldn't stay away from her. She didn't want a man loving her because he was forced into it.

Beltaine leaned her head against the windowpane and found the courage to reveal to her heart that she was lonely. No more lying to herself about being happy that there wasn't anyone waiting at home for her at night or no one special in her bed to hold her when nightmares came to haunt her. She wondered when she had started telling herself she was happier alone.

She thought of the day when she'd been fourteen and had ended her father's life. Killing him had been easy at the time. Her anger had grown into a raging beast, and she had lost control of it. She remembered wondering why her father hadn't killed her when she was a baby. He might not have fallen nearly so far so fast if she hadn't been around to serve as a reminder of his sins.

Two strong arms snaked around her waist and pulled her back against a warm, naked chest. Kalan's moist breath caressed her ear as he asked, "What has you thinking so hard?"

The urge to laugh and make a joke flitted through her mind, but she didn't want to lie to him. Whatever was going on between them was honest and real, even if it only lasted until the Veil was repaired. "I was wondering why my father didn't kill me when I was little."

He drew a sharp breath and stiffened behind her. Tightening his grip around her waist, he said, "Maybe he just couldn't kill an innocent baby."

A bitter laugh burst from her lips. "He never thought I was innocent. I think he believed I plotted the whole thing with my mother before I was even born. I think he kept me alive so he had someone to blame. With me dead, there wouldn't be anyone he could point at to show that it wasn't his fault he sinned."

She allowed his lips access to her neck. He nibbled his way down to her collarbone, where he sucked on her skin. She gasped, and he licked the mark with his tongue.

"Are you leaving your mark?"

"Just making sure the other guys know you're taken." His hands slid up to cup her breasts.

"What other guys? I don't see a line of them waiting." She arched her back and pushed her nipples against his palms.

"Well, you are a little scary, Beltaine."

She gasped, pressing her ass back toward his groin. "Yeah, having a demon for a mother puts a whole new spin on the scary mother-in-law tale."

He ground his erection into the crease in her ass. "I'm sure that's a part of it, but you don't let anyone close. You've got a huge wall built between you and the rest of the world. It's made of brick and topped with barbed wire. A guy could hurt himself trying to climb it to get to the real you."

"The real me? How do you know that what you see isn't the real me?" She spread her legs to give his questing hand better access to her pussy.

"Oh, I believe most of what I see is the real you, but there's a part you keep hidden, and I think it's to keep it from getting broken." His hand slid into her curls, fingers rubbing over her clit, and she moaned.

It was getting hard to concentrate on their conversation. "Can you blame me?"

He shook his head. "Your father sounds like he was an asshole, and why risk your heart again on someone who will betray your trust?" His fingers thrust into her, and she cried out.

"Kalan," she gasped.

"Why do you trust Roger as much as you do? He's a man and a priest. As far as I see, he has two strikes against him." He pushed at her back and she leaned over, placing her hands on the windowsill.

"He's been there, almost from the beginning, and he's never turned from me. No matter what I asked or did, he accepted me." She moaned as the blunt head of his cock teased her slit.

"So all a man has to do to make you trust him is be there for you, no matter the circumstances or where his loyalty lies."

They both sighed as his cock sank into her hot, wet pussy. She braced herself and arched her back to give him a better angle to fuck her. His thrusts were slow and gentle to start with, and she murmured her appreciation.

"Mmm…that's nice." Her body tingled. She showed her enjoyment of the activity by clenching her inner muscles to keep him in each time he started to pull out of her.

"Answer me, Beltaine. No matter where my loyalties lie, if I stood by you, would you trust me?" His next thrust was deeper and hit her sweet spot.

"Yes!" she screamed as he rode her faster and harder. "No more talk, Kalan. Fuck me now."

She heard him chuckle as he proceeded to do what she commanded. One of his strong hands caressed her spine with sweeping touches. The other crept around her hip to burrow and find her throbbing clit. He tugged at it with a firm grip. She cried out as desire rippled through her, centering in the place he fucked with force.

Lifting her head, she caught their reflection in the glass of the window. The sight of the ecstasy on Kalan's face as he watched his cock slide in and out of her brought her orgasm burning through her. She screamed, and her pussy clamped down on his cock as her body shuddered. Three fierce thrusts, and he was crying out her name as he shot his seed into her.

He barely managed to pull out of her and get them to the couch before they collapsed. Snuggling tight to him, she listened to his heartbeat and breathing slow down. His fingers ran through her hair, untangling the knots and soothing her. She struggled to stay awake as her eyes grew heavy. A kiss brushed the top of her head, and she heard him whisper.

"Sleep for a little while, love. I'll keep watch over both of us."

She knew he would and allowed sleep to take her.

* * * *

Creeping into St Benedict's, Richard tried not to alert Father Paul, who was still in the priests' office. A surge of excitement raced through him. Johnson had come through and was waiting for him in the catacombs with the whore and the other members of his army. He found the door in the wall and opened it. Slipping into the stairway leading down to the cellar, he reached out and felt the weight of the book in his pocket. It was time to strengthen the spell and see if he could rip the Veil even further.

Chapter Twenty

A violent knocking on Beltaine's door woke Kalan up. She murmured something as he lifted her off him and stood up. He tucked a blanket around her and found his pants. Sliding them on, he made his way to the door. Taking the time to check through the peephole, he saw Father Paul standing in front of the door, wearing an anxious expression.

"Who is it?" Beltaine asked as she sat up.

He turned to look at her and smiled. The blanket had slid down, leaving her breasts uncovered. "You might want to put some clothes on, love. Father Paul has come to pay us a visit."

Her eyes widened. "You're kidding, right?"

"No, he happens to be standing right outside your door. So put some clothes on." He chuckled as she stood up and raced to where the bed was behind the hanging blanket. "Good evening, Father. It's a surprise seeing you so soon after our visit."

"I know." The priest seemed agitated. "I remembered what you asked about anything strange at the church. And before tonight, nothing had been going on."

"But?" Beltaine asked as she slipped from behind the blanket.

Father Paul's eyes bugged out, and Kalan turned to see what she was wearing. He couldn't help but laugh. She was wearing her usual uniform—black leather pants and a red tank top—but there was a knife strapped to her left thigh and a handgun holstered on her right hip. Her amber eyes were flashing flares of red.

Turning back to the priest, he drew his attention. "But tonight?"

"Um…right. Tonight I was working late in the office when I heard a noise out in the sanctuary. The small outside door makes an unusual sound when it's opened. I heard it, so I went to investigate. I saw a figure make its way down one of the side aisles. I don't know whether it was a he or she. It was too dark, but it went about halfway down and then just disappeared."

"Disappeared?" Kalan glanced over at Beltaine and raised his eyebrows.

"He had to have disappeared. He never came out the other end of the aisle. I waited to see if he did and then went to search around. There wasn't anything there and no evidence anyone had been there, but I know what I saw and heard." Father Paul seemed to be trying to convince Beltaine because that was who he was staring at.

Kalan stood quietly, not wanting to disturb either of them. Beltaine studied the priest with a piercing gaze. It was almost as if she were staring directly into the priest's soul. Finally she nodded.

"I believe you. We know something's going on at your church. We just haven't been able to figure out what. So if you'll let us, we'll go back and take a look around. Maybe we'll see something you've overlooked." She gestured for the priest to lead the way out of the apartment.

"What do you think is going on?" Kalan asked, as they followed Father Paul down the stairs.

She shrugged. "Don't know. It took a lot of courage for him to come here. He came to see me alone. I have a reputation for not being very nice, so imagine how scared he was. Even if it turns out to be nothing, it doesn't hurt for us to go look." She gave him a smile and leaned in to whisper, "I was planning on checking the church out later tonight anyway."

He managed to give her a shocked look, even though he'd figured that had been her plan. "You were going to break into a church?"

She laughed. "Why would that shock you?"

"It doesn't, actually. I was going to ask you about it, but we got sidetracked." He grinned at her.

He was surprised to see a slight blush stain her cheeks. She smiled back at him, and he saw desire flare in her eyes.

"Are you coming?" Father Paul called from the corner of the sidewalk.

Kalan leaned down and whispered in her ear, "Yes, but not the way I'd like to be."

She pushed him away with a chuckle. "Stop it. Your halo's going to be tarnished by the time you get back to Heaven, angel boy."

"Probably, but I can't think of a better way to tarnish it." They caught up to the priest, who was shifting nervously from foot to foot. They stayed close as he led them back to the church.

* * * *

"This is the aisle the shadow moved down. I'm not sure where it disappeared at exactly. It's so dark through this area that he could have just stood there until I left and then moved." Father Paul gestured down the side aisle.

Beltaine checked how far the altar was from the aisle. A memory nagged at her, but she couldn't grab a hold of it. Pushing it to the back of her mind, she decided to let it stew — it would come to her. She made her way into the shadows, one hand on her gun. Kalan was right behind her, holding his sword in his hand.

"Father Paul, why don't you wait in your office? We'll give you a report when we figure out what's going on here."

The priest didn't say anything, but he did move away from them.

A pulsing wave rolled over her, and she gasped. A sharp curse came from Kalan, and she knew he had felt it, too. Stopping, she turned to him. "If the pressure starts getting bad, you get the hell out of here."

"You need someone to back you up," he protested.

"Yes, I probably do, but you're no good to me if you can't breathe. Get out if you feel like you're choking." She punched him slightly to drive home her point.

"Ok, but I think I can handle it."

He might have agreed with her, but she knew he wouldn't leave her. It wasn't in the angel's code to run from trouble. The energy got stronger and heavier the farther down they moved. They passed the center point of the wall, and the energy lessened the closer they got to the altar. Turning around, she made her way to the spot where the waves were the strongest.

"Somehow it's coming from here."

"Yes." Kalan's voice sounded like he was gritting his teeth.

"How are you doing?" She didn't look at him. She was running her hand over the wall, looking for a depression or something. She felt a crack in the stone. "I think there's a door here."

"I'm fine. I'm managing to siphon some of the pressure off. It isn't bad yet. Can you open it?" Kalan's breathing was shallow.

"Yeah. Here we go." She fit her fingers into a depression and pulled.

The door swung open on silent hinges. She didn't have a flashlight, but she could see almost as well in the dark as she could in the light. Kalan pressed up tight against her as she led the way down the stairs. They were heading in the right direction, because the energy was growing. Reaching behind her, she felt for Kalan's hand. He grasped hers and squeezed, letting her know he was fine for now.

They reached the cellar and looked around. The walls were made of the same stone the church had been made from. There were lanterns flickering in the dark shadows. Someone had come down this way before them.

"You go to the left, and I'll take the right. Search along the walls and look for anything unusual. I'd say we're looking for another hidden door." She gestured to Kalan to move off to her left.

He nodded and went to run his hand over the stones. She did the same, splitting her attention between the walls and Kalan. The angel looked like he was dealing with the pressure, but she wanted to be sure he wouldn't try to be macho on her and end up hurting himself. She was halfway around the cellar when she heard Kalan call her name.

"Beltaine, I think I found something." He gestured for her to come over to him.

He was pointing to an inverted cross carved into the stone. She reached up and kissed him on the cheek.

"Good going, angel boy. Let's see what's behind this wall." Pushing on the stone, she watched the wall swing open. Again the hinges were quiet and she had the feeling that someone had made sure they were well-oiled so nothing would draw attention to them.

After entering the tunnel, she made her way through the darkness.

Chapter Twenty-One

Kalan's lungs started to close off. The pressure was greater the farther down the tunnel they traveled. He wanted to say something to Beltaine, but he couldn't get the breath to do it.

A scream rent the air, and he saw her stiffen in front of him. He tensed, afraid she would take off without knowing what was going on ahead of them. Grabbing her shoulder, he pulled her tight up to his chest. Her hand fell on his chest right over his heart and the pressure seemed to ease.

Leaning down, he whispered in her ear, "Do you know what this place is?"

"These are the ancient catacombs. They run under all of Ericksberg. In the days before the church, pagans used to bury their dead down here. There are legends about the spiritual power of these catacombs." He felt her shrug. "I don't know if I believe that, but there is some kind of energy down here."

"Yeah. So who do you think was screaming?" He found drawing a deep breath was easier when she touched him.

"If I was a betting woman, I'd say the bad guy has gotten Betsy."

"Shit," he said softly.

"At least we know she was still alive a few minutes ago. We had better get down there to make sure." She stood on her tiptoes and brushed his lips with hers. "Are you okay?"

"I'm better. Your touch seems to lighten the pressure." He wrapped his arms around her and crushed her mouth to his.

She moaned and sucked on his tongue as he stroked hers. She pushed away from him, and he could see she was panting. "Now isn't the time. Keep that thought, though, and we'll pick up there later."

"I'm counting on that." A new sound swelled through the darkness. "Is that chanting?"

"It seems our villain won't be alone. I should have known it wouldn't be easy."

A smile skated across her face, and he saw her reach down to release the catches on the knife and gun.

"If he really is planning on invading Hell, he'd need an army." He tightened his grip on his sword.

"Should we crash their little party?" Her voice shook with excitement.

He laughed softly. "You're hopeless, love."

"And that turns you on, doesn't it?" She swung around and crept up to where a flickering light danced in the shadows.

Yes, it did, he admitted to himself. Her recklessness and enjoyment of danger made him burn with desire, but he pushed the passion deep inside. This wasn't the moment to allow that free rein over his body. He needed to keep his head and hope they got out of this situation without injuries. He snuck up behind her and, leaning over her, peeked around the corner.

The sight he was greeted with made him gasp. It was a circular room with an altar in the middle of it. The stone was stained black with what he imagined was old blood. The power throbbed in time with the chants of the masked figures in the room. A sick feeling burned like acid in his stomach. Blood rituals had been conducted on that altar, and he was afraid they had arrived too late to stop another one.

A blonde woman hung by her hands above the slab. Betsy was naked, and blood dripped from various cuts on her body. She didn't look like she was breathing. He heard Beltaine growl under her breath as they saw Betsy's body twitch. Pressing his lips to Beltaine's ear, he breathed, "She might still be alive."

"Not for long. Let's get in there and stop them before she dies."

Before he could stop her, Beltaine rushed into the middle of the chanting figures. Her knife came out of its sheath, and she jumped to the top of the stone slab. He stared at her, as did the other startled people in the room. Her eyes were burning red as she challenged the robed figures to come and get her.

"Come and pick on me, cowards." Anger was vibrating from her and her fangs lengthened.

"A demon," said a voice from amid the crowd of chanters.

Kalan used their distraction to make his way around the outside of the circle. When he was opposite her, he rushed and joined her on the table. He reached up and cut Betsy down. Allowing her to slide to the floor, he hoped she had enough strength to get under the table. It wouldn't be long before the figures broke free of their surprise and attacked.

Backing up, he looked down and saw a basin polished into the top of the altar. There was blood pooled in it. He made sure not to step in it, but reached out behind him to find Beltaine. His hand connected with her back, and she stiffened for a moment.

"Betsy's down." He didn't take his eyes off the men in front of him, even though he thought he saw a shadow slip down one of the tunnels radiating out from the main room.

"Good. Okay, gentlemen, I want to know who the guy in charge is. Let's make it easy on all of us and give him up without a fight." Her voice was strong and commanding.

One of the men glared up at them. "Who are you? Why should we fear you?"

"It doesn't matter who I am. You know *what* I am, and you should fear me because I'll kill you." She snarled at him.

Kalan spared a glance over his shoulder to see the man's eyes widen. He laughed harshly. "She will kill you. She has no reason to keep any of you alive and no one will stay her hand."

The same man moved slightly to stare at Kalan. The man pulled off his hood, and his scarred face registered shock. "You're an angel."

"Very observant. Can we get on with this?" Beltaine tossed the knife from one hand to the other.

"What is an angel doing with a demon?"

Kalan didn't answer. He wasn't sure if the man really wanted to know or if he was trying to distract them from the others. He kept his eyes on his half of the circle and allowed Beltaine to do the talking.

"I've corrupted him, and now he does my bidding. Stop with the questions. I only asked you one, and you never answered me."

The man made the mistake of coming too close to her. Beltaine reached down then grabbed the man by the front of his robe. Kalan swore he could hear the man's teeth rattle in his head as she shook him. He couldn't help but chuckle as the man whimpered.

"Where is the head lunatic?" she demanded.

The man's feet were dangling above the floor. His eyes searched franticly through the crowd, probably looking for some support, but for the moment, the other figures were quiet, watching and waiting to see what would happen.

"How dare you come and interrupt my ritual," another voice rang out.

Beltaine tossed the man she was holding across the room with a flick of her wrist. Kalan heard the crunch as the man's body slammed against the stone walls. He tried to find the owner of the voice, but it seemed to be coming directly from the walls.

"Sorry to crash your party, but not everyone is thrilled about you kidnapping women and bleeding them dry." Beltaine's voice was nonchalant, but Kalan could feel her tension.

"She's only a whore, and her blood is going to a good cause." The voice seemed to be fading away.

"A good cause? It's not exactly like you're raising money for cancer research, asshole. There's nothing good about what you're doing."

Again Kalan was content to let Beltaine do the talking. He was having a hard enough time filling his lungs with air. He caught a shimmer out of the corner of his eye and turned to look at a wall of pulsing energy. The holes in the wall were growing bigger as he watched. So, this was what he and Beltaine had been sent to protect.

"I'm cutting out a cancer that feeds upon our youth and preys upon their weak minds. He must pay for my son's death."

Kalan shared a glance with Beltaine. Did this man truly believe the Devil was responsible for the death of his child?

"I will take away the most important thing the Devil has, just like he took my son from me. I will take over Hell and destroy the creature who rules it." A cruel laugh rang out. "You won't be around to see it, though. My men will stop you."

It was like a spell was broken with those words. The robed figures surrounding them cried out and charged the altar.

"I don't think we should stay on the stone and fight. It's slick, and I don't want to step in the basin of blood," he pointed out to Beltaine as he sliced his sword through the air, holding the men at bay.

"You're right. Do we go my way and let your guys climb over or around the altar?" She was busy kicking whatever head got closest to her.

"Yeah, sounds like a plan. I'm going to need to stay close to you, though. You're the only thing keeping the pressure from overwhelming me." He felt her reach out and grab his waistband. He stepped back when she tugged. Soon they were pressed back-to-back, balancing on the edge of the stone.

"When I say three, jump with me. I'll keep us together. Don't be merciful, Kalan. Kill them."

"But..."

"I know you're an angel and killing mortals isn't in your code, but you're also a warrior and destroying your enemy is. These men are your enemies, and they'll show you no mercy if they get their hands on you. One. Two. Three."

When he felt her tense and jump, he went with her. Shock rippled through his legs when his feet hit the floor. Her grip broke, and they rolled away from the altar. Somehow they ended up beside each other. Whirling, they stood back-to-back again, facing the men who were trying to kill them.

"Why don't you shoot them?" He skewered one on his sword.

She lunged and gutted another. "I can't risk the bullet ricocheting off the stone and hitting one of us. Our blades will have to be enough."

Surrounded by fifteen men, Kalan wasn't sure steel would be enough. "Close your eyes for a second," he told her.

"What are you doing?"

"Just do it." He threw his hand up in the air and drew his power to him. A flare of light burst into the room, temporarily blinding the men standing around him. He cut two more down before their eyesight returned.

"Very good. It's nice to know you angels have useful powers," she teased.

He couldn't believe she would be joking around at a time like this. His feet were getting heavy, and gray was flirting around the edges of his vision. The energy from the Veil had begun to take its toll on him.

"Beltaine." He sounded desperate. Her hand gripped his wrist for a minute, and the gray receded.

Three men rushed him at once, and he forgot about not being able to breathe. He didn't concern himself with Beltaine. He knew she could take care of herself, and he needed to keep his focus on the men attacking him. When he was finished with them, the power slammed down on him and cut off his air. The gray turned to black, and he fell to his knees, gasping.

"Shit," Beltaine swore as she chanced a peek over her shoulder and saw Kalan fall to the ground. Looking around, she counted five men still standing. The others were on the floor, dead or dying. Shuffling back, she moved until her feet ran into Kalan's legs. She didn't take her eyes off her attackers. Snarling, she bared her teeth at them. "Come and get me. Just one against five. Those are pretty good odds for you, aren't they?"

Taunting them probably wasn't going to calm them down, but she was angry and she was scared. She had to save both Kalan and Betsy, and she wasn't sure she could do that.

Use your power, a voice in her mind suggested.

She didn't want to. She had never used her power to kill mortals. It was something she usually reserved for the demons she sent back to Hell. She had always thought if she started using it to kill mortals, she wouldn't be able to stop, and she didn't want to massacre them.

"What good is having this power if you don't use it to save yourself and that worthless angel of yours?" The voice was sarcastic.

Well, that certainly wasn't her inner voice talking to her. She didn't think Kalan was worthless. Sighing, she realized the voice was right, though. What good was having this power if she wasn't willing to use it?

Keeping her hand on Kalan's shoulder, she began to gather her power. An enormous wave rushed over her, and she gasped. She must have been getting energy from the Veil. Fire raced through her veins, and she held out one hand toward the men stalking her.

"Burn," she whispered. As fire shot from her hand, she closed her eyes.

Screams filled the air, and the smell of burning flesh made her gag. *Damn, it couldn't get much worse,* she thought. She allowed the fire to flow through her, even when she could no longer hear anything but the roar of the flames.

A voice shouted over the fire. "Beltaine, stop!"

Lifting her head, she saw Father Simon, Father Paul and Roger standing at the edge of the circle of fire she was still feeding. Slowly she drew the fire back to her. It fought her, yearning to be free to devour anything in its path, but she mastered it and put it out. As the flames died, the energy disappeared, and she fell to her knees next to Kalan.

He reached out to her and wrapped her in his arms. She rested her head on his shoulder for a moment then pushed away from him. His face was pale, and his breathing was extremely shallow.

"Damn. Roger, get over here."

Roger raced to them, ignoring the charred remains of their attackers. When he reached them, Roger took one look at Kalan and urged the angel to his feet. "We need to get him out of here."

"Yes, take him right outside the church. He needs fresh air and time away from the Veil." She helped get Kalan over to where the other priests were waiting. "Father Paul, you help Roger with Kalan. Father Simon, I need you to get Betsy out of here. Hopefully, we got here in time. She's lost a lot of blood, and I don't know if she'll make it."

Simon followed her to where Betsy was hiding under the altar. Beltaine reached under and lifted the whore off the floor. Simon wrapped her naked body in his cloak and took her into his arms.

"When you get her upstairs, call an ambulance. I'll be up after I take a look around."

Simon nodded and started out. Turning, Beltaine began to search the room.

Chapter Twenty-Two

Richard stared at the woman covered in the blood of his army. How had such a creature managed to destroy all of his men? His cause was just. No demon spawn should have been able to stop him. The book would help him figure out a way to stop her. He patted the pocket of his coat where he had always placed the book. There was nothing there.

Panic ripped through him. Where had the book gone? He couldn't have lost it. He still needed to know how to take over Hell.

"Ah-ha." The woman's voice floated over to where he was hiding in one of the alcoves just outside the altar room.

He cringed to see her bend down and pick something up off the floor beside Johnson's body. Damn, he'd forgotten he had given the book to the man to hold while he'd gone to change his clothes.

Starrer wanted to scream. His anger boiled inside him. All of his plans had been ruined. He had no army now to invade Hell. His son's death would never be avenged. He gritted his teeth and slammed his fist into the wall.

A cold voice entered his mind. *"The Veil is still ripped. You could make your way into Hell when you are ready and kill the Devil. I'm sure he can be destroyed just like any other man."*

Ah, yes. He could kill the Devil instead of taking over Hell. He glanced back once as he made his way down the secondary tunnel leading to the outside of the church. The woman was staring back at him, almost as if she knew he was there. A shudder raced down his spine. There would be time enough to find her and kill her as well.

Beltaine couldn't shake the feeling that someone was staring at her. She tucked the book under her waistband at the small of her back. The shimmering of the Veil drew her, and she reached out to touch it.

"I wouldn't do that if I were you." Azubah crouched just inside the chamber.

"Where did you run off to, you little monster?" Beltaine stepped back. Now that she knew the barrier was there, she could come back and test it.

"I followed Betsy around, waiting for her to get grabbed by the bad guys." The demon shuffled a little closer.

"Why didn't you help her get away?" Beltaine moved to the entrance of the chamber.

Azubah looked surprised. "Why would I?"

"I realize that staying out of the problems of mortals is what demons are supposed to do. You came to me to get help for yourself, but you're not willing to help some poor girl." She shook her head and went back down the tunnel toward the cellar.

"Well, it really doesn't matter why I chose to ask you for help, except in this respect it's my life that's in danger, not just that silly whore's."

Beltaine whirled around, and Azubah held up a clawed hand.

"Don't waste your time arguing with me about Betsy. You were in time to save her. Why worry about the reasons I chose not to save her?" The demon waved at the door leading back into the church. "Your angel is waiting for you. Take him home and let him sleep. Hell is safe from a madman, and mortals are safe from demons — for tonight, at least."

Beltaine nodded and raced up toward the sanctuary, where everyone was waiting for her. Azubah was right. They had the book, and for now, anyway, everyone was safe. It was time to rest up and formulate their next plan of attack.

Once they were all back at her apartment, Beltaine stared down at the small book in her hand. Who would have guessed that such a small thing could bring about the destruction of the world?

"So is it done? Have we completed our mission?"

She looked over to where Kalan sat on her couch. His gold skin was pale, and there was a tired glaze to his eyes.

"I don't think so. The Veil's visible, and the holes were there. We never learned who did it."

"You're right," he sighed.

She moved to sit beside him. He wrapped his arms tightly around her and pulled her to his chest. Sighs came from their lips. She had never been held by anyone else who could make her feel as if she'd come home. Resting her head on his shoulder, she relaxed into his warmth.

"I guess we should figure out how to contact my mother." She hated the way her voice held a hesitation.

"You don't know how to?" He sounded surprised.

"No. I've never wanted to talk to or see her. She always finds me, usually to annoy me." For the first time, there was a pang in her heart when she thought about her mother, and it wasn't heartburn.

"Maybe if we contact the Commander, he would know how to find her." Kalan ran his fingers through her hair.

"Bad idea. The Commander dislikes my mother even more than I do. We'll find some other way." She shuddered at the thought of her mother and the Commander being anywhere near each other.

"I'll save us all the trouble and take the book now." An elegant, aristocratic voice entered the room, along with the strange and compelling smell of burning wood and cinnamon.

Beltaine almost fell off the couch as Kalan jumped to his feet. Her angel stood in front of her, brandishing his sword at the being standing by her window.

"Beltaine, could you tell your bodyguard to put his sword away?" The Devil's thin hand fluttered in Kalan's direction.

Kalan growled and stalked forward.

"Kalan, put your sword away. He isn't going to do anything to us."

Kalan charged the Devil. A blinding light flashed and she heard Kalan cry out. She waited until she could see again. Kalan was kneeling in front of the slender creature, clutching his burnt hands to his chest. Turning, he stared at her with accusing eyes.

She went to the kitchen. She slid oven mitts on and pulled a bottle of holy water from the far reaches of a cabinet.

"What are you doing, if I may ask?" The Devil appeared at her shoulder, gazing curiously at her.

"I'm soaking some towels in holy water for Kalan to wrap his hands in."

"Okay." He backed off. "Why are you being nice to him?"

"He's not so bad, once you get to know him." Shrugging, she smiled slightly.

The Devil reached out to stroke her cheek. "And you know him well."

His voice was soft, and unlike so many others she had met during her life, there wasn't any scorn or disgust in his voice. There was only a quiet, desperate understanding.

Nodding, she walked to where Kalan was kneeling. Lowering herself to the floor beside him, she wrapped the soaked towels around his hands. Pain shined in his eyes. She pulled off the mitts and captured his face in hers. Beltaine kissed him, nibbling on the bottom one until he gasped. Taking advantage, she slid her tongue in to tease his.

"Beltaine," he moaned.

Pulling away, she stared into his eyes. "Jackass." Her voice was low and amused. "I told you to put your sword away. The Devil isn't here to cause us harm. What did you think you could do to him anyway? A lone angel—even if he is a member of the Host—can't defeat the Devil."

"He's evil," he ground out.

Disappointment flooded her for a moment. "After everything we've been through so far, you still don't get it."

She gripped his elbow and helped him stand. After leading him to the couch, she settled him on the furniture and waved the Devil to a chair.

"Don't get what?" Kalan eyed the creature with suspicion.

"He isn't good or evil. The Devil just is." She caressed his cheek and sighed.

"He'll never understand, dear. Angels see the world in black and white. They don't comprehend gray." The Devil shook his head at her.

"We've spent so much time together the past couple of days I was hoping he had figured something out." She shrugged.

"I'm not sure the time you've spent together is conducive to changing his mind about the good or evil of demons, dear." The Devil perched on a chair and crossed his legs with prim perfection.

"*He's* in the room with you," Kalan pointed out, an annoyed tone in his voice.

They ignored him. Beltaine narrowed her eyes at the ruler of Hell. "Why'd you kill the guy who stole the book?"

The Devil shrugged. "It was mine. No one is allowed to take what's mine." His eyes skated to the book resting on the couch.

Kalan glared at him and put his hand on the book. A smile raced over the Devil's face.

"Do you really think that'll stop me from taking it? It's mine and no one has the right to take it. I don't give anything away."

"Especially if it can lead to your destruction." Kalan seemed determined to push the Devil's buttons.

Beltaine sat back, allowing them to chat. If he wanted to annoy the fallen angel then she wasn't going to save him from his own stupidity. She didn't have the energy and Kalan was a big boy. He should know better.

"Ah, well, it's better for everyone if I'm not destroyed."

She could tell the smug certainty in the Devil's voice bothered Kalan.

"Better for everyone? How can you justify that statement?"

A frown crossed the Devil's face. The creature's gaze shot to her then back to Kalan. "Why would I want to justify it to you or anyone else, for that matter?"

She hid her smile. The Devil truly didn't understand why anyone would doubt or question him.

"I would think you'd want to convince me there is some purpose to you still being here." Kalan glared at him.

"Is he serious?" the Devil asked her.

"Yeah, I'm pretty sure he is." She laughed.

The Devil huffed and stood, grabbing the book from Kalan's grip. "I don't have to explain myself to anyone, least of all some angel who's under the delusion he can question me."

The Devil's hands were waving around as he turned to her. "You make it clear to him that it doesn't pay to question me."

Before she could say anything, he disappeared.

Kalan stared at her as she chuckled.

"What's so funny?"

"I think I'm rubbing off on you." She wiped the tears of laughter from her cheeks.

"What are you talking about? You've been rubbing on me since we met." Kalan's blue eyes snapped at her.

She stuck her tongue out at him. "I thought I was the only one who managed to piss off people who could kill me, but you seem to have developed a knack for it." Shrugging, she stood and strolled to the window. "Of course, I think my enemies are a little more dangerous than yours."

"The Devil isn't dangerous?"

She looked back at him. "He isn't nearly as dangerous as your Commander is."

Kalan's face held a confused look. "The Devil isn't deadly or vicious? You really fear the Commander more than him?"

She leaned against the windowpane, staring out into the darkness. While she thought about how to explain it, she had the strangest feeling that someone was standing out in the night, watching her. Hostility rolled in waves over her. Her skin crawled and a shiver raced down her spine.

"Beltaine?" Kalan touched her shoulder and she jumped.

She'd been so focused on the watcher, she hadn't heard him approach. Sliding into his arms, she put her head on his chest and tried to think about the question he'd asked.

"Lucifer is deadly and dangerous. I'm not denying that, but he tends to stay away from mortals. He has no real use for them."

"But is he trouble for me?"

"Not if you take him seriously. Don't treat him like a child or an idiot and you'll be fine." She rubbed her forehead on his skin.

By his hum, she could tell he liked what she was doing. "I'd never say he was an idiot, but he does come across as a spoiled child."

She agreed. "He's a very spoiled child with a lot of power. He's inclined to dismiss everyone, unless they enter what he considers his kingdom."

"Or take what's his." He traced a pattern over her back.

"Oh yes. He's very possessive. That's why we need to find the person who ripped the Veil."

"Why?"

"If the Devil gets him first, he'll kill him and we'll never know how to fix the Veil."

Chapter Twenty-Three

She pressed her lips to his. The kiss started out gentle, as if neither of them was interested in anything other than the soft give and take. His firm lips rubbed against hers while his hands reached down to cup her ass.

Forgetting about the watcher outside, she wound her arms around Kalan's neck and pulled him closer. She was addicted to his taste. She had figured out she couldn't last long without it.

"I'm mad at you," she said, leaning back from him.

A puzzled frown skated over his face. "How was I supposed to know the Devil wasn't going to hurt you?"

"I'm not mad at you for that. I'm angry because you scared me to death back in the catacombs."

"Sorry, Beltaine. I didn't know it would hit me like that."

"Maybe it's a matter of what side of the Veil you come from. When I'm near it, I'm energized, and I want to draw its power into me." Her body tingled, remembering the rush she'd experienced when she tapped into the Veil to destroy the rest of their attackers.

"All I feel is oppression and pain." He bent down and nibbled on her ear.

Purring, she tilted her head to allow him a better angle. "Was that really from the Veil, or could it have been from all the rituals and sacrifices committed in the altar room?"

"Not sure. It could have been from both." His voice was distracted as he trailed his lips down to the base of her throat. He was taking his time tasting her.

She was in the mood to let him. There wasn't any protest when he gathered the edge of her tank top in his hands and ripped it in two. Beltaine was happy the holy water had healed his hands so quickly. She braced herself against the window and thrust her breasts up toward him.

He licked over one shoulder down to the pink tip of her right breast. Kalan nibbled there before he moved to her other shoulder and did the same to her left nipple. Shivers traveled her spine as he fastened his teeth around it then tugged. Moaning, she allowed the pane of glass and the windowsill to support her weight. She threaded her fingers through his hair and urged him to take her breast deeper into his mouth.

A gasp tore from her throat as he bit her hard, then soothed the sting with long swipes of his tongue. She watched as he sank to his knees and placed his mouth on her. He teased Beltaine with teeth and tongue. He nipped, sucked and licked her flesh until it was red, aching and tender. Letting go of the left nipple, he moved over and fastened onto the right one.

"Shit, you're going to make me come," she cried.

She had never felt this way before. Not one of her former lovers had ever tried to ensure her own pleasure first. Well, she admitted to herself, she'd never been involved in their enjoyment, either. As long as she came, she didn't care if the man she was screwing got off.

His hand came up and began to play with her aching left nipple while he sucked the right harder. Each tug shot to her pussy, keeping her wet. Pleasure began to build. With a bite from his teeth and a pinch from his fingers, she came.

Her orgasm exploded over her, causing her to arch her back and clench his head tightly. While she was still coming down, he unbuttoned his pants. He stripped her quickly, not wasting a movement. Before she could say a word, he was naked and sliding into her. His head dropped to rest against her shoulder as he took a deep breath.

Beltaine wrapped her arms and legs around him. She ran her hands over his shoulders. "What are you waiting for?" She couldn't hold out any longer, tilting her hips to take him deeper.

"I'm savoring the moment," he said in a hoarse voice. "I love the way you feel around me."

"Good thing, since I love the way you feel inside me. Now move," she ordered.

Chuckling, he stroked into her then slowly pulled out. It was a slow loving. Deep emotion ran between them, and the wall she had built around her heart and soul began to crumble.

There had only been one person who was welcomed beyond that wall. Roger bullied his way into her life, and nothing she had done had pushed him out. Now, almost from the beginning, her body had recognized Kalan as a mate, but her heart wasn't willing to give him a chance. Yet the more time they spent together, the more she realized that he was trying to move beyond the lessons he'd been taught about her and her kind.

Laughing, she lifted her hips to encourage him to ride her harder. It wasn't the time for deep thoughts. Her heart might want to claim him, but she wasn't going to allow it any control at the moment.

Soon all thought rushed from her mind as the blunt head of his cock hit the spot that made her second orgasm crashed through her. Her pussy held him inside and the contractions of her muscles drove him over the edge. He grunted as he spilled into her.

Pressing her cheek to the cool glass, she felt the anger and insanity of the watcher roll over her. She stood up slowly, clothing herself with a casual wave. Since her back was toward the window, she didn't worry about the watcher seeing her lips.

"There's someone out on the street watching us." She grabbed Kalan's chin to keep his gaze on her. "I'm going to see if I can flush him out."

"I'll go with you."

Shaking her head, she moved them away from the window. "I want you to stay here. I don't want him to figure out that I've left the apartment."

He frowned, but Beltaine didn't care. She was better suited to stalking prey in the dark.

"I don't have a choice, do I?"

"No. Don't worry. I've been kicking demon ass for years. A crazy mortal isn't anything to sweat about." She kissed him as she strapped on her knife.

"I hate being left behind," Kalan complained as he followed her to the door.

"Imagine how women throughout the ages have felt when the macho men went out to save the world, leaving them behind to tend the children and make dinner." She snickered as he smacked her ass when she went out of the door.

Beltaine slipped down the stairs. She was lucky the entrance to her building was on the other side of the block. The watcher wouldn't know she'd left.

Slinking out of the doorway, she focused her power to pinpoint where the stranger stood. An odd emptiness came from the spot where he hid. Something absorbed her power instead of bouncing it back at her. The emptiness caused an uneasy shiver to run down her spine. All creatures—mortal or not—caused a ping in her power. She wondered what creature was out there.

Drawing her knife, she made her way from shadow to shadow, trying to sneak up behind the watcher. She masked her own approach with some of her power. It was reacting sluggishly. She'd have to visit a cemetery soon.

Glancing up, she found her window and every once in a while Kalan would cross in front of it, talking. A smirk crossed her face because she figured he wasn't saying nice things. She hoped the person on the street couldn't read lips. Across the street from her building was an alley. That was where the emptiness and anger came from. With every sense on high alert, she moved into the alley. Beltaine wasn't sure what she expected to find, but she was surprised when she didn't find anyone. Searching the entire alley, she didn't see a single person. There was no way the watcher had got past her and the alley was a dead end.

Pushing her power out beyond the alley and finding no trace of the person who had been watching them scared her. Her power had never failed her before, yet if the stranger had anything to do with the Veil, he must be protected by someone more powerful than she was. She headed back to her apartment.

* * * *

A shadow parted from the darkness of the alley's dead end. Gleaming eyes held hatred for the demon spawn. Beltaine and her pet angel had foiled his plans and they would pay for that. He still had Starrer, and the mortal would serve his purpose — then true power would be his.

Thunder cracked and the sky opened with a torrent of rain. The shadow looked up and if he hadn't known better, he would think God wept.

Chapter Twenty-Four

When Beltaine returned to her apartment, Kalan wasn't alone. Father Simon and Roger chatted with the angel.

"Gentlemen." She nodded at them, taking off the knife sheath and tossing it on the end table.

"Did you find anything?" Kalan asked as she sank down to sit on the floor beside his feet.

"By the time I got there, he must have left. Strangely enough, my power didn't see him."

The men looked confused.

She explained. "When I send out my power, the essence of another creature makes a ping, in a way, and comes back to me."

"Like radar?" Roger asked.

"Right. Any being will do this, even demons or angels, but this stranger didn't. It was like he absorbed my power."

"Do you think it was the man you're searching for?" Father Simon looked tired.

"Did you get any rest?" She didn't wait for him to answer. "If it was, he's protected by something more powerful than I, and that concept scares me."

Roger and Father Simon nodded. Kalan frowned.

"I didn't think anything scared you."

She flipped him off and everyone laughed. "There are few things that scare me, but beings more powerful than me are creatures you should fear as well."

"Who are they? Besides God and the Devil." Kalan stroked a hand over her hair.

"The Commander and the Master. Trust me when I tell you to have respect for God and the Devil, but don't fear them. Their motives are rather clear." She rubbed her eyes and sighed.

"The Devil's motive is to collect souls and ruin people's lives." Kalan sounded confident.

Roger, Father Simon and Beltaine shook their heads.

Roger said, "The Devil's motive is to rule Hell and to make sure he's never bothered with trivial things. God's motive is truly known only to Him, but we know it isn't to harm us."

"With the Commander and the Master, you never know if they're out to help you or hurt you. If you can't trust them, you should fear them, especially since they have the power to kill you," Beltaine pointed out.

"But the Commander is an angel, one of the most powerful angels in Heaven. I'd think you'd be able to trust him to do God's will," Kalan protested.

"Maybe he does do God's will, Kalan, but I've felt there was another purpose behind what he does." Father Simon pinned the angel with a glance. "Are you telling me angels never have any other motive besides God's will?"

Kalan blushed and stammered.

Beltaine decided to let him off the hook. "We could discuss this all night and never convince him about anything." She patted him on the knee. "How's Betsy?"

"She's resting comfortably at the hospital. Father Paul was with her when we left. I see Lucifer's come and collected his book." The priest leaned back in his chair with a sigh.

"Been here and left all ready. He wasn't inclined to stick around when Kalan started questioning him." Beltaine looked at Father Simon with concerned eyes.

The priest was the only example of a father figure she had. Or at least what a real father might have been like. She'd watched him age over the years, but had steadfastly ignored the thought of his death. Now, staring at him under the harsh lights of her apartment, she could see the priest's death hanging over him. Tears she'd vowed never to cry welled up in her eyes.

Father Simon smiled with gentle understanding. "It seems I'll be joining our Father sooner than we had hoped."

She scrambled to her knees in front of him and took his gloved hands in hers. As much as she wanted to deny his words, she knew lying wouldn't stop the hurt and she nodded.

"What are you talking about, Father Simon? You've got a lot more life to live." Roger's voice held panic and pain.

"Son, there's no point in lying to ourselves. Each new episode with the stigmata takes away a piece of my soul. I'm losing the energy to live." The priest took Roger's hand and held it, along with Beltaine's.

"Why would He do that? Why would God give you the stigmata and allow it to kill you?" Beltaine's question was low and fierce.

Father Simon chuckled. "You're always questioning Him, child. You've never been content to accept the answer 'Because He's God'."

"Damn right. Everyone in this room is accountable for what he does. Why shouldn't God be? 'Because He's God' is such a cop-out. It's bullshit to be scared of asking God questions. If He didn't want us to know, He never would have given us free will." She jumped to her feet and smiled down at them. "You're not going to die tonight. I'm heading out to replenish my power. I'll be back."

With a simple wave of her hand, she disappeared.

Kalan stood, ready to follow her. Father Simon stopped him.

"Let her go. Confronting death is never pleasant, especially for Beltaine."

"Why? She kills demons all the time." He sat back down.

"Demon killing isn't the same as someone dying."

"How is it different?" He stared at the priest.

"When she kills a demon, she's destroying his corporeal form and its tie to the earth. The demon reforms in its true shape in Hell. For her, when a mortal dies, he dies. There's no reforming anywhere for him."

Kalan was puzzled. "What about Heaven? Most mortal souls reform in Heaven."

"Heaven is a vague concept to her. All she's known her entire life is the hypocrisy of Earth and the dangers of Hell. She can't stretch her imagination far enough to believe in a place of peace." The priest shook his head, sadness taking shape in his eyes.

"What kind of place would have beings so intolerant they would rather she be dead than alive?" Roger inquired, his gaze fighting with Kalan's.

Wincing, Kalan couldn't argue with them. He had been one of these angels who'd thought everyone would be better off if she were dead. Yet somehow, in spending time with her, he had come to realize there was more to Beltaine than the hard-nosed, kick-ass demon slayer. She had depths she didn't show others. He had entered some of the closed rooms in her soul, and he hoped she would allow him more access.

Kalan snorted. He wasn't sure how much more access she could give him. He loved her body and enjoyed it every chance he got, but it was her soul he wanted.

"I've changed," he said quietly, standing and moving to the window. "I see her as more than a demon."

"So angels aren't as rigid as we're led to believe." Roger smiled to take the sting out of the words.

"Only in some ways." He winked at the young priest and watched the man's cheeks flush. "I'm going to look for Beltaine. You're welcome to stay here for the night." He bowed slightly to both of them and disappeared.

* * * *

Beltaine sat in the potter's field. She gathered power from the souls confined in the cemetery, one of the few places she'd come to in Ericksberg.

"Is the woman all right?" Azubah asked from next to her.

Keeping her eyes closed, she held the thread of power. She wasn't interested in talking to the demon.

"I would've thought you'd be happy to hear me ask about the whore."

She could almost feel the demon staring at her. Opening her eyes, she gazed over the plain wooden crosses marking the graves of the poor. Would she even get an unmarked grave when she died? Would there be any mourners at her service? A laugh broke from her. There wouldn't be any sort of service because except for Roger, no one would really care.

A sharp pain drew her gaze back to the demon standing beside her. Something wet trailed down her arm. She snarled when she saw a long, thin scratch running along her skin.

Azubah's red eyes widened as he stepped back. Beltaine clamped her hand around the demon's neck and jerked it close enough for it to see the fire in her own gaze.

"What the hell do you think you're doing?" She shook the creature and pushed it away from her.

The demon cowered and whined. "You weren't paying any attention to me."

"Did you ever think I might not want to talk to you?" She watched with narrowed eyes as the scratch healed.

"Why wouldn't you?" Azubah stuttered as she glared at it. "Anyway, you were wallowing in self-pity."

Her eyebrows shot up. "Wallowing in self-pity?" Climbing to her feet, she considered punching the creature, but decided it wasn't worth it.

"Sure. You were thinking no one would mourn you if you die."

"How'd you know that?" A suspicion skated through her mind.

"I didn't read your thoughts. I'm a lesser demon. I can't do any of that, even with the power I have. You had a sad look in your eyes, so what else would you be thinking in a cemetery?" The demon shrugged.

She didn't want to talk about it. "Betsy's fine. Father Paul is staying with her at the hospital for tonight."

"Great." The demon dismissed the whore with a flap of its hand. "What are you going to do now?"

"Do? Why would I do anything more?" She started to move down the stone path leading out of the graveyard. "Maybe I've changed my mind about helping out any further."

"Wait. You're joking, right?" The small demon skipped after her.

"Am I? I got the book back for the Devil. The idiot who ripped the Veil can't do any more damage." Standing at the gate, she looked in both directions before she stepped off hallowed ground.

Azubah reached out to stop her and having thought twice about touching her, drew his hand back. "What if the mortal tries to sneak into Hell? What if the Veil falls?"

"Do you always worry about 'what ifs'?" The same strange feeling of being watched made the scar her father had left on her neck itch.

"Only if they involve my very existence. Aren't you scared? If the Veil falls, beings like us are screwed."

She stopped suddenly, causing Azubah to run into her back. Whirling around, she grabbed the demon and shook it.

"We're all screwed, you stupid demon. Every creature on Earth is doomed from the moment it takes breath. It's only a matter of time before God gets His head out of the sand and realizes how fucked up this world's gotten."

The demon was a little wild-eyed. "If you believe that, why try so hard?"

Pushing Azubah away, Beltaine started to walk off. The demon didn't follow, but another voice let her know someone else had arrived.

"Why try so hard?" Kalan's question made her stop and turn to look at him.

The angel leaned against the low stone wall surrounding the cemetery, his muscled arms crossed over his chest. His white leather pants lovingly outlined every bulge and her mouth watered. She tried to ignore the part of her body that wanted to jump the angel and ride him until they were both crying out with pleasure.

"Beltaine?" Kalan waved a hand in front of her face.

She hated when people did that. "What?" She'd forgotten he had asked her a question.

"Why did you fight so hard to find the book and save Betsy if you believe we're all doomed anyway?"

It was a good question, but she didn't have a good answer. "I never said angels were doomed—just mortals and demons. I can't tell you why, for sure. Maybe it has to do with the human part of me I try to forget exists. Mortals fight so hard to survive and to live. Do you think it could be coded in their genes or something, and I got some of it from my father?" She grimaced, not wanting to think about getting anything from her father.

"If you have this will to live, why do you have such a negative outlook?" Kalan took her hand and pulled her close to him.

"There's more than enough demon blood to counterbalance any optimism I might have. As a mortal, I want to live, even if this world's screwed up. The demon in me says, 'What's the point in even trying anymore, because we're all doomed anyway'."

"That's a depressing way to live." Kalan frowned as he cupped her cheek.

She was feeling a little more bitchy than normal. Instead of soothing, his touch irritated her. She jerked away and moved toward the village center.

"Maybe it is, but it's the outlook I'm happiest with at the moment. I've lived with it all of my life and I don't see why it's any of your business whether I believe we're doomed or not."

He blinked, and she could tell he was unsure why she was attacking him. Beltaine longed to scratch her scar and her neck was burning. Shooting a glance back up the street, she saw Azubah standing in front of the entrance to the cemetery. A large black shadow formed behind the demon.

"Azubah, get the hell out of here," she cried as she raced up the sidewalk.

The demon's eyes widened, and he didn't take the time to look to see what was behind him. It disappeared as Beltaine skidded to a stop before she ran into the figure emerging from the shadow.

Chapter Twenty-Five

The creature was tall, reed thin and pale. Its fangs dripped some noxious fluid. She didn't want to know what it was. Snarling, the vampire lunged for her.

"Shit," she swore, as she managed to dodge her attacker.

"What the hell is that thing?" Kalan's voice came from behind her.

"It's a vampire." She kept her eyes on the Hell-born creature. She needed to grab it without getting any of the poison on her. She had seen a man's skin melt off his body when he got a drop of the vampire's slime on him.

"A vampire? Amazing. I never thought I'd get to see one. It's interesting how its head can spin around on its neck like that."

"Now's not the time to discuss this, Kalan. Stay away from his saliva. It'll melt your skin off." She danced to the left side of the vampire and drove her foot into the creature's ribs.

It shrieked and shambled toward her. She fought her gag reflex. God, the creature reeked. The thing was literally a walking dead man. She shouldn't expect it to smell like roses. The vampire hissed and she swept her foot out to connect with his ankles. The creature went flailing past and into the downswing of Kalan's sword.

Now the vampire was beheaded and not moving. She didn't have to worry about dodging the flinging drool. Gathering her power, she held out her hand and said, "Burn."

Fire engulfed the body and severed head. She tried not to watch as the flames turned the pale flesh into ash. When everything—bone and flesh—was gone, she turned to glare at the angel.

"What the hell were you doing?" She shoved him.

He blinked his pretty blue eyes at her with an innocent smile, but she saw a hint of wickedness hidden in them. "Doing?"

"You were gawking at that thing like a damn tourist."

"I've never seen a vampire before. I knew you had him under control. I'm surprised you're not yelling at me for helping you." He leaned against the stone wall with an insolent wink.

Snarling, she pinned him to the wall with her body. "Your way of killing him was more effective, but don't push me, angel."

"Or what? You'll beat me up?" he teased.

Beltaine's adrenaline raced. She grabbed his head and brought it down to crush their lips together. He grunted as her tongue demanded entrance to his mouth and took it.

Kalan tensed.

She knew he fought the urge to take over. Well, she wasn't going to let him. Reaching down, she unzipped his pants and burrowed her hand into them, cupping his balls. He moaned when she squeezed them. Nipping his bottom lip, she tugged on them a little harder.

"Hey, be careful," he yelped.

She grinned up at him as she sank to her knees in front of him.

He looked down at her. "That's becoming one of my favorite positions for you."

A mischievous grin appeared on his face, then disappeared quickly when she took a tight grip on his balls and flashed her fangs at him.

She stared up at his pained expression and tried to decide if she should continue what she planned on doing or if she should walk away.

"Please," he whispered.

Beltaine wasn't sure if he was begging for her to release him or if he wanted her to pleasure him. In the end, it didn't matter, because her body demanded its own release, and Kalan was the only way it wanted to get it.

No mercy. She sucked his cock into her mouth and went to work. Rolling his balls in her hand, Beltaine licked Kalan's shaft. She nibbled the throbbing vein on the underside of his rod. She teased the slit in the blunt head and tasted the salty pre-cum leaking from him.

The tip of her tongue found the sensitive spot right below the crown, and Kalan cried out.

"Beltaine." His voice rang through the night air.

She stroked a fingertip over the soft skin behind his balls. Wrapping her other hand around the base of his cock, she slid her mouth up and down the shaft along with it. He threaded his fingers through her hair to keep her from pulling away. Humming, she continued to work him until his hips were snapping and he was fucking her mouth.

"I'm going to come, love," he ground out between clenched teeth.

She pulled off him with a pop. He wasn't going to come until he was inside her. She squeezed her fingers tight around the base of his cock. "Not yet."

With a burst of power, she willed her clothes away and climbed his body. He leaned against the wall to support her weight while she entwined her legs around her waist. Sighs filled the air as her wet, hot pussy sheathed his throbbing cock. It wouldn't take long for either of them to reach their climax. He thrust up while she pushed down and he went deep. One more hard, deep thrust and their orgasms overwhelmed them.

She rested her limp body on his chest while he managed to keep them upright. She felt a chuckle well up in him before he spoke.

"I think we need to get into fights more often. It doesn't take much to get you off when your blood is racing."

Angling her chest away from his, she stared. "Do you really want to rile me up, angel? I can do things to you that would tie you in knots."

A gleam came into his eyes. "Are we talking about bondage?"

She slid to the ground and clothed herself with a casual wave. "Yes, and not in a fun way either."

A wild-eyed look crossed his face.

"Don't worry. I don't have any interest in tying you up." Glancing at the scorched earth where the vampire's body had been, she shivered. "It's not looking good."

"What do you mean?" Kalan tucked his cock away and did up his pants.

"First, it was zombies. Now, it's vampires. The Horde is mustering its troops. The demons are already making forays into this world." She moved toward the center of Ericksberg.

"The Devil and the Master will keep the others in check, won't they?" Kalan inquired as he followed.

"The Devil might, because he'd be out of a nice cushy job if the Host destroyed Hell. I'm not sure what the Master would do. He's the one unknown in this whole affair." Beltaine stopped at an intersection. "Every move we make, we're being watched. Who's watching? I don't know."

"What do we do now?" Kalan stood beside her and she enjoyed the solid warmth of his presence.

"I'm going to St Benedict's to look over the Veil. You can go back to the apartment and rest." She cut off his grumble. "You can't be in the presence of the barrier for very long. It puts too much pressure on you. Nothing's going to happen tonight. Whoever's watching us is hiding while he rethinks what he's going to do. I need to assess what's going on with the Veil."

She knew he couldn't argue with that. After kissing him, she headed off to the church.

Chapter Twenty-Six

Beltaine stood before the large oak doors carved with angels and a stylized picture of St Benedict. She studied the patron saint of war. Had the bad guy picked this church on purpose? Had he known what he would cause when he started the process? Or had the whole thing gotten out of hand?

She stroked a finger over the fierce expression of the saint. She found herself wondering what type of person would suffer persecution and pain for a belief or a religion. She didn't know if she would be strong enough or crazy enough to become a saint. Laughing quietly, she went into the sanctuary. She'd have to change quite a few things in her life to come close to being a saint, and she wasn't willing to do that.

Not really paying attention, she made her way down the aisle toward the altar. A body slammed into her. She grabbed the man's arm to keep him from falling down. Once he settled, he shook her hand off his body.

"Are you okay?"

"You should watch what you're doing." He snarled at her.

Surprised, she shot the man a quick glance. His suit was wrinkled. The shirt underneath was dirty. His hair stood straight up, as if he had been running his hands through it. A deep sorrow shined in his eyes, but a twitch in the lid told her he was on the edge.

"Mr Starrer, what are you doing here so late?" Father Paul came from his office.

The priest nodded at her, so she decided she was going to let Starrer's comment pass.

"I needed to pray, Father. I was leaving when this woman ran into me." Starrer gestured to her.

As much as she wanted to tear into Starrer, she had the feeling he wouldn't be listening to her.

"St Benedict's is always open to the hurting." Father Paul touched Starrer's arm.

Starrer tilted his head, but Beltaine didn't think he was hearing the priest. He seemed to be hearing something else in his head. "I have to go." Starrer left in a rush.

Both Beltaine and Father Paul watched Starrer leave. Turning to look at her, the priest smiled and shrugged. "Mr Starrer's son committed suicide earlier this year. He's still trying to come to terms with it."

Nodding, she didn't pretend to understand what the man was going through. She'd never lost anyone she cared for. A vague tingle of uneasiness shot through her, but Beltaine couldn't put her finger on what exactly caused that feeling.

"I want to thank you." Father Paul's voice showed his nervousness.

"For what?" Surprise raced through her. No one had ever thanked her for doing her job.

"For stopping those men from killing that woman."

"You're welcome." What was she supposed to say? Father Paul had no idea what Betsy really was. She wondered if Roger or Father Simon had explained what was really going on down in the catacombs.

"I need to go back down there, Father. There might be some clues. Unfortunately, I'm not sure this is over." She stalked to the wall where the entrance to the tunnels was.

"Certainly. Is there anything I can help you with?"

"Just pray, Father."

Slipping through the opening, she made her way into the cellar and found the hidden door to the catacombs. A rush of power flowed over her. She fought the urge to open up and allow the Veil to fill her. She didn't want to find out what all that power would do to her.

Dismay swamped her as she walked into the altar room. The Veil was a solid barrier across the room, but there were large holes in it. Some of the holes were big enough for the higher lords of Hell to come through. She reached out to touch the shimmering barrier. A screech tore from her throat as a hand came through the Veil and wrapped around her wrist. Before she could free herself, she was jerked through the barrier into Hell. Shock rippled through her body.

Blinking, Beltaine met the sardonic gaze of the Master. As always, he was impeccably dressed in a double-breasted gray suit. He gestured for her to follow him. She wobbled when she took a step. Looking down, she stopped in horrified shock.

"What the fuck is this?" She waved a hand at the calf-length skirt, sensible black flats and button-down shirt.

The Master sat down at a café table in front of a coffee shop. He laughed. "I believe this is your version of Hell, Beltaine." He waved her to a chair.

"It'd have to be, because I'd never be caught alive in this outfit. What am I doing in Hell?" She flopped on to the chair and glanced around.

People walked the sidewalks of the picture-perfect city. If she didn't know better, she'd think the people were mortal. In a glimpse of their eyes, she saw sparks. These were demons, and none of them looked happy to have her there.

"Why am I here?" She sat up, keeping a wary eye on the demons.

"By virtue of who your mother is, you're capable of crossing into Hell without any side effects. You can return whenever you want. Your pet angel would suffer greatly if he came over." The Master's eyes gleamed deep red.

"Good thing he's not planning on vacationing here." Beltaine knew poking the demon wasn't smart, but she couldn't change who she was, and showing fear wasn't her way.

He bared his fangs at her. "Are you sure you want to mouth off to me?"

"No one's ever accused me of being smart. Why did you bring me here?" She shifted while holding the demon's gaze.

"I believed self-preservation was the most important thing to you, but you seem to have found a conscience somewhere." The Master leaned back and crossed his legs.

"It's not my conscience. My self-preservation kicked in. If the Veil falls, the Horde rides into the mortal world and the Host is unleashed. Who gets stuck in the middle of that fight? Me. I'd rather risk my neck to stop it than stand by and watch it happen."

He nodded. "I believe I understand what you're saying, but trust me when I say there are more who want you to fail than there are who hope you succeed."

"I can probably guess who they are."

She thought about the high lords of Hell. For centuries, they had chafed at the limitations God and the Devil put on them. They, along with the Master, would love to show mortals how inferior humans were.

"Maybe you can. You might be surprised, though. Don't trust anyone." He stood and bowed slightly. Turning, he walked away.

"I never have," she murmured. The burning sensation started in her scar. She needed to get out of Hell.

There were creatures she didn't want to face. Not in Hell, on their home turf. Beltaine rose and made her way to the barrier. She tried not to rush. Never show fear, or the demons would attack like wild animals. Before she could reach the Veil, a voice she didn't want to hear called out to her.

"Beltaine." Her mother appeared next to her.

"Great. Now I know I'm in Hell." She moved to step around the demon.

"That's no way to talk to your mother."

"We've been over this before. You might have carried me in your body, but you've *never* been my mother."

The demon shrugged. "I'm selfish and a terrible creature. All you can do is hate me. I've come to terms with that." Her mother wiped an imaginary tear from her cheek.

Beltaine grimaced. "Quit the bullshit, Mother. What do you want?"

"I see you got the book back and gave it to the Devil already. I wish you had contacted me before you returned it."

"So you could get the credit for retrieving it?" Beltaine moved, as tension seeped into her body.

"Of course, dear. Why else? You don't need the Devil's goodwill. He won't bother you. On the other hand, I need all the help I can get with him." Her mother was very nonchalant about cheating her daughter out of any credit.

"My friends and I almost got ourselves killed because of that stupid book. I would like to add that you were the one to lose it in the first place. I don't think you deserve to get any brownie points from it. That would be truly fucked up." Beltaine turned to make her way to the spot where she had crossed over.

"Darling, you're the one who has always claimed I had no maternal instincts. Why are you surprised by anything I do? I didn't know you had any friends." Her mother stopped to think. "Except for that odd priest you hang around with. That's a strange relationship."

"Why would it be strange?"

Her mother shot her a puzzled glance. "Considering who and what your father was, I would have thought you'd run as far away from a priest as you could."

"I don't run from anyone. Roger might be a priest, but he's never hurt me, so I'm willing to give him the benefit of the doubt."

"Very open-minded of you." Her mother smirked.

"Unlike either of my parents." Trying to be casual, Beltaine asked, "Since Father's dead, do you see him often?"

"See your father? Why would I? He wasn't that great a fuck." Her mother shook her head. "I don't even know if he's anywhere in Hell. Just because he was an asshole doesn't automatically mean he came here when he died."

Beltaine wasn't sure how she felt about that information. Would she prefer knowing he suffered in the afterlife? Or was not knowing better for her?

"I have to go. It's been great chatting with you. I hope we don't repeat it any time soon."

The time had come to leave. Hell wasn't a place she wanted to stay in and she needed to get away from her mother. Taking a deep breath, she stepped through the Veil. The tingling chased up and down her nerve endings. She could swear the energy recognized her and let her absorb it. Time to head back to the apartment and talk to Kalan.

Chapter Twenty-Seven

Kalan headed back to Beltaine's apartment. He wasn't thrilled with the fact that she was right. Until he could figure out how to control the effect the Veil had on him, he wasn't going to be very useful to her. It bugged him to know she was going somewhere dangerous and he couldn't be there to save her.

Yet she had to save your ass in the catacombs, his conscience reminded him.

He didn't deny that, but Beltaine was female and the urge to protect her was strong. He wondered if his growing feelings for her were short-circuiting his good sense, because she'd proven she was more than capable of taking care of herself. She'd done it when she was fourteen and time had only given her more experience. In truth, she had more experience than he did when it came to dealing with demons.

"Excuse me," a hesitant voice interrupted the conversation he was having with himself.

Turning, he saw a young woman standing a few feet away from him, her eyes scanning the night.

"Yes?" He didn't move closer to her. She was twitchy enough that he realized any sudden moves would cause her to bolt.

"Are you the one who is working with the demon slayer?" The woman stepped closer.

"Demon slayer? You mean Beltaine?" He nodded. "I work with her."

"Tell her the person she's looking for is seeking revenge." She took a small step in the opposite direction.

"Revenge?" He reached out to keep her from moving further.

"Something was taken from him he thought was so important, he needs to blame someone for the loss. He needs to punish someone for it. It's unfortunate he chose the Devil." She shook her head.

"Unfortunate? Why would you say that?"

She looked at him as if he were a fool. "Who else would God defend without question, if not the Devil? There would be no God without the Devil."

Before he could reply, she disappeared into the night shadows. Damn, he had forgotten to ask who the man was, though Kalan didn't think she would have told him.

He thought about what the woman had said. Was there truth in her statement? Would God defend the Devil because His own existence depended on it? He wanted to talk it over with Father Simon. The priest had a rather unique outlook on religion and God. He'd never met a priest who didn't hate the Devil. Father Simon talked about the creature as if he were a silly, spoiled child.

Kalan made his way to Beltaine's apartment, hoping to find the priest still there. He opened the door and disappointment rushed through him when he realized the priests had left. A note on the table let him know that Father Angelo had called to ask Father Simon and Roger to return to the city. There went his chance to talk to the priest.

He was settling down to nap until Beltaine returned, when someone knocked on the door. Frowning, he stood up and went to the door. Misha St Largent stood in the hallway. A shock of surprise raced through him. What was the head of the Board doing here? Board members should be too busy running all the commerce and criminal trade in the city to take a chance on bothering Beltaine.

"What are you doing here?" He didn't move out of the doorway.

"I came to see what Beltaine's found out so far." Misha's voice was husky, and she stared at him like he was a piece of meat.

"She told you she'd report in when she knows anything," he reminded her. "How did you find this place?"

"I have my ways. I'm not stupid enough to believe that bitch would tell me anything."

Misha stepped closer to him and ran her finger down his chest. He shivered in disgust, but he could see she thought the shiver was from desire. Another step and her breasts pressed against him. Fighting the urge to gag, he stepped back, only to realize too late that was what Misha wanted.

Gliding into the apartment, she glanced around and curled her lip. "Very sparse."

"What do you want to know, Ms St Largent?" He made sure he wasn't close enough for her to touch him.

"Have you found anything yet?" She wandered around the room.

He stayed silent and watched her circle like a shark. Two large men stood to each side of the door.

"Who are they?" Kalan nodded toward them.

Dismissing them with a wave, she said, "My bodyguards. Has the demon-spawned bitch discovered anything?"

He shrugged. "I don't work for you, so I don't have to tell you anything, Ms St Largent."

"Please, call me Misha. You might want to rethink your statement. Telling me will be healthier for you in the long run." Her smile was all teeth.

Incredible. "Are you threatening me?"

"I wouldn't call it a threat. Just a strong suggestion."

He laughed and took a step toward her. "I'm a member of the Host. There's nothing you or your bodyguards can do to force me. If Beltaine chooses not to talk to you, I must honor her wishes."

She flashed him a triumphant smile and flung herself into his arms. Before the shock wore off, she crushed their lips together. When he pushed her away, he saw her glance shoot over his shoulder. With a sinking stomach, he turned around to see Beltaine standing in the doorway.

"Beltaine—" he started to explain.

A glance from her closed his mouth, and he took a huge step away from Misha. Beltaine's eyes glowed red. When she opened her mouth to speak, her fangs gleamed. Squeaking, Misha gestured to her bodyguards. Kalan shot a look at them, and they didn't look inclined to come to her aid. He moved to cover Beltaine's back.

"They won't help you, Misha. You never told them they'd have to go up against me." Beltaine stalked toward the other woman.

Fear showed in Misha's eyes, but the woman didn't back down. Kalan couldn't decide if that was brave or foolish. He knew Beltaine had been looking for a reason to quit working with the Board, and Misha's hitting on him provided the perfect excuse.

Beltaine reached out a finger tipped with a claw. A thin scratch appeared on Misha's cheek.

"How dare you," Misha gasped.

Beltaine snarled. "I dare because you've never understood what I am. You and the Board have been so smug as you send me here and there, doing your dirty work."

Misha's eyes were wide. "You're a demon. You're nothing but a mad dog."

"You've been jerking my chain long enough." Beltaine pointed at him and said, "He's mine."

Kalan didn't protest because Beltaine was right. He was hers as long as she wanted him.

"You control him like we control you?" Misha glanced between him and Beltaine.

"No. Kalan does what he wants to do."

"Then how do you know he doesn't want me?" Smugness wasn't attractive on Misha.

"Kalan has better taste than to fall for a cold-hearted bitch like you."

Misha snorted. "I'm not as cold-hearted as you. At least I didn't kill my father."

Shit! Kalan moved to grab Beltaine, but wasn't fast enough. Beltaine had Misha by the throat and had slammed the woman against the wall. Misha's feet were dangling above the floor.

"You never personally killed anyone, but you've hired someone to murder for you. At least I have the guts to do my own killing. I guess your way lessens the nightmares you have." Beltaine shook her like a rag doll. "Remember what happens when you jerk on a dog's chain long enough. It'll turn around and bite you. Believe me…my bite is much worse than my bark." Leaning, she bared her teeth and ran the tip of her tongue over her fangs. "Since I had no problem killing my father, I'll have even less of a problem killing you, and I won't feel guilty about it either."

The two men started to move forward. Kalan blocked them as he said, "Let them handle it between themselves."

Misha must have seen something in Beltaine's eyes to convince her Beltaine was serious. Misha dropped her gaze in submission. Beltaine shook her hard then tossed her across the room toward her bodyguards.

"Get the hell out of here. *Never* threaten me or any of my friends again. You know how easy it is for me to kill you, and it would be *you* I came for." Beltaine stalked by him to stand in front of the trio. "If and when I decide to come and tell you what happened, you had better be prepared to pay me for my time."

Misha reached to touch the scratch on her cheek. Her face went white when she pulled her finger away and saw blood on her skin.

"You'll have a scar to remind you what I'm capable of. Don't push me."

They left and Beltaine turned to him. The fire in her eyes dimmed.

"I'm sorry. She must have heard you coming up the stairs or something. One minute she was threatening me then she threw herself into my arms and kissed me."

Beltaine allowed her anger to drain away while she listened to Kalan apologize. Her claws and fangs disappeared. When she had control over her power, she reached out and cupped Kalan's cheek.

"Shut up. Don't apologize for that bitch." She pressed her other hand to his chest. "As strange as it may seem, I trust you on this. You don't strike me as the type of person who'd jerk me around."

He looked surprised. "You trust me?"

Shrugging, she stroked her hand from his cheek into his hair. "Maybe not in every way, but I trust you when it comes to women."

"Confident of yourself, love?"

"Not really. You're an honest angel. It has nothing to do with me." She pulled his head to hers. Nibbling on his lips, she soothed him.

He wrapped his arms around her waist and drew her tight against him. Laying her head on his chest, she listened to his heartbeat. They rested against each other and absorbed each other's warmth.

His finger levered her chin up and their lips met again. She ran her tongue over the crease of his mouth, begging for entrance. Kalan's mouth opened and she slid in to tease him. A moan filled her mouth as she nibbled on his bottom lip. She entwined her legs around his waist.

She didn't stop kissing him as he carried her to the bed. Laying her down, he pulled away.

"Hey, I didn't say you could leave," she protested.

He chuckled. "Don't worry. I think you'll be happy with what I'm going to do."

Before she said anything else, he stripped her. He kissed her then made his way down her neck to where the tendons met her shoulder. She gasped and arched her neck when he bit her there. The wet kisses he trailed over the curves of her breasts cooled in the night air, making her skin tingle.

His teeth scraped over her nipples as he split his attention between them.

She threaded her fingers through his hair and held his mouth to her.

He lowered his body onto hers. His teeth closed around one tip, and he flicked it with his tongue. One of his hands cupped her other breast. His thumb and finger plucked at the hard nub.

Writhing on the bed, she begged for more. "Harder, Kalan. I want to feel it deeper." Her voice urged him on.

He sucked her in and with each tug, her desire surged. Each nip raced down her body to center in her pussy.

"No," she moaned, when he pulled off her.

"Shh," he whispered against her stomach.

Spreading her thighs, she gave him more room to settle between them.

He spread her pussy then blew a puff of air over her throbbing clit.

Clutching the sheets with her hands, she lifted her hips up.

He slid his tongue on each side of her pussy, but didn't touch her clit. Pointing the tip of his tongue, he dipped it in.

"Please." She fought the urge to pull his face tighter to her.

He pinched her hard clit between his thumb and finger. Thrusting his tongue deep into her wet pussy, he twisted her clit gently.

He picked up the pace until her pleasure built to a climax. Her orgasm burst through and her back arched as she cried out.

Kalan crawled up her body and thrust his cock into her. Reaching down to cup his ass, she tugged him deeper.

"I can't get enough of you," he whispered in her ear as he rode her fast and hard.

"Good. I think I'm addicted to you." She smiled up at him.

Squeezing his shaft with her inner muscles, she angled her hips and encouraged him. His smooth rhythm became jerky while his climax moved closer. A grimace graced Kalan's face as his cock rocked in and out of her. She watched his desire bloom in his eyes as he spilled his cum into her.

Collapsing, he managed to roll so he was lying beside her. She kissed him and snuggled close. Discussing their next move could wait until morning.

* * * *

"It's time."

Starrer shook his head. There was no way he could go back to St Benedict's. Father Paul was starting to become suspicious. He had never spent as much time in the church when his son was alive.

"The Veil is weak, and the Devil's vulnerable. No one's expecting you to move so soon."

The voice was insistent. He wasn't sure. How could the Devil be killed so easily? A mere mortal wouldn't be able to do it. He wandered into his son's room.

He had left everything the way it had been when his son died. Such a bright, talented boy, yet Starrer had never known how tortured the young man was. Picking up a photo, he stared down at the smiling face of his son. Why would he kill himself?

"The Devil made him do it. The evil creature was jealous of your son."

The Devil had no need to be jealous of any mortal. Starrer turned to look at the wooden cross hanging on the wall.

"The Devil coveted what your son had. You must make him pay for what has happened. God believes in your quest. He would never have sent me to you if He didn't. He understands losing a son. He has chosen you to take revenge."

The voice made sense. A bond had formed between him and God because of their mutual loss. He hadn't been misled yet. The setback of the destruction of his army was his fault. He had chosen wrongly.

"I'll do it. You're right. The time has come for me to destroy that monster and make him suffer."

Closing the door to his son's room, he went to his own bedroom to cleanse his soul. Tomorrow night would be the night the Devil died.

Chapter Twenty-Eight

A hard rod poked Beltaine in the ass as she woke up. Sighing, she rubbed against it. Kalan's hand reached around her and cupped her breast.

"Hmm, I think I like waking up this way," she purred as she arched her back to press her nipple into his palm.

"It's better than getting kicked out of your bed." Kalan massaged her chest while stroking his cock between her ass cheeks.

"If you hadn't been such a jerk, we could've spent that first morning like this."

She groaned when his hand slid down over her stomach and into the curls covering her mound. Angling her hips, she encouraged him to dip his fingers into her pussy. His fingertips pinched her clit and twisted slightly.

She jerked, causing the head of his shaft to leave a wet trail along her ass. Kalan moved to ease his cock between her thighs. His lips attached to the tender spot behind her ear. They both gasped as the blunt head hit her clit.

"On your hands and knees," he ordered.

Rolling over to her stomach, she rose and supported herself with her hands and knees. He knelt behind her and traced her backbone with his finger. He ran his cock from the top of her ass to her clit, where he applied pressure by circling it with the head of his shaft. She pushed back, wanting to rub harder against him.

He teased her by inching just the tip of his cock into her pussy and leaning over to bite the nape of her neck. Whimpering, she tried to get him to thrust farther into her, but he wasn't letting her control how much of his cock she got or how deep he went.

"What do you want?" A wicked chuckle sent hot air over her ear as he nibbled on her earlobe.

"You. Deeper. Harder." Coherent sentences were slowly getting beyond her capabilities.

"I don't think I can get any harder than I already am. Maybe I can get deeper, though." A roll of his hips and he slid in an inch farther.

Hissing, she demanded his entire length. "All of you in me, now."

"You're rather demanding for being on the bottom, love." Another roll and two inches filled her.

Heaving, she twisted. Suddenly he was on his back and she was straddling him. Bracing her hands on his chest, she lined her pussy up with his cock then took him in. They both cried out as she sheathed him.

"God," Kalan breathed as his hips twitched.

She pressed down to keep him from moving. "Never tease a demon about sex, angel boy. We tend to take it very seriously. Now don't move. I'll do the work."

Lifting herself off his cock until only the tip fitted in her, she contracted her inner muscles to massage the blunt head. He tensed, and she figured he was getting ready to put her on her back. Smirking at him, she slammed back down on him.

His cock throbbed inside her. Her fingers plucked at his flat nipples as she rode him with quick, deep moves. The room filled with their groans and the sound of their flesh slapping together.

Her orgasm burst through her and she cried out. Kalan grasped her hips to keep her moving. The inner muscles of her pussy urged his pleasure from him. Wet warmth spilled into her as he thrust deep and came. Rocking, she soothed him until his climax died away.

"Can we stay in bed all day?" Kalan asked, after he caught his breath.

Chuckling, Beltaine rolled to sprawl next to him. "I wouldn't mind that, but your Commander might have something to say about it."

He grimaced at the thought of explaining to the Commander why he hadn't found the mortal who'd torn the Veil. He didn't think the Commander would be amenable to him fucking Beltaine all day.

"Did you find anything interesting in the catacombs?" He climbed out of bed and padded into the kitchen for a glass of water.

She was dressed when he returned. Staring out of the window, she said, "I talked to the Master."

"Really?" After pulling on his clothes, he sat on the bed to watch her.

"He repeated the same thing he told me before. There are people who want us to fail." She shot a grin over her shoulder. "Like we didn't know that."

"Did he name anyone specific?"

She shook her head. "Of course not, but we know who they are."

He nodded. Yes, they did know. He wouldn't be surprised to find out the higher lords of Hell were lined up on the other side of the barrier, waiting for it to fail.

"I talked to a young lady last night before I got back here. She approached me on the street. After she asked me who I was, she said this whole thing is about revenge."

"What was her name?" She moved toward him.

"I didn't have time to think about her name." He fought an irrational urge to duck his head.

"You're an angel. Why didn't you read her mind?"

"I didn't think about it." He stopped her next statement with an upraised hand. "I was thinking about something else she said to me."

"What did she say to make you forget about her name?"

"'Who else would God defend but the Devil? Without the Devil, there would be no need for God.'" He glanced at her. "Do you think that's true?"

"I can't say I've ever thought about it, but it makes sense. How can you understand evil without having good to compare it to?" She reached out to stroke his shoulder. "Are you having a problem with the idea that the Devil might have a purpose for being in the world?"

He nodded. "Of course. I can't believe God would willingly allow evil to exist."

"Mortals are different from angels. We tend to take things for granted. If nothing bad ever happened to us, we'd end up forgetting how good we've got it."

"I still don't get it."

"Without the Devil, we have nothing to thank God for."

Silently he nodded. Her statement made sense. "So what do we do now?"

"We go out and ask questions. There are other people who know who is to blame for this. Shaking a few trees might drop something at our feet." She pulled him up, allowing him to get dressed before leading him from her apartment.

He stayed quiet as they walked down the street. She shot him a glance, and he smiled at her.

"I met a man at St Benedict's. He gave me an odd feeling."

"Sweetheart, I thought most men gave you a strange feeling." Laughing, he protested when she slugged him. "Hey, why'd you hit me? Wasn't I telling the truth?"

"Jackass," she muttered. "You're right. I like men for one thing and one thing only, but I wouldn't even do that with this one."

"What was wrong with him?" He was intrigued because there didn't seem to be anything that made Beltaine nervous.

"I can't put my finger on it really, but when I brushed against him, there was a feeling of something else being in there with him." She shivered.

"Like a possession?"

"No. I can tell when there's a demon involved. I'm not sure what it was. There were moments when I felt like he was listening to something inside his mind. Father Paul introduced us."

"So who was he?"

"His name was Starrer, I believe. His son died earlier this year by suicide. He was at the church praying for the hurt to go away."

He heard the disgust in her voice. "Why do you sound like that? God can remove the pain if you ask."

"Bullshit. The pain's always going to be there. It might get duller over the years, but it's never going to go away. I've never lost anyone I cared about, but even I know that much." She headed toward the bad end of Ericksberg.

"Have you ever asked God to take the pain and guilt away?" He hesitated before he asked, but curiosity got the best of him.

She stopped and turned to glare at him. "Guilt?"

He waited for her to either hit him or flay him with her tongue. She shut her mouth and seemed to think about it for a moment. Shrugging, she started walking again.

"I guess I do feel some guilt for killing my father, but I'd do it again."

"Would you? Even knowing what you've been through since then?" He didn't believe her.

"Yes, I would. I didn't have anyone to protect me."

He pulled her to a stop with his hand on her shoulder. "Why didn't you ask your mother for help or go to the church?"

She stared down the street. "I was fourteen, Kalan. My mother dumped me with that crazy, abusive man. Also, she was a demon—he very thing my father had tried to beat out of me." She turned to look up at him, her eyes bleak. "My father was a priest. Why should I trust the church?"

"I thought he was excommunicated after you were born."

"He was, but he still believed in the teachings of the church. Father needed a scapegoat and I was the perfect one. No one from the church came to help me until it was too late. He was dead and buried before Father Simon came to help me. I believed the church was as much to blame for my pain as my father."

"How did your parents meet?" They had grown closer than he had ever thought they would, but he wasn't sure she'd tell him.

Gesturing to a small café, she said, "Let's sit. I want to get something to eat if I'm going to tell you my life story."

"You don't have to tell me anything, Beltaine. You're not obligated to say anything," he assured her as they moved to a table.

"Do you really think I'd tell you this if I didn't want to?" She laughed. "I thought you knew me better than that."

Wrapping his arms around her waist, he hugged her close. "I don't know that, but I wanted you to understand I don't want you to feel uncomfortable with trusting me."

She kissed his cheek and smiled. "If you're thinking of sticking around, you need to know the story."

Chapter Twenty-Nine

After they ordered breakfast, Beltaine watched the people walking by in front of the café. She wondered how many of those happy families were hiding dark secrets behind their smiles.

"My first memories are of my father kneeling in front of an altar and praying. I was in a crib or maybe a cage. I don't know. The reason I say that is because my view was blocked by bars."

Kalan frowned. "Do you really think he kept you in a cage?"

"I'm not sure. It wouldn't surprise me. He never thought of me as a real child. I was a wild animal."

"You were an innocent child. It shouldn't have mattered who your mother was."

Reaching over, she grasped his hand and squeezed. "It shouldn't have, but it did. My father was looking for a reason to hate me. Being half demon was all he needed." She closed her eyes for a moment. "When I was old enough, I hid. I'd go anywhere I could where he couldn't find me. That's how I met Roger." A warm feeling welled up in her at the thought of her friend.

"The pain and anger festered in me and I looked for someone else to hurt." She sent him a questioning look. "You understand the concept of 'paying it forward'?"

"Sure. Someone does something nice for you. Then you go out and do something nice for someone else." It was a basic concept most angels lived by.

"Right. Well, that's a wonderful idea, but have you ever wondered what might happen if you applied that same concept to abuse or evil?" She watched as confusion showed on his face.

"The evil you do doubles and the effects are worse for the next person. My father caused me pain and even as a young child, I searched for a way to release my anger by hurting others."

Disillusionment showed on his face. "You hurt Roger."

Chuckling bitterly, she shook her head. "No, he was the one person I couldn't hurt. When we first met, a group of men was getting ready to kick his ass. I was a pissed-off child and even as a half-demon, untrained and young, I was more than capable of taking them on."

"What did you do?" Fascinated horror rang in his voice.

She waited until their waiter finished delivering their meal. After he left, she continued, "I mowed through them. Destroying mortals is easy when you've never been taught the sanctity of life. I killed them without remorse or thought. When I was finished, Roger and I stood among the pieces of human bodies. He looked down at me with those beautiful blue eyes and I swore to myself nothing would hurt him. There was an innocence in him that

I'd never had in my young life, so I've spent the rest of the time since then protecting him."

"But how did your parents meet in the first place?"

"It was Beltaine night—a particular celebration my mother can't resist. Father heard stories of the rituals and celebrations that go on during this night. Even though the church frowned upon it, he decided to go. It's never been clear to me whether he went to find a woman to have sex with or if he went because he wanted to see what the church was condemning." She smirked. "I never felt the need to go into detail about why he was there. Maybe he felt the call of the old gods."

"Why was your mother there?"

"A pagan ritual celebrating sexuality and fertility? She wouldn't miss it for the world. The more interesting question would be, what made her pick my father as a partner that night?"

"All right. Why did she pick him?"

"Don't know. She never told me. She's treated the whole thing like a joke from the beginning. I mean, if she was serious about me, she would have never dumped me." There was no compassion or willingness in her to understand why her mother fucked her father that night.

"Maybe she didn't think a baby should grow up in Hell."

She knew he was trying to think the best of her mother, but there wasn't any forgiveness in her about that. "She didn't want to be tied down with a baby. Maybe what she thought was true. Maybe she did think my father would take better care of me, but she never came to see me. I was inconvenient for her. She forgot about me once she dumped me."

Beltaine leaned back in her chair. Anger built in her. She had always been mad at her parents for that.

"How was she to know she'd get pregnant? Has there ever been another half-demon child born?" At the shake of her head, Kalan said, "See, she had no way of knowing it would happen, and like any unsuspecting mother, she panicked."

Beltaine was willing to let him talk. Even though she didn't believe a word he said.

"Besides, isn't there a legend that says a child conceived on Beltaine night is a gift from God?" He grinned at her.

"I think my father considered me a curse, not a gift. Anyway, my mother seduced my father and got pregnant. Four months later, I was born." She wanted to finish the story.

"Four months?"

"It seems demons have accelerated pregnancies. As soon as she could, she dropped me off at my father's. I was a helpless babe, and that's what I never understood."

Kalan waved to the waiter to get the check. "You didn't understand that you were a helpless babe?"

She stared at a couple walking by. They were laughing and holding each other. "Why didn't he kill me when I couldn't fight back?"

"He was a priest. His conscience wouldn't let him kill an innocent child." After standing, Kalan paid the bill, and they moved away from the café.

"Bullshit. He couldn't kill a baby, but he abused me until I finally fought back? I'm not buying that."

"He was a bastard, but you're more than he thought you'd be."

"I had Roger. I used him as my moral compass." She winked at him. "Of course, I'll admit I do a lot of things he wouldn't, but he's done more to keep me honest than anyone else."

"You love him." It was a statement, not a question.

"For a very long time, he was the only one I loved." Beltaine cupped his cheek and pulled his mouth down to hers.

Inches away from her lips, he murmured, "Is there someone else you might be willing to love?"

"Maybe."

Their lips whispered kisses between them as they wrapped their arms around each other. Tasting and teasing, they leaned on each other. They moved apart and walked toward the rough end of town.

"Enough about my depressing childhood. Let's find the creep who's trying to kill the Devil."

* * * *

Starrer strolled into St Benedict's. He wasn't going to do anything but draw energy from the Veil.

"Why not go now? No one's watching."

He shook his head. It wasn't time yet. He needed to scope the catacombs and make sure the Veil was still weak. He needed those holes to make his way into Hell. Without checking to see who might be watching, he opened the door to the cellar. It didn't matter if anyone saw him now. God had ordained he would be the one to end the Devil's reign. The voice had told him the truth. He headed down toward the catacombs.

Power rolled over Starrer, driving him to his knees. He stared at the shimmering barrier in front of him and felt a swell of pride. He had done it. Only a few more hours to wait, and the Devil's hold on terror would be over.

He fought his way upright and moved toward the Veil. The voice in his head urged him on.

"Go on and cross over. You can kill the Devil and be in control of Hell before anyone knows."

Starrer's hand trembled as he reached out to touch the gleaming Veil. The holes were bigger and he could see horrific images flash by as the tears fluctuated. He gasped as his hand slid through. A burning sensation raced up his arm and exploded in his brain. He needed to get his hand back. Jerking it free, he cried out at the sight of his charred flesh.

"It burns," he wailed.

"A cross. You're marked with a cross. It's a sign from God that you're meant to achieve greatness."

"Yes," Starrer whispered, as he stared at the brand seared into the palm of his hand. "God has chosen me to avenge the deaths of our sons." Raising his hand, he shouted, "I will prevail. The Devil will die tonight." Starrer shook his fist defiantly at the barrier and spittle sprang from his mouth.

Turning, he stumbled from the catacombs, his mind filled with the voice and their plans to assassinate the Devil.

Chapter Thirty

Kalan and Beltaine stopped to regroup. They had spent most of the day terrorizing the lesser demons for information. None of those creatures would give anyone up, not even with Beltaine threatening them. Somehow, they knew she wouldn't send them back to Hell.

"What do we do now?" Kalan looked at her.

She shrugged. "I'm not sure if they know something and don't want to tell me or if they really don't know. All we have are hints, but nothing concrete. I'm starting to get pissed."

"It's frustrating. This guy shouldn't be so hard to find. I don't know why people and demons aren't standing in line to lead us to the culprit." He kicked the crumbling bricks of the wall beside him.

She smoothed her hand over his shoulder. "Most of them don't understand what's going to happen if we don't solve this problem. They're too caught up in their own lives. The bigger picture eludes them." A twinge of unease rushed over Beltaine, making her step closer to Kalan. She leaned in and murmured, "Someone is watching us."

"Have you got a bead on where he's standing?" He turned to hug her, pressing his lips to her ear.

"I think he's in the alley across the street and a few feet to our right."

"You want me to take him?" He tensed.

"I've been feeling this same person all day. Not sure when he started following us." Twisting, she crushed their lips together.

"Is it the same person from last night?" Kalan eased them into the shadows cast by a doorway.

"No. Not nearly the same level of anger and madness. This one feels unsure. Maybe he wants to approach, but isn't sure how." Her hands grasped his ass and tugged his hips tight to hers.

"Do you think he wants to talk to only one of us?" He rubbed his erection against her mound.

"It'd have to be you. I've been alone a few times when he could've talked to me." She slipped one of her hands around to fondle his hard-on.

"So if you disappear for a while, he might talk to me." He nibbled her ear.

"Take a walk to St Benedict's. Maybe he'll feel more secure talking to you in the church." She gave him a quick kiss then pushed him a few inches from her.

"Where will you be going?" He stepped back.

A twinge of disappointment and frustrated lust crept through her. Desire sat strong in her and she wanted to finish what they had started.

"Later," he said, like he knew what she was feeling.

"I'm doing a little more shaking down before heading back to the apartment. Meet me there afterwards." She winked at him as she strolled off.

Kalan watched Beltaine walk away. He wondered if his warrior angel status would be revoked if his Commander knew he was far more interested in kissing Beltaine than finding the man bent on revenge.

"Doesn't matter," he muttered. "Keep your mind on the job and once this is over, maybe you'll have some time to spend with her."

He headed toward the church. Without Beltaine's presence distracting him, he could feel their watcher following him. He didn't like the idea of not confronting the person trailing him, but he didn't want to scare away anyone who might have information.

Father Paul was rushing from the church as Kalan rounded the corner. The angel started to call out to him then decided to let the priest go. Father Paul looked like he was in a hurry.

Stepping into the vestibule of the church, all the tension and worry he'd been carrying slipped away. With the peaceful calmness of the sanctuary, one would never have guessed the horrors that had gone on below in the catacombs.

He knelt in front of the altar and bowed his head. He needed to clear his mind. Focusing on the mission before him, he knew he had to find a way to control his overwhelming lust for Beltaine. She was distracting him with her body and attitude. A rueful smile skated across his lips. It wasn't like he was fighting too hard against the attraction. Some emotion had been there from the moment they had met, even when he'd hated her for what she was.

Someone knelt beside him. He didn't acknowledge the person at first. Silence made people nervous, so he figured the watcher would spill his guts without much encouragement from Kalan.

Shifting closer to the other person, he asked, "Why have you been following us?"

"I wanted to watch the great Kalan work with a demon. I wanted to see if your intolerance for anyone different than you could stand up to Beltaine's sensuality and her smart-ass mouth." The voice was filled with sarcastic amusement.

Startled, Kalan shot a glance over to the person next to him. A pair of hazel eyes stared at him with barely disguised disgust. He jumped to his feet and faced off with the other angel.

"Jasper, what the hell do you mean?" Kalan demanded.

Jasper rose to his feet and strolled over to the front pew. Sitting, the angel grinned at Kalan. "What do I mean? Come on. You've got to know what your reputation is in the Host."

Kalan frowned. He had never paid attention to what the other angels said about him. It was all about serving God, not winning a popularity contest. He shrugged. "I don't pay attention to gossip."

"Of course not. You're the Commander's favorite and on the fast track for success. That's why you were chosen. We all know it." Jasper smirked as he leaned back.

"I doubt the Commander has a favorite," Kalan stated.

Jasper shook his head. "So oblivious to anything that doesn't directly affect you and so intolerant of those less perfect than you."

"What have I done to you, Jasper?" Kalan was puzzled by the angel's anger toward him.

"Aside from making the rest of us look bad, nothing really." Jasper lifted a lazy shoulder. "Maybe it's jealousy, but I've always thought you felt like you were better than us."

Shocked, Kalan couldn't believe what he was hearing. He'd never thought anything like that. He never concerned himself with the others. "Do you have anything worthwhile to tell me?"

He didn't want to listen to Jasper anymore. He admitted silently that Jasper's tendency to whine irritated him.

"Ah, don't want to listen to your faults dissected and listed. Close your ears and turn away from anyone who might be reaching out to you for help." Jasper's hazel eyes flashed.

"When have you ever reached out to me?" Kalan's own anger was growing.

Jasper's gaze slid to the crucifix behind Kalan then back to him. "I couldn't reach out because you're perfect. Do you realize how hard it is to reach out and ask for help or understanding from a person who never does anything wrong?"

"Nothing wrong? You need to talk to Beltaine. I'm sure she could give you a list of things I've screwed up." Kalan paced as he waved his hands around. "I'm fucking a demon, for God's sake."

"I don't think God has a thing to do with it." Jasper chuckled at Kalan's snarl. "When I first heard the rumor going around the Host about you and Beltaine, I didn't believe it. I thought it was a lie someone started to discredit you. Imagine my shock when you two started sucking face on the street." The angel shook his head with a disappointed grimace. "I really thought she had better taste."

"I'm not sure either one of us had a choice," Kalan muttered. At Jasper's puzzled glance, he continued,

"There was an instant attraction and neither of us seemed to be able to fight it."

"You couldn't fight it?" Jasper shook his head. "You can't convince me you lost control."

"Believe it. Within five minutes of meeting her, she was wrapped around me like a boa constrictor, and we were trying to devour each other. Beltaine's not the type to deny herself."

"Except instead of a regular guy, she kissed an angel," Jasper pointed out. "She doesn't have a death wish. There's no way she'd risk touching you, because you could've killed her."

"See what I mean about not having control? Self-preservation is important to her. Beltaine isn't going to do anything that could result in getting herself killed, so having sex with me shouldn't be high on her list."

"It shouldn't be on her list at all." Jasper sounded confused.

"Exactly. I hadn't been particularly nice to her before that. I'm sure her first inclination was to kill me, not fuck me." Kalan stopped when he heard a gasp. Looking at the back of the sanctuary, he saw a parishioner standing there with her mouth open in surprise.

"You're ruining your image. Swearing in a church isn't something the Commander's prize angel would do." Jasper winked at the woman who ducked her head and hurried out.

"I know, and God knows I'm sorry." Kalan sent a silent prayer for forgiveness to the Father.

"I never thought we'd live to see the day you would willingly breathe the same air as a demon, even one as enticing as Beltaine." Curiosity brightened Jasper's green eyes.

Kalan flung his body down on to the pew next to his fellow angel. "I know. Before I met her, I believed the only good demon was a dead one."

"You were spoon-fed that drivel by our illustrious Commander, who bears a deep hatred for the Devil and his demons," Jasper commented.

"Even half-demons." Kalan thought of the last encounter between the Commander and Beltaine.

"I thought it was her abrasive personality he couldn't stand." Jasper joked.

"No. The last time they met, I really thought he was going to kill her, but he can't touch her. God won't allow it." Kalan frowned. "It's strange, though."

"What is?"

"That God would protect a half-breed demon." Kalan jumped to his feet and started pacing again.

"Not when you consider He allowed her to live in the first place." Jasper moved from the pew to stand in front of the altar. "Maybe He has a plan for her, like He does for all of us."

"What sort of plan would allow for her killing her father?"

Jasper was quiet for a minute. "I guess I have to fall back on the tried but true saying, 'God works in mysterious ways'. There was something seriously wrong with her father to begin with."

"What sort of plan does He have for you?" Kalan inquired.

"Who knows? It's not like He tells any of us the future." Jasper glanced up at the crucifix.

"Do you know anything about what's happening here?" Kalan was tired. He wanted to talk to Beltaine and hold her in his arms. He wanted to hear her tell him that all this was bullshit.

"The man you're looking for is Richard Starrer." Jasper shrugged, as Kalan stared at him. "It doesn't matter if I tell you or not. Being a rebel, I believe in helping whenever I can, even if it's against orders."

"No shit?" Kalan was so surprised, he forgot about not swearing. "I wonder if he's the man Beltaine ran into yesterday. She had a feeling something was wrong with him."

"Something *is* seriously wrong with him. Losing his son put him straight over the edge, and now getting revenge on the Devil seems to be all he can think of."

"I've got to get to Beltaine." Kalan turned away then whirled back to Jasper. "How do you know so much about Beltaine?" The question had been bothering him since they'd started talking.

"We've met at some of the clubs in the city." At the skeptical quirk of Kalan's brow, Jasper laughed bitterly. "They're clubs no self-respecting angel would go to, but since I have no self-respect, I fit right in."

Kalan didn't know how to react. He made a mental note to talk to Beltaine later about Jasper. "Thank you. I know you weren't supposed to help me. That you did, especially with you hating me as you do, means a lot to me."

Jasper smiled with a sad glint to his eyes. "I don't hate you. Helping you and Beltaine ultimately helps me. Find the bastard and stop him before he screws everything up."

"We will." Kalan focused his attention on Beltaine and disappeared.

Jasper glanced up at Jesus hanging on the cross and winked. "He might turn out okay after all."

Chapter Thirty-One

Starrer stared down at the girl sprawled in his living room. Her blood pooled into a dark burgundy puddle beneath her head. Dispassionately, he thought how beautiful it looked against the bright pine of his hardwood floor. Her brown eyes stared up into the fluorescent bulbs piercing the darkness. He pushed one of her legs with the toe of his polished shoe. When she didn't move, he shrugged.

The slack jaw and drooping skin gave her face a half-witted look. He knew she had been intelligent when she was alive. His son had never suffered fools or stupidity, and the boy had loved this silly girl. Starrer remembered how she had sobbed on his shoulder during his son's funeral. How she had talked incessantly about why he'd killed himself and how much she'd loved him. Richard had fought the urge to backhand her and tell her she could never have loved his son as much as he did.

"You are a loving father. You sent your son his girlfriend to keep him company in the afterlife."

The voice grew stronger every minute. There were times when Starrer thought the voice compelled him to do things.

"She was innocent, and as such, her place in Heaven is secure. You have done nothing but ensure your own spot in Hell." Another voice broke through the static in his mind to berate him.

"She was no innocent. She got my son involved in drugs. I know it was her and she is as much to blame for his death as the Devil is."

Starrer remembered his shock when the doctor had told him traces of cocaine and heroin had been found in his son's bloodstream.

"That's right, Richard. She knew about the drugs and did nothing to stop him or even to tell you about them. Her negligence makes her just as guilty and you've made her pay. Now it's time for the Devil to be destroyed."

"You're right," he muttered as he headed to his room. "This is the last day the Devil has lived to see. He will taste death tonight at my hand."

Opening his closet door, he pulled out his red silk robe. It should have stayed down in the catacombs, but running away from that bitch and her partner hadn't given him a chance to leave it behind. He hoped the mortal world hadn't contaminated it too much. Maybe soaking it in the blood of that silly girl would ensure the power was sealed in. He stripped and wandered back to the living room. Kneeling, he dipped it in the drying blood. When it was saturated, he folded it and stuck it in a bag. There was enough sanity left in him to realize he couldn't wear it out in public. Leaving the bag next to the door, he strolled back to the bedroom to retrieve a black cotton robe. Slipping it on, he glanced at his reflection in the mirror. A maniacal laugh ripped from his throat. He looked like a priest.

"That's what you are in the truest sense. Those priests in the church give lip service to God's words. His Word says not to listen to the Devil, yet they have allowed the creature footing in their world. The Devil turned from the Father and Heaven. His punishment should have been death, not banishment. God chose mercy. We will choose justice. Justice for all the souls he has claimed. Justice for all those lives he has ruined in his arrogance. When we are through with him, there will be only one powerful being in the world, and that will be us."

The room shook as if the earth reacted to the voice's words. Starrer braced his body against the dresser. His eyes widened as a large crack shattered the mirror he was staring into. Minute shards broke off and landed to pierce his hands. Running the palms of his hands over the dresser, he didn't flinch at the flaying of his flesh or the lines of blood streaking the wood.

"Your blood is offered as sacrifice and a good faith gesture that you will accomplish the goal God has set out for you. One being's blood was spilled for another's arrogance. One being's blood will be spilled for atonement. Go and take Hell for God."

Starrer nodded and stalked from the apartment, ignoring his son's girlfriend, whose body grew cold on the living room floor.

* * * *

Beltaine was strapping on her knife when Kalan returned to her apartment. Father Paul jumped and whirled to stare at him.

"I know who ripped the Veil," Kalan announced when he appeared.

"So do we." She smiled at the priest. "Father Paul came and told me. That's why I'm getting ready."

She laughed as Kalan shot the priest a glare. She decided to leave the gun behind. She didn't think she was going to have to kill Starrer.

"How did you know?" Kalan asked Father Paul.

"I followed Mr Starrer down into the catacombs." The priest nodded toward Beltaine. "You told me to come and see you if there was anything strange happening at the church. While Starrer was in the altar room, he slid his hand through the Veil."

"Father Paul said when Starrer pulled his hand back, there was a burn on it. Starrer was saying he was ordained by God to avenge the deaths of their sons."

"That's what my informant said as well. It all comes down to the fact that his son committed suicide, and instead of taking any of the blame for it, he picked the person least likely to care about the entire episode." Kalan followed her and Father Paul out of the apartment.

She glanced back at him. "I forgot about our follower. Who was he?"

"Jasper. He's a fellow angel of the Host. He followed us to see if I had learned to tolerate people. He doesn't have a real high opinion of me, but he seemed to like and know you." He shrugged.

"Jasper? We've met at a few clubs in the city. I didn't know your fellow angels could, or would, help us." She turned to look at Father Paul. "Where does Starrer live?"

"He lives uptown. I'm not sure if he would be there when we arrived. We might be better off heading back to the church." Father Paul directed them.

"It isn't that hard. We could pop over there and check. We need to catch him before he causes more damage," Kalan commented to her.

She thought about it. Would the use of power be worth catching Starrer before he headed to the church? She didn't know how much of a fight the man was going to put up. "Maybe one of us should head over there, just to check."

Kalan agreed. "I'll go with Father Paul. You know where to go in Ericksberg. Plus, I trust you to do what's needed to stop him." A rueful grin crossed his face when she glanced at him. "If he has to die, I'm not sure I could do it."

"You didn't have a problem with the vampire." She wasn't sure she believed him. The warriors of the Host were fierce and at times more violent than the Horde of Hell.

"It was evil. Nothing could redeem it or change its nature. Starrer is a mortal, helpless and worthy of my protection."

She speared him with an incredulous look. "Helpless? I'm not sure that's the word I'd use for him. Crazy. Totally fucking nuts. Lost touch with reality. Look what he's done. We don't know how many women he and his silly army might have killed. The idiot believes he's ordained by God to kill the Devil. I know Starrer isn't worth any sort of protection." She snarled.

"Exactly. That's why you need to go. Father Paul and I will meet you in the catacombs."

She watched the two men walk away. So she was relegated to be the assassin—she shouldn't be surprised. In the grand scheme of things, killing was what she was good at. Plucking Starrer's address from

Father Paul's mind, she gathered her power and disappeared.

* * * *

"Damn."

Beltaine couldn't believe it. Starrer had the Devil's own luck. Considering what the man was attempting, it didn't bode well for the Devil. She hoped the crazy man didn't get close to the ruler of Hell.

Kneeling, she felt for a pulse at the girl's wrist. "Dead," she muttered. "The big pool of blood should have given it away, you idiot."

She stood and shook her head. Another life ruined in Starrer's psychotic crusade. She thought about making a list, but it would be an overwhelming number if they didn't stop him. Glancing around, she frowned. Starrer must have put something in the blood puddle because there wasn't the quantity she'd expect to see if the girl had bled out, and there were drops leading to the door.

Curiosity got the best of Beltaine. She knew Kalan and Father Paul could hold down the fort back at the church for a few minutes more. Looking at the living room, she saw all the accoutrements of wealth. Beautiful works of art decorated the dark tan walls. Leaded crystal lamps and bits of sculpture graced the high-end furniture. She wondered if he'd bought any of the things legitimately or if he had gotten them from the black market.

Wandering down the hall, she stepped through a door and shock raced down her spine. The large ornate mirror hanging over the white pine dresser had shattered. Shards of glass littered the top. Moving closer, she wiped a finger through the red streaks on the wood. She brought the tip to her tongue and grimaced at the metallic taste.

"Blood." She spoke out loud.

Her gaze was caught by her fractured image in the mirror. *This is who you really are,* a small voice echoed in her mind. *Shattered beyond recognition.*

Had she always been cracked? Or had her personality developed small fissures, widened by the stress she'd lived under with her father? A tremor caused more pieces of the mirror to drop to the dresser and she blinked. Who the hell cared why she was fucked up? She couldn't go back and fix the past. She didn't even know if she wanted to. Another tremor shook the entire room and a piece of glass impaled itself in her hand.

Hissing, she picked the shard out and flung it onto the floor. Something was happening. She needed to get back to the catacombs. Beltaine started to make her way back to the living room, but a strange force pulled her to the closed door across the hall from Starrer's room. Pushing open the door, her mouth fell open. She stepped inside and contemplated the space around her.

It was a shrine to a dead son. It didn't look like anything had been moved for months. The layer of dust on everything was thick. A picture tucked into the corner of the plain dresser mirror captured her gaze. Reaching out, she tugged it free and pulled it closer. A young man around twenty years old posed with his arms around the very girl who lay dead out in the other room. Their faces held smiles, but where the smile showed in the girl's eyes, only darkness reigned in the boy's dark stare. Starrer had to have been blind to miss the despair in his son. She ran a thumb over the paper, stroking the kid's face. What had sent the boy on the path he chose? What had been so broken in him that he'd thought killing himself was easier than living? She couldn't help but compare herself with him. Why had she chosen to kill her father instead of herself? Was it her demon blood that turned the anger outward?

Studying the girl in the photo, Beltaine smiled. The girl must have been a cheerful person and a joy to be around. A rare twinge of sadness hit her at the most recent image she had of the girl. Those laughing brown eyes were empty now. The grin was gone from the slack face. It was rare for Beltaine to be disheartened about not having met someone. She would have enjoyed getting to know this girl.

"Beltaine, where the hell are you?" Kalan's shout broke into her thoughts.

Shocked, she dropped the picture. No one had ever been able to break down her barriers enough to communicate with her mentally—except for the Commander and the Master, but those two creatures disregarded any wall blocking them.

"What's wrong?" She shot back as she drew her power in.

"Somehow Starrer got past us. He's passed through the Veil and is in Hell."

"Damn."

The time had come to deal with the bastard. She would make him pay for killing the girl and for taking the world to the brink of destruction.

Chapter Thirty-Two

Kalan released the breath he'd taken when Beltaine arrived in the catacombs. He barely hung on to consciousness. There was no way he would have been able to survive going through the Veil if she hadn't shown up.

"Thank God you're here." He hugged her.

An eyebrow shot up as she frowned at him. "I don't think anyone's ever thanked God for me. What's got you all worried? As long as he stays in Hell, we'll be able to take care of him."

"What if he finds the Devil and kills him?" Father Paul's voice shook as he questioned her.

Kalan shivered at the coldness in her laugh.

She said, "Dear Father, there's no way he will get close enough to do any harm to the Devil. Do you think all those demons and the Horde of Hell are just for show? They serve as his bodyguards and will rip to shreds any mortal who dares to invade their domain."

"You are going after him, aren't you?" Kalan led her closer to the Veil. He had qualms about sending her into Hell, but since she'd been there once already and hadn't suffered any ill effects, he figured she'd be fine.

"Why would I? The Master and the Horde will take care of the problem without our getting our hands dirty." She leaned against the altar and smiled wickedly.

Kalan's stomach roiled. He had seen what demons could do to a body, and that image was seared into his brain. "We can't let that happen to him. He's mortal and one of God's creatures."

"Ah, but see, so is the Devil. Have we any right to keep the Devil from defending himself against attackers?" She pursed her lips in thought. "Maybe I should go and make sure they really do take care of him. We don't want him returning and causing even more trouble."

Disappointment rushed through Kalan. "I thought you were finally beginning to understand that everyone has the right to be judged by God. We can't play judge and executioner to Starrer. Only God has the right."

She reached out and drew a claw down his cheek, scratching a thin line into his skin. "I'm willing to suffer the consequences of his dying in Hell. You didn't see what I found in his apartment. You don't understand the level of depravity he has sunk to in his ridiculous quest."

He angled his head away from her claw. There was a wildness in her he hadn't seen in days. Anger turned her eyes red with fire. "What did you find?"

"A body of a young woman. She might have even been the one who talked to you. She was dead, her blood pooled beneath her throat. He cut her neck so deeply, he almost beheaded her. She was his son's girlfriend — the one person who might have been able to understand his grief and help him through it. Instead, he killed her and left her as if she were a mere side of beef at the butcher's shop. You look at the Devil and call him evil. You see a creature that serves only himself and has no concern for anyone else, and you say he's the one who should be destroyed." Stepping away from him, she gestured to the bloodstained altar in front of them and spat. "I look at Starrer and see a creature so evil that he doesn't deserve mercy. A mortal so far gone, he doesn't deserve justice. Richard Starrer is the true Devil and I have no sympathy for him."

"This is what you were born to do, Beltaine."

They whirled to see Father Simon standing in the entrance to the chamber. Hissing, she turned away from him. Kalan was relieved. If anyone could talk sense into her, it would be Father Simon. The priest was the only person she seemed to respect.

"You won't con me with that bullshit, Father Simon. I don't believe God created me to save some psychotic mortal."

"No, He didn't," Father Simon agreed with her.

Kalan figured he looked like a fish with his mouth gaping open. He'd thought the priest would be able to talk her into saving Starrer.

"I knew someone would see the light." Smugness tinted her voice.

"He created you to save demons and mortals alike from the consequences of Starrer's actions." Leaning on Roger, the priest moved into the room.

Kalan could see the toll this effort took on the old priest. He started to move forward to help them, but Roger shook his head.

She chuckled. "No way. If that's true, then God knew before all this started what was going to happen." She denied the words. "He would have never allowed it to start."

"As powerful as God is, He's bound by His own actions. He gave us free will and so has condemned us to the state we live in. He can only put in place things or people that could help ensure a better outcome." Father Simon placed a hand on her shoulder.

"Now I'm a simple game piece. A piece He ensured would be here at this moment. Someone He knows won't allow thousands to die for the idiocy of one." Shaking off the priest's touch, she moved closer to the Veil. "He's taking a huge chance I won't just decide to allow all of us to die. What if that's my choice…suicide by Heavenly Host?"

Father Simon didn't flinch from the burning glare she fired at him. "You chose not to kill yourself because of your father's abuse."

"Isn't it twisted that you see the fact that I killed my father instead as a good thing?" She moved away from them again. "I'm glad you find something good in the hell that my early life was."

"Beltaine, stop it. You have a chance to help the world out. You've always wanted to know the reason God had for making you," Roger admonished her.

"I hate it when you throw my words back at me." She didn't look at any of them and Kalan wondered what she was thinking.

The small glimpse into her demon side shook him. He didn't know why he was surprised and upset by it. She never tried to be anything other than what she was. Beltaine wore her truth like a badge. She might hate her demon heritage, but she wouldn't hide who she was from anyone. He respected that, yet complacence had grown in him when her hard edges had softened in the days he'd known her. The reappearance of her 'screw them all' attitude disheartened him.

"Please, Beltaine. I don't want to die yet." Roger's voice was soft.

A hint of jealousy rushed through Kalan as she cupped the young priest's cheek and smiled at him.

Jealousy gains you nothing and just makes you look like an idiot, his inner voice told him.

If there really was anyone she would listen to, it would be the young man she had grown up with and protected. Kalan doubted she would react the same way had he said anything like that to her.

That's because you can deal with things on your own. You don't need protection. You're an angel as well, so there's no danger to you.

He kept quiet as he watched Roger manipulate Beltaine.

"I know what you're doing, Roger. I've seen you guilt your parishioners with those innocent blue eyes." She kissed Roger's cheek and sighed. "All right, I'll do it and protest the entire way. It won't be my fault if he's already dead."

They watched as she strolled up through the Veil. Kalan turned to look at Roger and Father Simon.

"Can we trust her to bring Starrer back to us?" he asked them.

Father Paul stepped up to stand beside him. "I was wondering that as well. She doesn't really care if he lives or dies. What's to stop her from allowing the demons to kill him and then tell us he was already dead when she got there?"

Roger smiled. "She'll bring him back. Beltaine had made the decision to go get him before I said a word. There isn't a thing I could have done to convince her if she didn't want to go."

* * * *

"What the hell am I doing here?" Beltaine asked herself as she strolled down a deceptively quiet city street.

She chuckled. The men believed Roger had talked her into going after Starrer, and if anyone ever asked, that would be her answer. Truth be told, she had decided she wanted to make the man pay for what he had done to Betsy and the young woman he'd left on his living room floor. If Beltaine could kill him, she would, and there wouldn't be any guilt about it.

"Now to find the crazy bastard and drag his ass home."

She made her way toward what seemed to be the seamier part of the city. It was odd how Hell appeared to her like a city on Earth. There was nothing to distinguish it from Ericksberg or the city she lived in. As she walked, the buildings fell apart around her, marking that she was entering the rough part of Hell.

Who knew there was a bad section of Hell?

Angry voices came from ahead of her. Breaking into a jog, she wound her way through a growing crowd of demons and mortal souls. She stopped outside a seedy jazz bar, where the Devil stood complaining to the Master.

"You're telling me some mortal has come into Hell to kill me." A nasty cackle came from the Devil's throat. "Not only does he dare to do this in my realm, but he also does it on the night my favorite band is playing. Mortals have no manners at all."

The Devil saw her standing there and gestured for her to come forward. Without a tremble, she greeted him. She didn't want to show any fear, but she had to show respect for the creature in his own world.

"Sir," she said, as she nodded to the Devil and the Master.

"Do you know the arrogant whelp who has entered my world without permission?" the Devil demanded.

"Yes. His name is Richard Starrer and he believes you caused his son's suicide."

"If I caused every bad thing attributed to me, I wouldn't have time for myself — and that would never do." He paced in front of her, tugging on the cuffs of his suit.

"He's mortal, sir. He doesn't grasp how unimportant his son's death is to you. I'll be glad to take him back to his side of the Veil."

The Master hissed.

"Do you really believe you can waltz in here and take him from us?" The Master grabbed her shoulder and whirled her around to face him. "Did you really think it would be that easy?"

"I was hoping it would be, but I should have known you'd be an ass about the whole thing."

She cringed inside. Antagonizing him probably wasn't a good thing. Biting her tongue had never done anything except make it sore, so she would do what she did best. She had worked hard at being a smartass, and she was going to use that talent to her advantage to tick off the Master and get the Devil on her side. Those two creatures hated each other almost as much as the Commander and the Master did.

The Devil's thin eyebrows shot up and he laughed. "She knows you well, friend."

"An ass? A mere mortal dares to enter Hell without permission and she calls *me* an ass." The Master's voice dropped into a low growl.

The hair on Beltaine's neck stood up. The warning tone in his growl shivered up her spine. *Now would be a good time to back down and walk away.* It was good advice, but she had never listened to anyone's advice, not even her own.

"Listen, the man has some serious issues and personally, I'd let you rip him apart, but there's a disagreement on whether that's the merciful thing to do." She turned to the Devil. "Do I have your permission to find the bastard and take him out of here?"

A pleased smiled blossomed on the Devil's face and she knew she had him. Stroking his ego would get her farther than being a bitch to him. He beamed at her.

"Of course you can. I'm going to listen to the band. I don't want to be bothered by this mortal again." With a wave of his hand, the Devil dismissed both her and the Master.

"You think you're smart, scraping and acting like he's the important one here. Remember, I control the Horde. They do *my* bidding, not his. Don't think I'll let Starrer out of Hell alive," the Master warned.

"I guess it's a race then. If I find him first, I get to take him back to the other side. If you get him, you can kill him."

"Are you serious?" The Master stared at her with narrowed eyes.

"I don't tend to joke with beings that can kill me without thought." She eased away from him.

"Remember that when you're looking for your mortal." The Master gestured for the Horde to follow him.

Chapter Thirty-Three

"You do have a knack for upsetting demons and angels alike, dear."

Beltaine groaned as her mother appeared beside her. "You are the last person I want to see right now."

"Not true. The Commander would be the last person you'd want to see now. He'd pitch a fit and try to kill you." The demon giggled.

"Can't argue with you on that, but he can't touch me, so he'd be blowing hot air." She stared at her mother. "Is there a reason why you're talking to me now? I don't have time to deal with you."

"No reason. I wanted to say thank you for bringing the book back."

Beltaine was surprised. "Who are you and what the hell did you do with my mother?"

"No, I mean it. The Devil thanked me for sending you after the book. You made me look good. I appreciate it."

"Ah, I see now. You want to thank me because my almost getting killed made you look good. It doesn't matter what the Devil thinks. He's still going to screw you." Disappointment rolled over her.

"We both know he can't get enough of me." The creature preened. "He thinks I was awfully clever to get pregnant with you."

"It was all *your* doing. Father and God didn't have a damn thing to do with it," Beltaine sneered.

"They didn't carry you for four months. I looked like a whale. I should get some sort of recognition for that."

Before Beltaine could release her frustration by hitting her mother, Azubah appeared.

"What do *you* want?" Beltaine demanded of the small demon.

The demons spat at each other like alley cats then her mother disappeared. Azubah sniffed as it turned to look at her.

"I really don't have time for this. I have to find that lunatic before the Master gets him, or we'll have pieces of mortal strewn all over Hell." Crossing her arms, she stared down at the winged creature.

It nodded. "I know, and for some odd reason, you don't want that to happen. Why not allow the Horde to punish the man for his impertinence?"

"I'm a sucker for blue eyes and a body made for loving." She laughed at the demon's puzzled frown. "Roger wants me to bring Starrer back."

"A body made for loving? Roger's a priest." A look of horrified fascination crossed through Azubah's red eyes.

She shook her head. "It's Kalan's body I was talking about, sick creature."

It shrugged. "I'm a demon. Being sick is a rule or something for my kind. So you're obeying an angel now." Cunning slid onto its face.

"I listen to him when he tells me what he would like me to do, but I don't obey anyone, so get that look off your face." She started to walk away.

"Do you know where to find this man?" Azubah asked with an innocent grin.

"Hell no, but since I'm tired of talking to you, I thought I'd leave and see if I can trip over him." Her patience was wearing thin with everyone in Hell. She'd reached the point where she wanted to hide and say screw everyone.

"Well, I might know where he's hiding." The casual tone in the demon's voice belied the tension in its body.

She grabbed the creature by the throat. After dragging its trembling figure toward her, she lifted it so they were staring eye-to-eye. She bared her fangs and growled. "I should kill you here. You've been jerking me around while you go on a power trip. Don't fuck with me and you'll be a happier demon." She shook Azubah so hard she thought its fangs were going to rattle out of its head.

"Okay. Okay. No need to get all manic on me, Beltaine. I was just kidding." Waving its arms, the demon babbled.

"Sorry if I have no sense of humor at the moment. Tell me where he is and I won't tear your head off."

"Where else would a mortal who knows nothing about the Devil go?"

Beltaine dropped the demon and took off. "The throne room."

"Yep," Azubah said as it scurried along beside her.

"How did he find his way there without some demon seeing him?" she wondered out loud.

"I don't know. He's been hiding in a corner and mumbling to himself since he got there."

Stopping quickly, she turned to question the demon. "How do you know where he is?"

Azubah bared its fangs in a sick parody of a smile. "I've been keeping an eye on the Veil since you rescued that whore. When Starrer crossed over, I followed him. I was on my way to find you when I saw you talking to that thing you call 'mother'."

"Thing? She's a demon like you." Beltaine continued toward the throne room.

A snort of disdain came from the small creature. "I would never stoop to her level. She might be the Devil's favorite, but she's just a bitch in heat. Gives the rest of us a bad name."

She snickered. "My mother gives demons a bad name? You, dear Azubah, have some serious delusions if you think it's only my mother's actions making you look bad."

She skidded to a stop outside the Devil's throne room. The doors leading into the room were over ten feet tall and made of solid obsidian. Carved into the panels were tormented faces, dismembered bodies and creatures Beltaine had never seen before. The handles were glistening white leg bones.

"The Devil has a sick sense of humor." Grumbling, she pulled one of them open.

The atmosphere in the throne room was so oppressive she wondered how any creature—demon or mortal—could stand to be in the room for very long. Azubah ran into her as she stopped inside the door.

"Watch where you're going," Beltaine snapped.

"Sorry. I thought I saw a shadow in an alley before we came in," the demon apologized as it glanced back toward the street they came from.

"Do you think one of the Horde followed us?" She wouldn't put it past the Master to have one of his creatures spy on her.

Shaking its head, Azubah disagreed. "No, I think it was something else. I swore I saw a glimmer—like light reflecting off glass or something."

She barked out a laugh. "Right. Light off glass. There's no light here unless I imagine some. It's amazing how Hell looks a lot like Dark Town."

"Hell's what you want it to be. Your worst fears and memories create this place. The only place that doesn't ever change is the throne room. It's the base of the Devil's power."

"And the one place he never goes." She moved with careful steps across the wide room to where the Devil's throne rested.

Again, obsidian had been used to create the chair. Elaborately carved skulls formed the chair's feet and armrests. The back of the throne rose seven feet in the air and had a gold sun etched into the face of it.

"Lucifer, the Daystar," she whispered. It saddened her to see the symbol of what the Devil had once been. She wondered if that was why he chose to spend his time elsewhere in Hell.

Azubah shivered as the demon settled beside her and stared up at the throne. "I've never liked this room. It's so gloomy and depressing here."

Beltaine shot a confused glance at the creature. "Are you sure you're a demon?"

"Yes. Why?" The question held a defensive edge.

"You don't sound like any demon I know." A quick peek at the sun again then she spun around to look over the room.

Thirteen enormous pillars spaced in two rows guarded the aisle leading from the doors to the platform. Paneled with darkest ebony, the walls soared up into darkness. Blackness covered the ceiling, hiding the roof of the room. Fear crawled down her back at the thought of what might be shrouded in the shadows. She knew there were beings in Hell she had never seen and had never imagined existed. It was those creatures she didn't want released on unsuspecting mortals. The room freaked her out.

"Let's find the asshole and get out of here before something worse than the Master finds us." She pointed to the right side of the room. "You search that side. If you find him, give a shout."

Beltaine had been right about things hiding in the shadows. Even the strongest of creatures wouldn't have been able to see the stranger perched in the farthest corner of the ceiling. His power blocking their sight, he glared down at the demon whelp and the pathetic thing helping her. His anger grew until he was almost overwhelmed by it. He wanted to fall upon Beltaine and rip her to shreds. *How dare she try to stop this cleansing I've started? She can't stand between my goal and me, even if she takes my mortal. Soon the Veil will fall, and my power will be absolute. It won't matter that she bears His mark — I'll kill her.*

White teeth gleamed in the darkness as the watcher snarled in fury at Beltaine's triumphant shout.

"Azubah, I've found the idiot." Beltaine's shout echoed through the room.

Starrer huddled in a corner behind the throne platform. His brown hair stood up in spikes, and tufts littered the floor around him like he'd pulled hunks out. He muttered words she couldn't hear and wasn't likely to, since she didn't want to get any closer to him. The stiff robe he wore had a metallic smell to it. She was sure it had been soaked in the girlfriend's blood before the man had entered Hell. Reaching out, she stopped before she touched his shoulder.

Her skin twitched and her hand trembled. She wanted to believe it was because she was so angry at the senseless destruction the man had done, but she couldn't lie to herself. Fear caused her hand to shake. When she had run into Starrer the first time, a feeling of madness had swept over her. His attempt to find and kill the Devil proved her right, but at this moment, she knew by touching him, the madness would drag her into his mind, and she didn't want to go there. Insanity had dogged her steps for fourteen years of her life and she had chosen to kill instead of allow it to take her. She didn't know if she could willingly step into that abyss by touching this mortal.

Chapter Thirty-Four

"Why do you hesitate?"

The hoarse voice caused her to jump. Turning her head, she saw a transparent wraith standing beside her. She recognized the vague outline—she had held an image of the spirit in her hands earlier in the night. Starrer's son scrutinized the body in front of him. Then those eyes met hers and she saw the same emptiness in them that showed in the photo.

"You don't want to touch him. Is it possible you can see the madness that hides in him?"

She drew her hand back with a careful movement. Spirits didn't often linger in the throne room of the Devil. They were sent to their own specific Hell within minutes of arriving. There was something off about this young man. Taking a step away, she settled into a defensive position.

"I don't wish to harm you." A faint grin graced the phantom's face. "I'm not sure I could even if I wanted to. The mark upon your neck compels me to leave you alone."

Fighting the urge to touch the scar on her throat, she clenched her hands and kept quiet. The shade glided closer to his father. A wave of its hand in front of the fixed eyes elicited no response.

"Like in life, he doesn't see me. Why is he here?" The question was directed toward her without the son's gaze leaving the father.

"He believes the Devil caused you to commit suicide. He wants to avenge your death by killing the Devil." The words forced their way from her throat.

"Amazing. He had no time for me while I lived. Now he attempts great foolishness to atone for his own neglect." The son's voice held no concern or worry for his father. He knelt on the floor to look into Starrer's eyes without touching him. "You've come to take him back to face judgment from God, haven't you?"

"He'll face judgment from the mortal world first for all the women he has killed or attacked in his crusade. More than likely, he'll receive the death penalty. After they kill him, he will stand before the throne of God and be judged for what he was."

An ironic chuckle came from the son. "He will end up down here with me anyway. I never believed suicides went to Hell, no matter what the church said. Yet here I am, trapped in some strange room I can't leave."

"You can't leave the throne room?" Beltaine hated oddities because it usually meant someone else had a hand in what was happening. "You should have gone on to your personal Hell when you arrived without even seeing the Devil. He doesn't care who joins him, as long as they're dead."

The young man shook his head. "I'm sure that's the way it usually works, but for some reason, I have been stuck here. I can't walk out the doors even if they are open. I don't believe I was meant to be here."

"Everyone says that. All the people who commit suicide don't think they should be condemned for taking their own lives." She was thrilled to see that the spirit wasn't any different from others she'd run into.

"Maybe so. I knew what I was doing could kill me and I was fine with that. I was willing to die, since I didn't see anything to live for."

"Not even your girlfriend?" She couldn't forget the girl.

"She's a sweet girl. I've never been sure why she would hook up with someone like me, but I guess it's the attraction of a bad boy, huh?"

"She's dead. Dear old dad there slit her throat before he came to Hell." She pointed to the robe Starrer was wearing. "His robe is saturated with her blood."

There was no noticeable change in the wraith's visage. She couldn't tell if he was angry or really didn't care that his father had murdered his girlfriend.

"Unfortunate."

Azubah grabbed her wrist to stop her from jerking the spirit to his feet and throwing him across the room. She took a deep breath, trying to calm down.

"Unfortunate? I guess you could say that. The most unfortunate thing that ever happened to her was becoming involved with your fucked-up family. Don't you feel any sorrow for the fact that your insane father killed the girl who loved you?"

"It would make you feel better if I said yes, but why should I lie to make you feel better? She's dead and in Heaven, a place she is suited for." Glancing around them, the shade smiled and nodded. "I'm suited for Hell. Its darkness and torment touch a place inside me

I never knew except through the touch of heroin. I won't complain about coming here."

Shock rocketed through her. She'd never known any creature that wanted to stay in Hell. None of them ever felt it was home. Even demons made in Hell fought to get out. She couldn't kill a spirit, so she needed to get out of there before she killed the young man's father. Without thinking, she encircled Starrer's wrist and yanked him to his feet. The man blinked and his eyes focused on his son.

"Azrael," the man whispered.

Beltaine looked at Azubah. "Please tell me I didn't hear that name."

Azubah grimaced. "Sorry, he really did name his son after the Angel of Death."

"That could explain why the kid feels at home here in Hell."

Pulling away from her, Starrer tried to embrace his son. The phantom slid over to stand behind her, making his father go through her to touch him. Starrer stood, staring over her shoulder with puzzled eyes.

"Azrael, why won't you let me hug you?"

"This urge to hug me is weird when you consider the fact you never wanted to even talk to me while I was alive."

From the words, Beltaine thought there should be some sort of resentment coming from the son, but it was almost like the young man was reading lines of a play. They were words he had memorized for the moment he might meet his father again.

"I'm here now. I'm going to kill the Devil for you. The voice said I've been ordained by God to do it. If you've ever doubted I loved you, look at everything I did to ensure you were even given life," Starrer protested.

Beltaine didn't want to hear what was going to be said next. She tried to move out of the way, but a force greater than herself held her in place.

"Oh yes, I thought the blood sacrifice you made to make sure your wife got pregnant was a wonderful touch. I thank you for that, but the boy you knew as your son is gone. He's been gone for a while now. His soul was needed only to create a body for me. When that was finished, he was sent back to where he came from." Azrael thanked Starrer with flat words.

"I knew I didn't want to hear this," she mumbled under her breath and Azubah nodded.

A sound came from the doorway. They turned to see the Master standing just inside the door. His red eyes fastened on Starrer and he lunged for him. Beltaine tried to intercept him, but she couldn't move. Starrer was still in shock over his son's dismissal of his sacrifices and didn't seem to sense the danger. Right before the Master struck, the demon was flung across the room and pinned to one of the ebony walls. Beltaine didn't know where the power came from, but she was happy someone had stopped the Master.

"Beltaine found the mortal first. She takes him back beyond the Veil for judgment in his world." Azrael stepped from behind her and approached the snarling demon. The fragile-looking phantom challenged the Master with a direct gaze. "You know who I am, Master of the Horde."

Fear flashed in those angry red eyes—an emotion Beltaine had thought the Master didn't feel, no matter who he faced. She sent an inquiring glance at the young man. Who was Azrael? What kind of being was he that he could cow the meanest demon in Hell?

The Master growled. "Azrael, so nice of you to join us finally."

"I have been biding my time, waiting to see what you would make of this world you were given. I'm not impressed."

"Why haven't you been seen in the rest of Hell?" The Master was still arrogant enough to demand answers.

Azrael didn't seem bothered by the demon's insolence. "I've been trying to figure it out myself. But that isn't important at the moment. The demon killer will be taking Starrer out of Hell. We will get him soon enough, and once we do, his torment will last for eternity. We can afford to be generous." The spirit turned and gestured for her to take hold of Starrer again.

She twisted the man's arm up behind his back then forced him to walk toward the door. Things had gone over the edge into the downright scary and she wanted to get the heck out of Hell before she got caught up in it. She stopped before she stepped out of the door. Turning, she looked at Azrael.

"I don't know what you are and I don't ever want to find out. Thanks for this and for not killing me when I'm sure you could have at any point." As much as her mind was screaming for her to get out while she could, she knew she had to show respect to this being.

With a regal nod, Azrael accepted her thanks. "We'll meet again, Beltaine." The shade held out a hand toward her.

Heat blossomed on her throat. Pain burned in a spot directly in line with her other scar. *Great, now everyone is marking me. I hope we don't meet until after I'm dead,* she thought, as she hustled the stunned man from the throne room. Azubah followed right behind her.

The rest of Horde stood aside and watched her rush away. She wondered why none of them had gone in to help the Master when he'd confronted Azrael. No one impeded their progress as they made their way to the Veil. When she got there, she gave Starrer a hard shove and tossed him through the barrier before her.

* * * *

Kalan and Father Paul jumped to their feet when a ragged man came stumbling through the Veil. Kalan caught the man to keep him from falling. Beltaine popped out with a pissed-off look on her face. She glared at all of them.

"No matter how much you beg and plead, I'm never going back. They are sick, twisted people over there — not to mention some truly frightening things have shown up." She reached out to snatch the man from Kalan's grasp.

"Wait. What happened?"

There was a wild-eyed look to Beltaine, and he didn't think it was anger. A look of disgust crossed her face and she let go of Starrer so fast, the man fell.

"The bastard dragged that robe he's wearing through a girl's blood before he headed to Hell. It happened to be his son's girlfriend."

She scrubbed her hands on her pants while she stared down at the man kneeling before her. She grimaced as he blubbered all over her boots. She kicked him in the chest and Starrer fell over.

Appalled, Kalan knelt beside the man. Grabbing the man's chin, Kalan turned his gaze to him. "Why would you do that?"

"The voice said killing the Devil would be easy. I knew I needed blood to make my prayers heard. Blood seals oaths."

"The voice?" Kalan kept Starrer's chin in a firm grip. The man kept trying to look at Beltaine.

Starrer seemed to know where the danger would come from because she looked like she was ready to slap the man silly. Kalan couldn't help but wonder what idiot believed killing the Devil would be easy, and what kind of maniac listened to voices?

"It came to me at my son's funeral. Told me the Devil made my son kill himself. Said I should make him pay. It told me about the book and helped me. Now it's gone and I'll never get revenge," he sobbed.

"Shut the hell up. I doubt very much the Devil had anything to do with your son's death. That's just an excuse for ignoring your son until the boy thought there was no one left to support him." Beltaine glared at Starrer.

Kalan admonished her. "He's still grieving for his son. Cut him some slack."

"Some slack?" She shot the angel an incredulous look. "We come close to total annihilation of every mortal and demon in Hell and on Earth because this fuck-up can't take blame for his own actions and listens to voices. I can't cut him enough slack to keep him from hanging himself."

"How do we know he isn't telling the truth?" Kalan was serious.

"I have enough souls joining me in Hell every day, I don't need to go out and recruit more." The Devil appeared, his dark eyes studying Starrer as though the man were a fascinating bug. "Besides, God and I made a deal before I got sent to Hell. I wouldn't mess with any mortal's mind, and He wouldn't kill me. Very generous of Him, I thought."

"Who would try to convince this loser that killing you would be easy?" She shrugged when Kalan frowned at her. "What? Now you're mad at me for telling the truth. I'm sorry his son killed himself, but it's something that happens every day, and he shouldn't be looking for someone else to blame. Besides, I met his son. The boy's as fucked up as his dad."

The Devil looked at her. "You met this mortal's son in Hell?"

"Yes, he's in your throne room. Tell you what...that is one scary soul. He pinned the Master against the wall, and there was fear in the demon's eyes when he realized who had done it." Beltaine rubbed her arms like she was cold.

"Really? What was this shade's name?" The Devil stopped his inspection of Starrer to stare at Beltaine.

"Azrael." She breathed the name like she didn't want to bring notice to it.

The Devil's pale skin went chalky white as a fine tremor shook his frame. "Azrael is in the throne room," he whispered with a hint of panic. "I had better go and see what is going on."

The fallen angel disappeared. Kalan caught Beltaine's face in his hands before kissing her. She wrapped her arms around his neck with desperate strength. He tasted the acidic flavor of fear. In the back of his mind, he wondered who Azrael was and why Beltaine was afraid of him.

Chapter Thirty-Five

"Disgusting. Don't you see this is why I have to go back and finish the job? You can't stop me now!" Starrer yelled.

They broke apart to find Starrer holding Father Paul hostage. With one arm wrapped around the priest's neck, he held a knife pressed against the man's jugular vein. Kalan cursed. While he'd been reassuring himself and Beltaine, he had forgotten about the mortal who had started this whole thing. Beltaine stayed where she was and he took a step to the man's right. There was no way he could keep an eye on both of them. Kalan didn't think Starrer's brain would be able to cope with the two of them. He tried to reassure the priest they would save him. Father Paul wasn't looking at him. The priest's eyes were firmly fixed on Beltaine and the Father seemed to expect her to help him.

"What job? Even your son sent you back here with me. He didn't want you to take revenge for something he chose to do. He seems quite happy there." She moved in the opposite direction, forcing Starrer to make a decision about who to follow.

Starrer stuck with Beltaine, turning as she moved. Kalan smiled. It meant Beltaine was the scarier of the two of them. Maybe it was the fact she had allowed some of her power loose, so her fangs and claws were growing longer. Her eyes glowed an unearthly red. Kalan moved another step and Starrer started to look at him. She growled low in her throat and the man's gaze skated back to her. Kalan hoped they didn't push the man too far and cause him to cut the priest.

"No, Azrael is still under the influence of the demons. He doesn't want to stay there. He wants to come home with me and be a family again." Drool dripped from Starrer's lips.

"I don't think so. He seems very satisfied with Hell. Your son is seriously screwed up, Starrer. What the hell did you do?" Beltaine taunted him.

Go easy, love, Kalan thought. *Don't taunt him.*

"I didn't do anything. His mother and I tried to have children for years. Then one night, I got the idea of coming down here into the catacombs. I knew the altar had been used for rituals before. Blood oaths are needed to seal deals, so I picked up a whore to sacrifice. I performed the ritual, asking any being for help in having a son. The next month, my wife told me she was pregnant. I knew it was because of the ritual. I knew I had been blessed." Starrer gestured wildly with his knife.

Kalan tensed. He wanted to wait until Starrer faced away from him before he rushed the man. He didn't want to risk Father Paul being killed, or even injured, by this bastard. Sliding another inch behind Starrer, he tried to catch Beltaine's eyes, but her stare focused on Starrer and she didn't see anyone else.

"Ordained by God? Do you really believe God wants you or anyone else to kill in His name? What kind of God would do that? Someone lied to you and used you for their purpose. You've done nothing except earn your own place in Hell, and I can guarantee you, the Devil has a special spot all picked out for you." She paced closer to Starrer.

Kalan assumed she moved so Starrer's entire view would remain on her. She presented the scariest prospect. He was close enough to touch Starrer, but he didn't want to move yet. The knife was pressed tightly to the priest's neck. He ran the risk of Father Paul's throat being cut if he jerked Starrer away from him.

"The Father wouldn't allow that. I am avenging our sons, and you'll thank me for it when the Devil's dead." Starrer pointed the blade at Beltaine.

Now! In one quick movement, he snatched Father Paul from Starrer's grasp then pushed the priest across the room. With his other hand, he punched the lunatic in the jaw, dropping him where he stood. Turning, he saw Beltaine crouched next to Father Paul, talking to him.

"Beltaine, do we have any rope around here? I don't want to risk Starrer taking off through the Veil again."

Before she could answer, Jasper appeared. "Don't worry, Kalan. I'll take him. The Father wants to see him before the judgment seat."

Kalan felt a hint of suspicion rush through him. "You? Where is the Commander? He should be the one to take the mortal for judging."

The hazel-eyed angel nodded. "Yes, he should be, but no one can find him."

"No one?" Beltaine helped Father Paul climb to his feet. "Not even God?"

The angel strolled over to Beltaine, brushing a kiss over her cheek. "Good to see you again, Beltaine — though I do prefer to meet you in the clubs."

Jealousy rose like a hateful creature in Kalan's chest, but he didn't say anything. He didn't want Jasper to realize he was irritated. Also, he knew Beltaine wouldn't be thrilled with his jealousy issues.

"I'm sure God does know where the Commander is, but He's chosen not to tell the rest of us, and that's fine with me. The Commander is the last angel I want to run into." Jasper glanced down at the mortal lying on the altar room floor. "I'll take him."

Kalan started to protest, and those brilliant eyes caught him.

"Do you have something to say about that, Kalan? Are you the only angel who can perform his duties to the standards we're expected to achieve?" Bitterness coated the angel's words.

"It's not that, but how do I know I can trust you to deliver him?"

Jasper's narrowed eyes glared at him as the angel opened his mouth to reply. Beltaine broke in.

"Shut the hell up. Why are you acting like children? Jasper, take the asshole and when you see God, tell Him Azrael is in Hell."

Jasper's eyes widened with a hint of fear in them. "I'll tell Him, but I'm sure He already knows."

"Probably, but tell Him anyway." Beltaine handed Father Paul to Kalan before yanking Starrer to his feet.

Jasper clasped the man's arm in his hand and disappeared.

"Are you okay?" he asked the priest, as they walked out of the altar into the cellar.

"Yes, thanks to you and Beltaine. Is everything done now? Will things go back to normal?" Father Paul's eyes skated between him and Beltaine.

She shook her head. "No. I don't think anything will be normal again. The Veil still needs to be repaired, though I'm not sure how that'll happen. With the appearance of Azrael, I think things will get even more interesting for the rest of us."

Unease settled into the pit of Kalan's stomach. Something was telling him she was right.

* * * *

Beltaine stepped into her apartment with a sigh. She never thought she would feel this way, but it was good to be home. Hell was a terrible place to be and she didn't want to go back before she had to. She laughed as Kalan whirled her around then kissed her hard.

His teeth bit her bottom lip until it bled, and he soothed the wound with his tongue. She didn't fight as he tore her clothes off. It wasn't going to be slow and gentle this time. Fear and anger coursed through their bodies, and they needed to reassure themselves they were alive. There was love in each touch as well. She admitted she loved the troublesome angel. She poured all her feelings into the kiss.

They fell back onto the couch with his hips wedged between her thighs. Her hips arched up to allow Kalan's cock to slide in. She wasn't wet enough, so his penetration burned. Hissing, she reached down, grasped his hips and jerked him even deeper. A low growl came from his throat and Beltaine laughed.

She enjoyed their moments of slow lovemaking when Kalan took the time to tease and torture her into a climax. She wanted more of those times, but the rough and fast fucks were the ones she got the most pleasure from. He slammed into her as his hands bruised her skin.

"I can't slow down," Kalan panted in her ear.

"Then don't. I won't break." She allowed her nails to grow into claws and she raked them down his back, leaving welts on him.

Kalan cried out and arched, driving even deeper. Staring up at him, she saw his climax building in his blue eyes, and her own orgasm started to take over. Her thighs tightened around Kalan's waist. Her inner muscles stroked his cock as he rode her. Her orgasm burst through her, causing a blackness to darken her sight. Her fangs erupted and she bit Kalan's shoulder, drawing blood. Crying out, he threw his head back. Wet warmth spurted as his climax washed over him.

Her pussy continued to contract and encourage every last drop from Kalan. He collapsed on her, pressing her into the couch.

"Wow." It was all he seemed to have the energy to say.

Chuckling, Beltaine agreed. "Yeah, wow. Before you fall asleep, let's head to the bed."

They forced their bodies to move and made their way to her bed. Snuggling, she traced her fingers over the welts on his back.

"Are we done now?"

Kalan's question tore a tiny hole in her heart. "What do you mean?"

"We found the book and the man who ripped the Veil. Have we done what they wanted us to do?" His lips pressed against her hair.

"There's one more thing I think everyone is expecting from us. The Veil still needs to be repaired.

We'll have to figure out how to do that. So we're not done."

"Good. I don't want to leave you."

His whispered words sealed the hole temporarily. "We'll worry about it tomorrow, angel boy. Tonight, we get to rest."

Kalan's warm breath bathed her neck and eased her into sleep.

Chapter Thirty-Six

Standing in the altar room, the Commander stared at the shimmering Veil. The holes were big enough for the higher lords of Hell to pass through. He wondered where those demons were. With a shot to overrun the mortal world, he thought they would be fighting to get out. His lip curled in a sneer when a werewolf slinked through a hole.

Ah, yes, the scouts are arriving.

He thought about contacting Kalan, but decided against it. He no longer trusted the angel to have the Host's best interest in mind. He made the decision to keep watching. If things got worse, he'd make a move.

* * * *

"I'm going to come," Kalan grunted in her ear.

This is how it started, Beltaine thought as she straddled him. Filling her pussy with his shaft, she grinned down at the angel.

Kalan cradled her breasts and massaged them. His rough fingers plucked at her hard nipples. Reaching behind her, she grasped his balls in one of her hands and squeezed firmly. She teased him as she slid up and down his cock. His thighs splayed farther apart.

Clenching her muscles, she urged Kalan's climax to build. One of his hands trailed down her stomach to find her clit.

"Like that, do you?" A smug smile crossed his face.

"Yes, I do." Why lie when her body told him what he wanted to know?

Letting go of his balls, she leaned forward to brace her hands on his chest. She picked up the rhythm and Kalan grabbed her hips. With a surge of his body, he rolled them over to put her on the bottom. Placing his hands under her ass, he tipped her hips for a deeper angle.

"Kalan," she moaned as the blunt head of his cock scraped over her sweet spot. Pleasure skipped down her spine, flooding her pussy with moisture.

"Wrap your legs around me and hold on," he ordered her.

She did as he commanded and grasped the headboard. He slammed into her. Soon, the room filled with their grunts and the sound of skin slapping together. Her orgasm raced over her, causing her muscles to clamp down around his cock and milk his cum from him. Heat filled her as he rode his climax by nailing her to the bed.

After their breathing eased, they lay side by side. Her fingers traced random patterns on Kalan's sweaty skin. She gathered her thoughts to try to figure out what their next move should be. They had slept most of the day, recovering from the emotions of the night before. The Devil's spell book had been recovered, and the mortal who'd ripped the Veil had been captured before he could kill the Devil. They needed to figure out how to repair the Veil before the Horde and the higher lords crossed over. She wasn't sure how to do that.

A scream came from the night outside her window. The unearthly screech caused shivers of fear to chase down her spine.

Kalan's skin went cold and he tensed. "What the hell was that?"

Beltaine climbed out of bed and went to the window. Staring into the darkness, she contemplated what creature might have made that sound. Another wail came and a chill filled the room.

"Shit. It's a banshee."

"How do you know?" Kalan joined her in front of the window.

"I heard one the night I killed my father. They're the heralds of the Horde." She rubbed her arms to warm herself.

The memory of that night pulled her back into the past. All day, her father had yelled and beaten her. There wasn't anything she'd have been able to do that would have pleased him. The fact she was in the apartment bothered him and though her physical wounds healed as soon as they happened, the anger had built until she'd had to make a choice.

She'd decided then that she could either continue to allow her father to destroy her, inch by inch, or she could take her destiny into her own hands. It had been at the moment she'd lifted the gun and pointed it at her father that the banshee's wail had echoed through Dark Town. Ice had formed in her heart and she'd pulled the trigger.

"If the banshee is the herald of the Horde, why would it announce your father's death?" His question drew her back to the present.

"The Master showed up for the first time as my father bled out."

"Who's going to die tonight?" He wrapped his arms around her.

Shrugging, she leaned back into his warmth. "I'm not sure it's announcing any death in particular, but it doesn't bode well. It means the Horde is getting ready to come through the Veil."

"The Devil won't stop them?" Kalan rested his chin on her shoulder.

"Why would he? He doesn't really control any of the demons in Hell. They do as they please."

"I thought the Devil was the ruler of Hell." He sounded puzzled.

"It's a title, mostly. The other demons will listen to him usually, but if they want something, they'll take it, and most of them want to rule in the mortal world." She pulled away and headed toward the bathroom.

"So what do we do?" Kalan followed her.

"We gather everyone together and decide how we fix the Veil. Where did Father Simon and Roger go? I didn't see them when Starrer and I came back from Hell." She turned on the shower.

"Father Simon wasn't feeling well. He wanted to check on Betsy before heading back to the city. Roger told me you'd bring the bastard back. He didn't doubt you." He leaned in the doorway and watched her.

She raised an eyebrow as she glanced over at him. "You didn't think I'd return? Where's your faith?"

"I knew you'd come back, but I didn't think Starrer would be with you. How was I supposed to believe in you? You were so angry. I figured maybe you'd let the Master get to him and deal with Starrer for you."

Beltaine faced him. "First of all, I don't need anyone to deal with things for me. I was more than capable of kicking his ass if I wanted to. Secondly, I might get mad, but I can control my anger."

"Not too be rude or anything, but you said you were so angry at your father that you shot him. Why should I be confident enough in your control to believe you wouldn't do the same thing to someone who threatened your existence again?"

She wondered if she should feel hurt by his lack of trust. "Are you afraid I'll get mad at you and kill you?"

Beltaine tested the water. Finding it as hot as she could stand it, she stepped in.

Moving closer, he looked at her and shrugged. "I don't think you would. There's nothing in it for you. Killing me would get you more trouble than letting me live."

She poured shampoo in her hand and started washing her hair. His hand clamped around her wrist and pulled her to him. He lifted her chin and kissed her.

"More than that, I think you like — or even love — me. You'll cut me some slack when you get angry at me. How often have you gotten mad at Roger, and he's still around."

"Talk to Roger about my temper. I've learned to control it, and you're right. It's more trouble to kill people than to intimidate them." She wrapped her fingers through the wet strands of his dark hair and pulled his mouth down for another kiss.

One of his hands braced against the shower wall while the other slid around her thigh and pulled it up around his hip. She gasped as he rocked his hips and rubbed his cock over her pussy. The warm water and her cream made his passage smooth. She licked what flesh of his they touched. She nibbled her way from his mouth to his neck, where she tasted the throbbing pulse at the tender base of his throat. She trailed her hands from his hair down to his ass where she tightened her fingers to urge him to continue rubbing against her.

"We've never fucked in the shower before." She grinned at Kalan, as his cock pushed against her clit.

"We need to change that, then," he suggested as he took his hand off her thigh to grab her ass. Angling her hips, he used the water to ease his way into her pussy.

She gave a moan of contentment. "I've missed that."

He chuckled. "Missed it? It's only been ten minutes since I finished making love to you."

Shrugging, she winked at him. "What can I say? I like the feel of your cock inside me."

Kalan answered by thrusting into her. Wrapping her arms around his neck, she lifted her other leg to encircle his waist. He turned to lean against the tiled wall. His hands bit into Beltaine's skin as he raised her up and allowed gravity to bring her down on his cock. Groans filled the air over the pounding water as his shaft went deep. Kalan leaned forward to nip the tip of her breast. Her back arched at the sharp twinge of pain.

His tongue lapped water from her breasts as his hips jerked, pushing his erection deeper. She tightened her muscles to stroke him as he pulled out. His mouth fastened on a hard nipple and began to suck in time with his movements.

Her breasts ached with desire while he used his tongue and teeth on them. Pleasure built at the base of her neck and in her pussy. Flexing her body, she drew his entire length into her and squeezed. The head of his rod hit the right spot, and she cried out his name as her orgasm burst free.

"Kalan," she urged him on.

She could tell by the strength of his grip she was going to have bruises later on, but she didn't care. They were marks caused by pleasure, not by pain.

A sharp crack sounded when Kalan threw his head back and hit the wall. It didn't stop him from pumping hard and fast into her. She sighed as heat flooded her. His climax drained him until only the wall was holding them both up.

Beltaine slid off him and grabbed the soap. Lathering her hands, she smoothed her way down his chest and over his thighs. With exquisite attention to detail, she eased the sweat from his body, and any leftover tension drifted out of his muscles. Motioning to him to tilt his head, she washed his hair for him.

Chapter Thirty-Seven

Kalan watched Beltaine wash her own hair. He smiled when she swore as some soap got in her eyes.

"Don't you dare laugh, angel boy," she warned.

"I wouldn't dare, but you might want to slow down. Why are you suddenly in a hurry?" He reached around her to turn the water off once she rinsed.

"I was thinking how Roger has a tendency to walk in on us. He doesn't need to see you naked. It might give him ideas." With a wink, she headed to the closet where her clothes hung.

A bit nonplussed, he dried quickly then clothed himself. Heading out to join her in the living room, he asked, "Do we have a plan to fix the Veil?"

She reached into the refrigerator to grab two beers. After tossing one to him, she sat down on the couch. "Well, since the book we got back for the Devil caused the rips in the barrier, it should have a spell to fix it."

"Do we go and ask the Devil for it back?" He popped the top and took a swig.

"What's this *we* shit? We both know who'd have to go after it." She shook her head. "Father Simon has a copy in the church's archive, remember? I'll call Roger and see if we can go and look at it, or maybe he can bring it to us."

He handed her the phone and finished off his bottle. She swung her feet into his lap as she dialed Roger's number. Cupping her heel in his hand, he began to massage it.

"Hey, Roger. Yes, we got the bastard, but we need to look at the book Father Simon said he had." She listened for a moment. "Yeah, give me a call after you talk to him."

Hanging up, she sighed. "If we didn't need to check on things out in the village, I'd let you do that all night."

"Why are we heading out? There's nothing we can do until we hear back from Roger." He ran a finger over her ankle, up her leg to the crease where her hip and thigh met.

"There are banshees to be sent back and we need to keep an eye out for werewolves." She pulled away from him before slipping on her boots.

"Why werewolves?" He followed her out of the apartment.

Stopping, Beltaine looked at him. "Why did the Commander send you to help me when you've got no clue about the creatures in Hell?"

"I haven't figured it out yet. He showed up and told me I had to come down here to stop a war. He didn't mention you'd be half-demon or irresistible. No one ever told me about Hell and the creatures that call it home." Kalan shrugged.

"Talk about a crash course. You didn't have a chance," she pointed out as they started moving again.

"Not from the moment I saw you. So why are we watching out for werewolves?"

They stepped out onto the street and a screech echoed through the night. Goosebumps rose over his skin. She touched his arm and pointed toward an alley entrance on the other side of the street.

Squinting, he made out a rather vague shape lurking in the shadows. Unease swelled and he wanted to protest as she headed toward the banshee. As they moved closer, the shape evolved into an extremely thin, pale woman with long white hair. The banshee's eyes were black, without pupils. When she opened her mouth, Kalan saw fangs.

Beltaine gestured to the creature and stopped the sound before it left the banshee's mouth. "I think you need to go back home, my friend."

There wasn't any way to tell if the banshee had emotions, but he imagined it was surprised by Beltaine's statement. It tilted its head and stared at her.

"Who are you to tell me where I should go?" The banshee's voice was high-pitched.

"I'm Beltaine."

The banshee's head went back and its eyes widened. He could tell it recognized her name.

"I was warned about you." It shifted away from them.

"I'm sure you were. You should return to Hell on your own. If I send you back, it's going to hurt." The matter-of-fact tone Beltaine used told him she meant what she said.

"You don't fear us." It wasn't a question.

"Few creatures are scary enough for me to fear, and you aren't one of them." Beltaine moved closer to the banshee.

"I must stay. I proclaim the coming of the Horde. The Master will be furious if I don't do my job."

Kalan winced as the creature's high-pitched whine pierced his head. He wanted to cover his ears, but didn't want to give the banshee the satisfaction of knowing it bothered him.

"The Master was having a problem or two of his own when I saw him last." Beltaine shrugged. "Of course, I could let the angel take care of you, and that would mean instant death."

True fear took hold of the banshee's face when it got a clear view of him. He grinned, and by the way the banshee cringed, he knew it had to be a rather cruel smile. "I'll be glad to help you leave."

The creature screamed and several apartment windows shattered around the alley. Crouching down, it covered its head with reed-thin arms. "Please, no. I'll leave."

He backed off, but Beltaine stayed where she was. He knew she wouldn't back down for a silly banshee. As she said, few creatures ever brought fear into her eyes. Uttering one last haunting cry, the banshee fled.

"I hate those things," Beltaine grumbled as they made their way out of the alley.

"You had to threaten it with me. I thought you could handle anything." He couldn't help but tease her.

"I could have dealt with it, but it takes less effort to scare it with you." She smiled. "They might call me the demon killer, but I don't kill them. I send any demon that gets out of line back to Hell. My reputation is a little exaggerated. You really could destroy them, so any demon in its right mind doesn't want to tick you off."

"You were telling me about werewolves." He brought her back to the original topic because he didn't feel like pointing out that most demons weren't in their right minds.

Beltaine nodded as she led them into the center of Ericksberg. She would have a talk with the Commander about sending his angels into the mortal world unprepared.

"Werewolves are scouts. They're sent in advance of the Horde's arrival. With their stronger senses, they find the places where mortals are weaker so the higher lords of Hell can go to collect their souls. If we see a werewolf, it means their crossing is imminent. I'm not sure we could stop them once the Horde breaches the barrier."

"All Hell busts loose and we're in a shitload of trouble."

It was still a shock to hear her angel swear, but she couldn't argue with what he said. "Yes, a shitload of trouble. You'd be recalled and the Host would be unleashed to destroy mortal and demon." Stopping, she turned to stare at him. "That's what's so weird about this whole thing. Demons and angels alike know what's in store if the Veil is destroyed. Mortals don't know the danger because we protect them from the truth. We caught the person causing the trouble."

"What's bothering you, then?"

"Starrer kept saying he heard a voice."

Kalan nodded. "Sure, but he was crazy. It's not a stretch to think he invented the voice to explain why he did what he did."

"I'd be willing to believe that, but this voice told him very specific things. It told him about the book and how to work the spells. It convinced him that killing the Devil would be easy. I'm inclined to believe someone or something is behind this entire thing besides the man being crazy."

"Why would the Devil do it?" Kalan didn't sound convinced.

"See, there's your inborn prejudice sneaking in. Why do you assume the Devil did it? Why would he take us all to the point of annihilation?"

He frowned. "He wants to take over Earth. He's not content with ruling Hell. He wants to control everything. If he had the chance, he'd try to take over Heaven again. Ow," he complained as she slapped him upside the head.

"You've got to be one of the most stubborn people I've come across." She glared at him. "Maybe that's why the Commander sent you. Even when you learn something different, you'll stick with what you've been taught."

He rubbed his head and pouted. "Maybe, but you didn't have to hit me that hard."

"I think you needed that. You've met the Devil. Was your impression of him that of a power-hungry tyrant?"

"Well, no," he conceded.

"Of course not. Contrary to popular belief, he isn't plotting to take over Heaven. Judging from his reaction, I'd say he would be trying to stay as far away from Azrael as possible instead of planning anything against God or mortal." She fingered the burn on her neck. "Take a look at this and tell me what it is." She pulled back her hair to reveal it.

The touch of his finger caused a blade of pain to cut over her skin. She hissed, barely resisting the urge to jerk away from him. He was the one to pull away suddenly.

"Beltaine, where'd you get this?" His voice held shock, disgust and a hint of fear.

"Someone gave it to me while I was in Hell. What is it?"

"Why would you allow it?"

She dropped her hair and gazed at him. "It wasn't as if he gave me a choice. Now tell me what the hell the psychopath put on me."

"It's a symbol of destruction" Kalan shuddered.

Bile rose in her stomach. *Why me?* was all she could think. Why did God allow such cruel jokes to be played at her expense?

"The bastard marked me. Not only do I have the symbol of God on my body, I'm now carrying the symbol of Azrael. There are times when I'd love to chuck the whole damn thing and hide away." Crossing her arms, she stared down at her feet.

Kalan put his hands on her hips before tugging her close to him. "Hiding isn't in your nature, love. You'll fight this marking just like you fight the other one." He kissed her hair and smoothed a hand down her back. "Who is Azrael?"

"He looks like Starrer's son, but he said the boy's soul no longer lives in the body. I'm not sure who he is. I know Azrael is the name of the being many call the Angel of Death. I don't know what his place in Hell is." She stepped back from him and straightened her shoulders.

"The Devil seemed scared of him," Kalan reminded her.

"I know, and he pinned the Master to a wall. Azrael was the one who allowed me to leave with Starrer. It seems even the higher lords of Hell fear him." She tilted her head back to look at the sky.

"What kind of being would scare the Devil and his Horde?" Kalan's brow creased with a frown.

"I don't know. I've always had a theory that Hell existed before the Devil had his falling-out with God. When they chose to disagree about the Devil's place in Heaven, God allowed him to take over Hell. There are creatures far more evil living in those depths and I'm afraid Azrael is one such being."

"Why would he mark you? That doesn't make sense."

"Why would God allow my father to burn a crucifix into my neck? I'm beginning to feel like a game piece in a huge chess match. I move at the whim of either side."

He took her hand in his. "Ultimately you decide what you want to do. You're a wild card in the entire game." Tugging her hand, he said, "Come on. I want to see a werewolf."

"Trust me. You really don't." She laughed and let him lead her away.

* * * *

Rage burned in his eyes as he watched Kalan and Beltaine walk away. The chaos mark on her neck was going to cause a problem. It meant he wasn't supposed to touch her.

But touch her he would, if she continued to involve herself in his plans. He could feel the energies seething. When the time was right, they would explode, and he would be there to reap the benefits.

Chapter Thirty-Eight

Roger stared in horrified silence at Father Angelo. There was no way Father Simon could be missing. "I dropped him off. I even walked him to his room. Now you're telling me he's not anywhere?"

Holy shit, this wasn't good. Father Simon was the only one who could tell them where the book of spells was.

"We've searched the rectory, the church, even the surrounding cemeteries. Simon is nowhere to be found." Angelo sat down in a pew with a weary sigh. "We must inform the bishop."

"You tell the bishop. I have to tell Beltaine the man she considers a father is gone. It'd be almost as bad as having to tell her he died." Roger scrubbed his face with shaking hands.

"Make her come here. Call her and tell her Father Simon needs her. She has to use her powers, but don't tell her about his disappearance until she's here," Angelo suggested.

Roger nodded. Pulling a cell phone from his pocket, he walked outside to place the call.

"Beltaine." Her voice shot over the phone.

"Father Simon needs you, Beltaine. Right now. I suggest you use your power to get here." He hung up before she could say anything. Sitting on the steps, he bowed his head and prayed.

* * * *

Beltaine appeared in front of church to see Roger sitting and praying. She bounded up the steps to kick at his feet.

"What the hell kind of call was that? You could've given me more information." She moved to head around him, and he grabbed her ankle.

"Father Angelo suggested it. We've got a major problem, Beltaine."

Something in Roger's voice told her she didn't want to hear anything he had to say. Kalan's warmth at her back eased her a little.

"All right. What's wrong?"

Roger took a deep breath. "Father Simon's gone."

Her stomach dropped and tears welled in her eyes. "He's dead?"

"No, he's gone. We can't find him anywhere." Roger grimaced when she kicked him.

"You could've phrased it a little differently. How do you know he's missing?"

"I brought him home last night, even walked him to his room. After I got your call, I went to ask him about the book. Father Angelo told me Father Simon's door was locked, and he wasn't answering when they called him." Roger let Kalan pull him to his feet. "I picked the lock."

"Seems an odd talent for a priest to have," Kalan commented as the angel followed the other two into the church.

"Not if the priest is from Dark Town." Beltaine said, as she hugged Father Angelo and ignored the bishop standing next to the priest. "When you opened the door, what did you find?"

"Father Simon wasn't there. His bed hadn't been slept in. We searched the rectory and archives. We even searched the cemeteries. We can't find him anywhere." Roger filled her in.

"He just went for a walk or something. I'm sure he'll show up soon." The bishop didn't sound worried.

"He wouldn't have left. It's getting too close. Tomorrow, his stigmata will return." Father Angelo frowned at the bishop.

"Show me his room," she ordered Roger.

She was led to where the door of Father Simon's room stood open. Walking in, she glanced around. Someone had been in there besides Father Simon or the other priests. Someone with more power and less inclination to do good. There'd be a note, she was sure, but not an ordinary one.

"Kalan, look around. There has to be a note somewhere." She gestured for him to search the other side of the room.

"Why would you be able to find it when my priests couldn't?" the bishop asked.

"Whoever took Father Simon wasn't mortal. He knew you'd call me, so the message is for me, not you." Beltaine sent a blanket of power over her side of the room. Nothing flared. A touch of doubt ran through her.

"Beltaine," Kalan called to her.

She turned to see words appear, etched deep into the mirror over the dresser. The message flared when she moved closer.

"What language is it written in?" Roger moved closer as well, intently focused on the words.

"It's an archaic language used by angels before the Fall. Our kidnapper is trying to confuse us and make us think an angel took the Father." Kalan squinted and mouthed the words under his breath.

"Why? There are few people, angels or demons, who could read it. I don't think anyone but the Devil would know how to decipher this," Father Angelo pointed out.

Kalan shot her a triumphant grin. Shaking her head, she read the words out loud as the pentagram on her neck burned.

"'Don't attempt to find the priest. The book you search for is gone as well. The Veil will fall and a new order will begin'."

Everyone was staring at her as she finished. She pulled her fingers off the glass.

"It seems you've been holding out on us, Beltaine." The bishop inspected her as though she had been a dog that started talking.

"I don't know how to read it. It looks like gibberish to me." She remembered the burning sensation from Azrael's mark.

"I think I know how you read it, but it's not important. Not only does he have Father Simon, he has the book. So what do we do now?" Kalan looked at her.

They were all looking at her for the answers, and she wasn't sure she had them. Oh, the book was easy enough. As much as she hated to, she'd have to go back to Hell and ask the Devil for his copy. What to do about Father Simon was a different story.

"Since we know whoever took him was either angel or demon, I have to believe we won't find him until the kidnapper wants us to."

Roger protested. "What if the stigmata comes tomorrow? Without the proper care, he could die."

"We can only hope that God stops His torment of Father Simon for one week, or the kidnapper has enough compassion to take care of him." She cupped Roger's face in her hands. "That's all I can do for now, Roger. I have to get the book or we'll have more to worry about than a missing priest."

Turning, she kissed Kalan, ignoring the angry glare from the bishop. "Keep searching. As soon as I'm back with the book, I'll call you."

Kalan nodded. "Be careful."

She touched the chaos mark on her neck. "I think I've got a 'get out of Hell free' card."

Closing her eyes, she gathered her power. She placed the palm of her hand over the brand and thought of Azrael.

* * * *

"What do you want?"

Her eyes popped open when she heard the emotionless voice of Starrer's son. She was standing in the middle of the throne room, with only Azrael standing before her.

"Don't use my name often, Beltaine. For each time you do, I claim a piece of your soul."

Fear rolled over her in a cold wave. "I don't have a soul," was all she could think to say.

"Every breathing creature has a soul. Yours is divided, demon and mortal. It fights for one side to become dominant."

"Why has no one told me?"

He shrugged. "It has never mattered before. But now events have been put into motion that demand your soul be balanced."

"What are you, some sort of scary Zen master? Are you going to teach me to balance my two souls?" She fell back on her smart mouth.

Azrael shook his head. "It's beyond my interest to show you how to do it. You'll learn or you'll die."

"Simple." She shook her head.

"Why did you call my name?"

"I need the book of spells the Devil has. The Veil must be repaired and the other copy has disappeared." She hated having to ask.

"And so has the priest who had it. Interesting. What creature would be bold enough to kidnap a priest marked by the wounds of Christ?"

She startled a little at his knowledge of Father Simon being taken as well.

Azrael's gaze narrowed. "You may borrow the book, but don't use it for anything other than repairing the Veil."

"Are you sure the Devil will give it to me?"

In any other creature, it would be arrogance, but Azrael didn't have any emotion in his voice when he said, "Tell him I told you to take it."

"Okay." She turned to leave. The total confidence Azrael had, that a self-centered creature like the Devil would give her the book on his word alone, shook her.

"Before you go to see the Devil, there is someone I think you need to talk to." Azrael stopped her.

"Don't bring my mother into this. I've had enough bad news for one day," she groaned.

"It's not your mother." Azrael gestured to a shape cowering in the shadows behind him. "I believe it's time for you to confront your father."

Hissing, Beltaine crouched as her father materialized from the depths of the throne room. He shied away from Azrael, keeping his gaze downcast. It was the first time she had ever seen her father intimidated by someone. Of course, she didn't blame him for being scared of Azrael. The shade turned its dark eyes on her and a flame of hatred flared in them.

"He recognizes you, I see." Azrael settled on the platform where the Devil's throne rested.

"Are you going to watch us?" She didn't take her eyes off her father. It didn't pay to let her guard down.

"I certainly am. There is something compelling about a daughter confronting her father about all the bad things he did to her."

"You're a sick bastard," she snapped. "Why would I need to confront him? Don't you think killing him was confrontation enough?"

"No. There are unresolved issues between you. Mostly trying to figure out why he allowed you to live instead of smothering you as a child?" Azrael gestured to the phantom standing in front of her. "Here's your chance to ask."

Beltaine had thought she'd want the answer, but now that she had the chance to ask it, she didn't want to hear what he had to say. "I don't have time for this."

"Yes, you do. Time has no existence here in Hell. Why would we allow it to mean anything when we torment these souls for eternity? When you return to your world, only a few minutes will have passed, even if you spend a year here."

She realized Azrael wasn't going to let her off the hook. She would have to confront the one demon that had always haunted her. Squaring her shoulders, she stepped into her father's personal space and made herself meet his gaze. It took all her courage and strength to stare at him. When she was younger, he would beat her until she was bloody for daring to look him in the eye like an equal.

"How dare you?" His breath streamed over her face like a breeze of fire. "You insult me by acting like you are as good as me. You're demon spawn and have no right to be alive."

"Then why didn't you kill me when I was a baby? Why allow me to live and suffer when you could have gotten rid of me when I was at my most defenseless?" She spat the words at him.

"My life was destroyed because of you. There was no way I was going to allow you to die and leave me here to be miserable. If I hated my life, I wanted you to hate yours as well."

"You succeeded beyond your wildest imagination, but didn't you feel bad about abusing an innocent child?" She wanted to hit him, but he didn't really have any corporeal shape.

"You were never innocent. It wasn't like you were human anyway. You are a demon, no matter what any of these creatures say. You haven't got a soul and you'll never be anything but a monster." The shade's gaze burned into her.

The confused child Beltaine used to be fought to be free of the cage she had shoved it in. She knew if she let the child go, she would end up begging her father for forgiveness. There wasn't enough nobility in her to give him the pleasure of knowing she still feared him.

"I'm not a monster. I've got friends and people who care for me. I'll never be the selfish creatures you and my mother are."

A cold laughter came from her father. "You'll always be a product of us. Your mother was a selfish whore who tricked me into having sex with her."

"Bullshit. She didn't have to trick you. You were more than willing to fuck her. Don't try to lie to me."

"I'm not lying. Don't you raise your voice to me." He stepped closer to her and lifted his hand.

"Or what? You'll hit me?" She smirked at him as she reached out. "I killed you once. You can't do anything to me."

He shrunk from her touch. "Not true. I hurt you every time you think your demon side is evil. I've done my job."

Shit, he was right. All her life, she'd hated that part of herself. It was why she was so hard on her mother every time she saw her. Beltaine thought she had freed herself of his influence when she'd shot him, but somehow, like a parasite, he had wormed his way into her psyche. *What a sneaky bastard.* He'd known what his abuse would do to her. She shot a glance over at Azrael.

"You must accept both sides of your soul. The mortal part is selfish and arrogant, but holds the capacity to do great good. The demon part is just as selfish and arrogant, but it holds the part of you capable of great evil. You seem to have managed to control your different sides well so far, but there are things you need to learn. The repair of the Veil might rest upon you." Azrael shrugged.

"It's like talking to a damn oracle," she complained, as she turned her gaze back on her father. Azrael's comments caused more confusion than she could deal with at the moment. "I can't forgive you, but I can forget you."

"Easier said than done, girl. You haven't forgotten me in the fourteen years since you killed me. Do you really think I'll disappear just like that because you want me to?" Her father growled at her.

"Maybe not, but I can start today and not worry about what you thought of me. You were a crazy bastard and deserve everything that is happening to you here. I'm done beating myself up because of your inferiority complex. Your inability to accept blame for your actions isn't my problem anymore." She turned away from the phantom and addressed Azrael. "I'm going to get the book. If I have any trouble with the Devil, I'm sending him to you."

"I'll deal with him." Azrael's eyes rested on her father, and she could see the fear in her father's eyes. It was satisfying for her to finally see him scared of someone else. She couldn't blame him—Azrael scared the shit out of her.

* * * *

"You're kidding me? You want my spell book?" The Devil stared at her with incredulous eyes.

Beltaine nodded. She'd been going around and around with him for ten minutes about the stupid book. She didn't want to pull the Azrael card, but it looked like she was going to have to. The Devil turned to look at her mother, who stood snuggled close to him.

"Your daughter has the nerve to ask for the one thing that could destroy me."

Her mother glared at her, but she refused to get upset by that. She had made a vow after speaking with her father that she would never allow her parents to affect her again.

"To be honest, I don't need your permission. I already got it from Azrael." A cocky grin crossed her face.

"You didn't?" Horrified shock graced the Devil's face.

"Yes, I did. He told me to tell you he said I could have it."

The Devil scraped trembling hands through his hair. "You do know that asking Azrael for anything means you own him a favor in the future."

"I knew it. I'm pretty sure I can handle whatever he asks of me." She could deal with anything Azrael threw at her.

"Beltaine, dear, you don't understand who Azrael is. He'll take your soul if you allow him." Her mother reached out to touch her arm.

Stepping back, she realized she might have made the vow not to let her parents bother her anymore, but she wasn't going to get all touchy-feely with them. "I know that as well. He informed me when I showed up in the throne room. It's a little hard not to deal with him when he's marked me just like Father did." She lifted her hair to reveal the chaos mark.

"You poor thing." The Devil waved his hand and the book appeared. "I don't like the idea of you and that silly angel of yours having this, but if Azrael demands it, then I have no choice. Return it to me as soon as you can." He held it out to her, snatching it back before she could grab it. "You are going to be fixing the Veil with it and nothing more?"

"I promised Azrael and I'll promise you...I won't do anything other than repair the barrier. I won't even read any of the other spells." Clenching her teeth, she tried to find patience.

"Oh, fine. Take it then." The Devil tossed it to her and whirled around to take her mother in a passionate embrace. "Where were we when she interrupted?"

Beltaine closed her eyes and sent her body to the sanctuary in St Benedict's. There was no way she wanted to see the Devil and her mother kissing. She gagged just thinking about it.

"Kalan," she called out, knowing he would hear her. "I got the book."

Chapter Thirty-Nine

Kalan arrived to find Beltaine pacing in front of the altar. He genuflected to the cross before touching her shoulder. Whirling, she plastered herself against him and kissed him.

His mind protested furiously. They were in a church, for Heaven's sake. He shouldn't be allowing lust to overwhelm his control. His body thought the touch of hers was perfect. It wanted him to pull her closer and allow it to rub against her.

Her lips nipped at his, demanding entrance. He opened to tell her no, but her tongue slid in and he lost his voice. His arms slid around her waist to grasp her ass and tug her as tightly as possible to him. Climbing his body, she wrapped her legs around his waist and threaded her hands through his hair. Their tongues dueled and thrust, each trying to gain supremacy over the other. Her hips began to rock, pushing her mound hard into his erection. When the urge to strip her naked and take her on the sanctuary floor hit him, he pulled his mouth off hers and took a breath.

"We can't do this here, Beltaine."

She suckled the skin at the base of his neck for a second before she replied, "Why not?"

"For goodness' sake, Beltaine, it's a church." Indignation speared through his voice.

"So?"

"Have some respect for God, even if you don't have any for the church." His tone was harsher than he'd planned.

She dropped out of his arms and put her hands on her hips. Glaring at him, she said, "I have a lot of respect for God. I just don't think He's petty enough to worry about where you and I have sex, but if you have a problem, then come with me."

She grabbed his hand and dragged him toward Father Paul's office. "Where are we going?" he inquired as he stumbled along behind her.

"We're going somewhere more private." She let him get ahead of her then pushed him through the doorway.

He tripped over the threshold. Catching himself on the edge of the desk, he turned in time to see Beltaine shut and lock the door behind her. *I might be in trouble,* he thought as she stalked him. Her gaze pinned him and he couldn't find the determination to move.

"What's gotten into you?" Not that he minded or anything, but he wanted to know why she felt the need to jump him in a church.

"I had a very rough time in Hell and I need to release some energy."

Her wicked smile made his cock twitch at the thought of her mouth wrapped around it.

"We can't do that here. This is a priest's office." Kalan knew his protest was weak. What male in his right mind would refuse to take what she was offering quite willingly?

"Sit down." Her gesture toward the leather chair behind the desk was jerky.

"Yes, ma'am." Easing around the corner of the desk, he stayed facing her. His hand hit the arm of the chair and he flopped down in it.

Leaning over him, she rested her hands on the arms and effectively blocked him in. Her demon blood was heating, he could tell by the flare of red in her eyes and the hint of fangs in her smile.

"Should I strip first?" Encouraging her probably wasn't a smart thing to do, but he found there was a perverse need to give in to her.

"Yes." She backed off and sat on the desk. Crossing her legs at the ankles, she motioned for him to stand up. "Take it off – and do it slowly."

Rising to his feet, a part of him wondered at the sudden willingness he had to obey her. The other part of him seemed to be controlled by his cock, and it told him to hurry. It wanted to be buried deep in her as soon as possible.

He unhooked his sword and laid it on the cabinet next to the desk. Sliding his vest from his shoulders, he ran his hands over his chest and whispered his nails over his nipples. A shot of pleasure bolted through him. He'd never thought his own touch would excite him. Beltaine's eyes followed his hands as he trailed them to his waistband. Sucking in his stomach, he unbuttoned his pants and eased the zipper down, making sure not to catch anything in the metal.

She drew her breath in a hiss as his cock sprang out from the leather. Her gaze burnt brands into his skin. The rough palms of his hands scraped over the flesh at his hips while he pushed his pants down his thighs. He bowed over to take his boots off. With a flourish, he stood naked in front of her.

On every spot her eyes landed, a tingling started, until his nerve endings were strung tight. He longed to beg her to touch him. His muscles trembled with the need to run his hands over her, but he managed to control them.

"Touch yourself."

Beltaine's order shocked and embarrassed Kalan. He'd never done anything like that, but even while he thought that, his hand fisted his shaft. The thumb of his other hand swiped the pre-cum off the head of his cock, and he lifted it to her lips. The tip of her tongue shot out to lick the pad clean. Humming, she winked at him.

"Tasty. Now undress me."

This order he could handle. Grabbing the neck of her tank top in his fists, he ripped it from her. Her firm breasts glistened in the dim lighting of the office. He reached out to pinch her nipples in his fingers. She slapped his hands away.

"No touching. Just get me naked."

He frowned but did what she told him to do. Kneeling, he pulled her boots and pants off at the same time. He ran his hands up her legs to her knees and pushed her thighs apart. When he would have leaned in to taste her pussy, she thrust him away.

"Go sit down and stroke your cock."

"Why?" He sat down but didn't touch himself. He wasn't sure what she was trying to prove.

"Because I want to watch you pleasure yourself. Haven't you ever masturbated before?"

Shaking his head, he stared at her as she slid her hand over her stomach and between her legs. She spread her thighs wide so he could see what she was doing. His mouth dropped open as her fingers slipped into her pussy and came out glistening.

Holy shit. Without thought, his hand stroked his cock and spread the pearly liquid dripping from the slit in the head down the length of his shaft. He tightened his grip, thinking about how much he'd enjoyed it when Beltaine had fisted him firmly. Although his hand was busy jerking himself off, he couldn't take his eyes off her.

With her head tipped back and her eyes half closed, she looked wanton, sprawled over the priest's desk. His rhythm slowed while hers sped up. Her fingers speared into her pussy while she rubbed the heel of her hand against her clit. Moans came from her throat. He bit his lip to keep from groaning with her. When her hips started rocking to take her fingers, he started moving his hips as well.

He splayed his thighs wider and slipped his other hand down to cup his balls. He fondled them as he fucked his hand. His climax gathered at the base of his spine, and he knew it would be soon. His grip tightened to the point of pain, but he didn't stop. Beltaine cried out as her body rippled with her orgasm.

Watching her pleasure herself was one of the most erotic things Kalan had seen in his life. His back arched as his climax shot through him. Cum covered his hands and stomach. A metallic taste exploded in his mouth as he bit his lip to keep from crying out.

A chuckle from the desk drew him back to himself. He opened his eyes to see Beltaine staring at him with a smile on her face.

"Did you enjoy jerking off?" Beltaine clothed them with a lazy wave of her hand.

She climbed off the desk and straightened the papers then headed to unlock the door. Kalan watched her from under heavy lids. He smiled and nodded.

"I did, but I can't believe you talked me into doing it here." He laughed. "You press your body against me and all my good sense goes out the window."

Strolling back to him, she sat on his lap. She wiggled around to get comfortable and made sure to rub her ass over his cock.

"Beltaine," he growled.

She kissed him. "I got the book. We'll have to find the spell soon."

"I didn't think the Devil would give it to you." He was mildly surprised to see the book in her hand.

"He wasn't but Azrael forced him to." She couldn't stop the shiver racing down her spine.

"The more you tell me about Azrael, the less I want to meet him." Kalan wrapped her in the warm strength of his arms. She sighed.

"I hope you never meet him. Now let's start looking for the repair spell." He unlocked the door before they settled down to look through the book.

They'd been reading for several minutes when the door burst open and Father Paul raced in. Kalan felt his cheeks flush. Embarrassed, he couldn't meet the priest's gaze.

Beltaine touched his cheek and grinned. "You're going to have to get past it or you'll never be able to look him in the eyes." She kissed him then turned to Father Paul. "What's got you all worked up?"

"There's a demon in the sanctuary," the priest stammered and pointed back out the door.

"Really?" Beltaine sounded intrigued instead of worried.

Kalan let her climb to her feet. He shook his head when she offered him the Devil's spell book. There wasn't any way he was touching it. Following her, he was surprised to see Azubah perched on the back of one of the pews. The small demon smiled at them while the other priests fluttered around, trying to shoo it away.

"Father Paul, Azubah has been working with us. It won't bother anything, so tell your fellow priests to get out of here," Beltaine ordered the priest.

Nodding, Father Paul started ushering the others out. Kalan found it interesting that the priest accepted Beltaine and was more likely to listen to her than anyone else.

Beltaine turned to the demon. "What's the problem?"

"Oh, we've got a huge problem. Tariq has crossed over." Azubah shifted, its claws leaving scorch marks in the wood.

"Shit. That is seriously bad news." She stalked over to the pew and flung herself down.

"Who's Tariq?" Kalan could tell they both were troubled.

"He's a higher lord of Hell. There's a hierarchy within the demon world, especially if an invasion is about to happen. First, the vampires come. They're the spies for the Horde. Usually, werewolves cross next. Those dogs scout things out. You've met the banshee who cries out a warning about the coming of the Horde." She stopped to take a breath.

Azubah picked up the explanation. "Loosely translated, Tariq means 'he who pounds on the door'. He's the first member of the Horde and first higher lord to cross over. He goes out among mortals and tries to find the ones who would welcome the demons. He's at a small club in downtown Ericksberg."

"Which one?" Beltaine jumped to her feet.

"The Red Tie Club," Azubah informed her.

"Why would he go there?" She didn't wait for an answer as she headed out of the church.

"How does she know where it is?" Kalan asked the demon as they followed her.

"I would assume she's been there before." The demon shrugged.

Chapter Forty

They skidded to a stop in front of the club. It was eerily silent. Usually the doors of the club were open and dance music poured from the inside. The line to be admitted to the club should have snaked down the block, but no one stood there.

"Let's go." Beltaine gestured for Kalan to follow her.

"I'll stay out here," Azubah squeaked.

"I wouldn't expect anything else from you."

Pushing the door open, she was struck again by the void of noise. All the men in the club stared toward the stage where two beings faced off. She recognized the tall, thin blond. She should have known Jasper would be there. Tariq stood a foot taller and was much heavier. The demon's red eyes gleamed with malicious delight. He seemed to think he'd found the perfect spot to start his gathering of power.

Kalan ran into her as she stopped. Steadying him, she pointed to the two figures and said, "I guess we shouldn't have been worried."

A hiss burned in her ear. Looking up, she saw confusion skate over Kalan's face as he realized Jasper was the angel facing the higher lord.

"We should help him." Kalan started to push his way through the crowd.

Grabbing him, she turned him back toward the entrance. "We've got other problems to take care of."

"But he's facing a higher lord," he protested, trying to twist away from her.

"At the moment, Jasper's perfectly capable of handling him. Tariq still doesn't have a lot of power. The best way to help Jasper is to fix the Veil."

"He'll get hurt."

She pulled the angel to a stop and forced him to look at her. "Listen to me. There's no love lost between you and Jasper. He wouldn't appreciate you barging in to save him. He's a member of the Host, Kalan. Let him do his job."

He still didn't look convinced, so she shoved him outside. Before the door shut, she glanced back over her shoulder and saw Jasper looking at her. The angel nodded and winked. She didn't feel bad about leaving him.

When they got back to St Benedict's, Roger was waiting for them with a bloody bandage wrapped around his hand.

"What happened?" She glanced at the gauze around his wrist and raised an eyebrow.

"I got bit by some crazy dog while I was searching for Father Simon. It's nothing. We haven't found him yet. What's going on here?" He dismissed the wound.

"A crazy dog, huh?" She pulled the bandage off.

A putrid smell rose from the opening. The others gagged as she ran her fingers over the red, jagged edges of the tear.

"It shouldn't be infected already." Roger covered his nose.

"Breathe through your mouth. It'll go bad quick if it was a werewolf bite—which it seems it was."

"Is Roger going to turn into a werewolf?" Father Paul asked.

"Why do you ask?" She allowed a small amount of power to seep from her fingers. Roger hissed and she knew the healing was burning away the infection.

"Isn't that how werewolves are made? The legends speak of people getting bitten and turning at the next full moon."

Shaking her head, she sealed the bite. "A bunch of bullshit passed on by ignorant peasants. Werewolves are born, not made. It's in the DNA, not the saliva." She winked at Roger. "But if you get an urge to howl at the moon, let me know. I'll chain you up and feed you while you're a wolfman."

"It's not something to joke about." Kalan frowned at her.

"If you can't laugh at something like this, angel boy, you'll be crying all the time." She handed the book to Roger. "You gentlemen go through this and find the spell. I need to go and replenish my power."

Stopping at the door, she turned to see the trio staring after her. She hoped they'd find the spell before any other demons crossed over. She might have a chance against one or two of them, but if there were more demons than that, she'd never be able to defeat them, even with Kalan's help.

Sending up a little prayer for help in case God was listening, she set out for the potter's field.

Beltaine entered the small potter's field at the outskirts of Ericksberg. She had been in this cemetery before, but a strong spiritual presence had unnerved her enough that she'd chosen to use other sites around the village before all the excitement started. The power boost she got from this particular place outweighed the nervousness she'd felt just by stepping inside the gate.

Settling down on a boulder in the middle of the field, she closed her eyes and lowered the walls around her power. She sent tendrils out to collect what the souls were willing to give her. A surge of energy threatened to overwhelm her. She struggled to master it.

"Finally, you came back. I've been waiting." A voice startled her.

Opening her eyes, she saw a specter standing in front of her. A weak wave came from the spirit and Beltaine realized this soul was the source of her nervousness.

"If I'd known you were waiting, I'd have called."

"How rude. Your parents certainly didn't teach you manners." The phantom sounded female.

"My father did the best he could to beat them into me." Beltaine managed to keep the other lines of power open to build her reserves.

"He should have tried harder."

"Maybe, but since I killed him, he didn't have a chance." She glared at the soul. "What the hell do you want?"

"Revenge. I want revenge on the people who put me in here." The spirit's eyes blazed with hatred.

"Revenge isn't my thing, lady. You'll have to find someone else."

"But you're perfect. You've got tons of power and you wouldn't be intimidated by those hypocrites." The woman was so angry she was almost foaming at the mouth.

"What set of hypocrites are you talking about?" Curiosity had always been a problem for Beltaine.

"The Board and the men who run the church."

"Now wait a minute, not all of the priests are hypocrites. Some of them are very godly men." Beltaine thought about the priests she knew. "You're right about the Board, though."

"The men who run the church killed me, not those silly priests of yours. The Board stood by and let them because I couldn't pay for mercy." The woman spat on the ground.

"Why should that bother me? It's your problem, not mine."

"Someone on the Board and in the church is helping the being who wants the Veil ripped."

Beltaine shot to her feet. Letting go of the tendrils, she blocked off her power. "How do you know this?"

"When I have enough power stored, I can travel through the world. I've gone to the city. I've seen your conspirators meeting. I can give you their names." The woman had stepped back when Beltaine got to her feet.

"What else will you give me? Because if I wanted to, I could force you to give them to me without promising anything to you."

Maybe she was crazy for considering going into the revenge business for a silly soul, but the thought that the Board and the church helped to bring about the end of Earth and Hell made her furious.

"I'll give you my power. You're going to need more than you have now. Take all of mine. Just promise you will think of helping me," the woman bargained.

Beltaine inspected the woman with narrowed eyes. There were no warning signs telling here this was a double cross. The woman was right. Repairing the

Veil would take all of her power. "Okay. Give me the names, and let me take your power. I can't promise anything, but I might be able to help you."

She reached out and took the woman's hand. Power poured over her walls as if they weren't there. The energy was volatile and seething with rage. She struggled to keep it under control. Minutes later, she was vibrating with the overflowing coffers.

The woman had faded as she was drained. Before Beltaine let her go, she gave her the names. "Misha St Largent and the bishop of the city."

Fuck. She knew those two self-absorbed bastards would try to secure their own survival. It would explain why the bishop hadn't seemed concerned about Father Simon. The asshole knew exactly what had happened to the priest.

"Thank you," Beltaine said to the spirit.

"The best way to thank me is by dealing with those two. Most of the Board members are oblivious to what goes on around them. It's those two who actively go out and hurt people for their own gain." The last of the woman's power expired, and she disappeared.

"Trust me. I'll make them pay," Beltaine vowed to the night air.

Chapter Forty-One

The door slammed back against the wall. The three men looked up in surprise as Beltaine stalked in. Stopping, she placed her hands on her hips and glared at them.

"People suck," she announced.

Kalan could see she was strung tight. "You're just now figuring this out?" His tone was mild.

"Shut up. I've always known most of them aren't worth my time or trouble, but I've decided it would suit me just fine if two of them died."

"That's rather harsh." He wondered what had happened at the cemetery to make her so upset.

"It was bad enough the bitch came here and tried to seduce you. I scared her, and I was willing to leave her alone after that, but she better get ready to hide." Beltaine bared her fangs in a snarl.

Ah, Misha St Largent. "What did she do? I thought you were going to a cemetery."

"I did." She paced in front of the desk he was sitting at.

The priests stayed quiet and Kalan thought he should've keep his mouth shut as well, but since he'd already spoken, he might as well keep going.

"Did she bother you there?"

"Do you know what she's doing?" Beltaine threw her hands up in the air.

"Not a clue."

She shot him a glance. He ducked his head to hide his smile.

"She's working with the bastard trying to start a war. That bitch and our sanctimonious prick of a bishop are padding their pockets with our lives." She looked at him, daring him to argue with her.

"How do you know that?" He didn't really doubt her, but he couldn't figure out how she knew the information.

"There was a spirit in the potter's field I went to. She wants revenge against St Largent and the bishop. When her power is at its strongest, she can travel from her gravesite. She's seen them meeting and overheard them talking about this whole thing." Anger poured off her.

"Who's the mastermind behind this whole thing, then?"

"She could never see him. He had power, and it obscured her view. Damn, it has to be either the Master or the Commander."

Kalan protested, "How can you think the Commander would do something like this?"

She held up two fingers. "There are only two people besides God and the Devil with the kind of power this jerk has. I know the Devil has no interest in ruling Earth, and we both know God wouldn't take this roundabout way of getting rid of mortals and demons. The best thing about God is how straightforward He is." She shook her head. "The Commander and the Master use any means necessary to achieve their goals, even to the extent of killing people to succeed."

Kalan believed that of the Master, but he had a difficult time reconciling her view of the Commander with his. "I think your view of both of them is tainted by your upbringing. You have a hard time giving anyone the benefit of the doubt."

"I gave you the benefit of the doubt by allowing you to work with me." She was indignant, but she seemed willing to think about it. "You might be right, but I can't think of anyone else who has the power to hide himself from all of us like this person does."

"We found it." Roger's excited shout drew them away from the argument they were about to have.

Kalan and Beltaine joined the priests by the couch the men were sitting on. Father Paul held the book out to her and pointed.

"How to Repair the Veil between Earth and Hell," she read out loud. That was straightforward enough. She didn't take it. Gesturing for the priest to read the spell, she paced. Kalan mirrored her movements on the other side of the couch.

"The Veil hides the secrets of Hell from mortals and keeps demons safe. If the barrier is breached or torn, two people must repair the holes." Father Paul's voice shook.

"I'm sure we can find two people easily enough," she stated.

"These two people must trust each other with their lives," Roger read the next sentence.

"That might cause a problem." She knew such complete trust was so rare as to be nonexistent.

Father Paul glanced at her then over to Kalan. The look on the priest's face said she wasn't going to like what he had to say next. "Since the Veil was created using the power of Heaven and Hell, so the two who attempt to repair it must be from both worlds."

She jerked the book from Father Paul's hands and swore when she re-read the sentence. "Shit. If this doesn't take the cake. You and I are the only two creatures on the face of this Earth who can do it." She read the rest of the spell. "The Hell creature must stand on that side of the Veil. The Heavenly creature must stay on the Earth side. Placing their palms together with the barrier between them, they must connect their powers to rebuild the Veil."

Shutting the book with a thud, she headed out of the room. She didn't check to see if any of the trio was following her. She just assumed they were.

"Where are we going?" Kalan asked, as they stopped in front of the secret door.

"We're going to fix the Veil. There's no big ritual needed or sacrifice to slaughter. It's simple. We combine our powers and the Veil's good as new. Our bodies merge well, so why shouldn't our powers?"

Kalan stayed quiet while they made their way down to the altar room in the catacombs. His breath hitched, and she knew he was feeling the oppression from the shimmering wall—except it didn't seem to gleam as brightly. Large holes were scattered around it, including the one Tariq must have punched in order to come through.

Taking a deep breath, she steeled herself to cross over into Hell. Before she took a step, she was pulled into Kalan's arms. His mouth crushed down on hers. He seemed to be pouring all his anger, fear and fondness for her into the kiss. There might even have been love in the touch of his tongue against hers, but she wasn't willing to think about that yet.

He let her go and stepped back. Roger came up to wish her good luck.

"If you don't trust him completely, you could die. The power you expel will ricochet back into you and destroy you. Are you willing to risk it?" he asked her softly.

She looked up into a pair of blue eyes she knew as well as her own. "It would suck if it happened, Roger, but I've got to take the chance. Take care of him for me." Beltaine nodded toward Kalan.

"Of course I will." Roger hugged her.

She took the spell book with her as she crossed over. She might as well return it while she was there. Stepping through the Veil, she blinked at the darkness that greeted her. Was her subconscious already imagining the nothingness Hell would become if it was destroyed?

She turned and saw Kalan watching her through the filmy barrier. She could see the worry on the surface of his gaze. Walking back toward the Veil, she lifted her hand and placed it against his. Electricity rippled through her and the Veil then poured into him. She wanted to close her eyes and absorb the power rushing in and out of her.

"Open your eyes. You must be looking at him at all times."

Opening her eyes, she turned to see Azrael standing beside her.

"Don't look at me. Share your soul with the angel. If you truly wish the Veil to be repaired, you must do all you can to fix it."

Beltaine turned her eyes back to Kalan's gaze. She found herself swimming in a warm sea of blue.

Feelings of safety and love enfolded her. Gasping, she was swamped by those emotions.

She jerked her hand away. Kalan shouted something she couldn't hear over the rushing in her ears. Cold fingers gripped her chin and lifted her head. Her watering eyes met Azrael's infinite dark stare. The emotions had driven her to her knees.

"Why did you pull away?" he asked.

"I was drowning," she said. Her breath burst from her.

"Drowning? How?"

"I looked in his eyes and I fell into a sea of blue. There were all these emotions of safety and love. I was drowning in them."

"And this is a bad thing?"

Azrael's cold questioning made her angry.

"Yes, it's a bad thing because it's not real. It's an illusion." She gestured to where the angel stood on the other side of the Veil. "He could never love me."

"Ah, here's the true test of your faith, Beltaine." Azrael let go of her chin and moved away.

"Faith? I have faith. It doesn't need to be tested." She climbed to her feet and faced the creature.

"You have faith in the evilness of mortals, angels and demons alike. You have faith that someone will hurt you for their own personal reasons."

"Can you blame me? I've had plenty of examples of people doing that to me." She wasn't sure what his point was.

"Yes, you have, but you have also had examples of people loving you without any thought of what it could do for them. And in fact, their love of you has done nothing but gotten them in trouble." Azrael pointed to where Roger stood, trying to stop Kalan from coming across the Veil.

She shook her head at Kalan, hoping the angel understood that she could deal with Azrael. She thought about all the trouble Roger had gotten into from the church because of his friendship with her. Yet he'd never once walked away from her. There had been times when he should have run in the other direction. She thought on that night fourteen years ago when she had arrived at Roger's door covered in blood. He'd been seventeen and about to start seminary. He'd never blamed her for killing her father. He'd helped her make it look like a suicide. Beltaine had never been angry with him for telling Father Simon. She knew the burden of her crime was heavy to bear.

"I know he loves me," she admitted.

"You can believe the priest loves you, yet you don't believe the angel can? Tell me why."

She studied Kalan through the Veil. His blue eyes and superior smile had become as familiar to her as her own reflection. She'd mapped every dip and plane on his body.

"He's perfect. No one that perfect could love a demon spawn like me," she said.

"That's wrong." Azrael smirked.

"What's wrong?"

"Kalan isn't perfect. If he was, he'd never have allowed you to touch him, much less fuck him. He would've kept his mind closed to your possibilities. Yet he didn't. His flawed perfection gives him the strength to see beyond your demon heritage to the soul below." The creature tapped her chest. "He risks more than death to be with you. He risks banishment from the presence of God. For an angel, that is a fate worse than death."

Her gaze caught and held on Kalan's lips. He was saying something over and over. She moved closer to the Veil to read what he was saying.

"I love you" was what he kept repeating. He reached out a hand to her.

Their palms met on the barrier, and a shock raced through her.

"Now is the time to believe, Beltaine. You've trusted him with your body and your life. Maybe it's time to trust him with your soul." Azrael's voice faded as she focused on Kalan.

When she fell into that sea of warmth again, she didn't panic. She thought back through the week they'd known each other. There had been several times Kalan could've killed her or gotten rid of her somehow. He had judged her from the first, but his mind had opened to the truth. His arms had held her safe when she'd needed a shelter and had given her freedom when she'd needed to fly.

Azrael was right, as much as she hated to admit it. She needed to find the courage to believe an angel could love a terribly broken demon spawn like her.

It was hard taking that first step toward giving her heart away. She gave her body away all the time, but there was no danger in that. Nothing on her body would be permanently damaged if it was broken, but she'd never heal her heart.

A flare of power brought Beltaine's mind back to the business at hand. *Screw this maudlin bullshit,* she thought. *You're big enough to handle any problems if it doesn't work out.*

"I love *you*." She spoke the words out loud.

The energy was like getting struck by lightning. In a blinding instant, Kalan's pure golden power flooded her as her gray magic flowed into him. The spot where their palms met began to shimmer. The Veil started to heal itself.

Chapter Forty-Two

Half the tears were gone when Beltaine was ripped away from the barrier. She cried out as the power started to backlash. It felt like she was burning from the inside out. Fighting through the pain, she looked up to see the Commander standing over her, his blue eyes blazing with fury.

"I won't let a demon-spawned bastard and a bewitched angel destroy everything I've worked hard to do."

She wasn't sure if she could even speak. The pain made her head pound like it was going to explode.

"Why?" she forced out.

He drew his sword and raised her chin with the tip of the blade. "You wouldn't understand."

She wished she had the strength to wipe the smug smile off his face.

"Maybe I would." Kalan pushed through the barrier. The cost the Veil extracted showed on the sweat on his brow and the grimace of pain he wore. He forced the sword away from her and faced his Commander.

She wanted to scream at Kalan to go back to the other side. She could see the Commander had gone off some edge.

"You are my greatest disappointment. I chose you to go on this mission because I thought your inflexibility and habit of seeing things in black and white would block you from achieving anything. I figured you would be too busy fighting her that you would never see what I was doing. Instead you screwed her and fell in love." The Commander's scorn dripped from his words.

Beltaine could see Kalan's hurt grow with each comment by the Commander. There was nothing she could do except climb to her feet. Swaying, she stood beside Kalan and with a defiant lift of her chin, she challenged the Commander.

"So you've decided not to let your lover fight your battle for you. How brave, but foolish. You have no hope of defeating me." The Commander chuckled.

He was right and she knew it. Even with what combined powers they had left, they wouldn't be able to stop the creature from killing them.

"Maybe we can't, but I'm willing to die trying," Kalan said.

Beltaine wasn't sure she was as willing, but she'd back Kalan up. For one of the few times in her life, she sent a prayer to God for someone to help them.

"Why?" The Master strolled out of the darkness. "If you've gone to all this trouble to start a war, the least you can do is tell us why." His tone was casual, but his red eyes stared steadily at the Commander.

The angel focused on the Master, allowing Beltaine and Kalan to relax slightly. She wondered if the Master was the answer to her prayer, but she wasn't going to question it if he was.

"Why? Why would I want to destroy weak mortals and useless demons?" The Commander shrugged with a harsh laugh. "Power. It all comes down to power."

"Power. You want more power than you already have. How could that be possible?" Kalan spoke up.

Beltaine wanted to slap her hand over his mouth to keep him quiet. She didn't want the Commander's attention drawn back to them.

"God's attention is divided. His love for mortals makes Him weak. If there were no mortals, He could focus on His angels — on those beings who have stuck by Him and never questioned Him. It isn't right that mortals should be regarded more highly than angels." The Commander gestured wildly, almost hitting Beltaine with his sword.

"But why try to destroy demons? The Father has chosen to ignore us. We're not bothering you or taking power from you," the Master pointed out.

"You should have been destroyed when you chose to leave Heaven. He showed you mercy. By causing the Veil to fall, I can rectify that mistake."

"God made a mistake? How is that possible when He's perfect? Who are you to determine what decision is a mistake or not?" The Master moved a step away from where she and Kalan stood. He seemed to be drawing the Commander's attention from them.

"I know what I've seen. He pushes angels aside as if we were nothing. He lavishes extraordinary amounts of love and energy on mortals and demons. With all of you gone, angels would be the most important beings and I would be at God's right hand. Only He would be more powerful than I."

She could see the madness filling the Commander's eyes, and for the first time, she knew what true insanity looked like.

"It doesn't matter how many people you destroy on this quest of yours—innocent people who have never bothered you. Angels are supposed to be the guardians of mortals. Your duty is to take care of them, no matter what." The Master's face distorted into a frown of disgust.

"I should protect weak mortals who've never shown any interest in thanking God for anything? When bad events happen, they are quick to scream at God for not being there for them. Yet when good things occur, they thank themselves and each other, but never God. They don't deserve to exist."

Beltaine couldn't believe what she was hearing. Who would've thought the Commander of the Host would condone slaughtering millions of people? She knew he had been on the edge, but she'd never imagined he would turn evil.

"And everyone believes *I'm* the evil brother." The Master's eyes held a touch of sorrow.

"What?" Both she and Kalan reacted to that statement.

"Yes, the Commander and I are brothers."

"Used to be brothers. I stopped thinking of you as related to me when you chose to leave Heaven and turn your back on God," the Commander informed the demon.

"I was known as Rasul, the prophet. It was my job to deliver messages to mortals blessed by God. It was a thankless job because most of the mortals chose to ignore what I was telling them. They wanted to hear something different." The Master shrugged. "I chose to leave Heaven because I was getting tired of the whining. It's easier as the Master. People fear me, making them listen to me when I talk to them." He shot a glance at Beltaine. "Well, most mortals anyway."

She shrugged. She never listened to anyone, so it didn't really matter what he'd tried to tell her. "And the Commander?" she couldn't help but ask.

The angel hissed and lunged at the Master. Dodging him easily, the Master wound up farther away from Kalan and her. She knew that was deliberate.

"The Commander was once known as Husam—the sword. He was one of the best warriors the Host has ever had. True and honest, he never questioned God or His orders. Husam had my respect for never losing faith or love for the Father." The Master stared at the Commander. "I don't know you. You aren't the angel Husam. You have become more of a demon than I could ever dream of being."

The Commander attacked, and a sword appeared in the Master's hand. Beltaine and Kalan crouched, trying to stay out of the way. Who would have thought the first battle between the Commander and the Master would be over the fate of the world? And that the Master was the one trying to save it.

Each blow shook the ground. They were equals in strength and skill, so there were no advantages for either one. The Master drew first blood then the Commander retaliated. A thin scratch traced its way down the demon's cheek. He stepped back and touched his fingers to the blood seeping from the wound. Touching the tips to his tongue, he growled at the Commander. He took a sweeping swing that the Commander dodged.

The battle raged on, but neither side was gaining any advantage. Beltaine noticed the Master had several opportunities to disarm the Commander, but for some reason had never taken them. He didn't seem to be capable of harming his brother. The Commander seemed determined to destroy the Master. One well-timed blow sliced across the Master's chest caused him to drop his sword. Falling to his knees, the Master clasped his hands to the wound and looked up at his brother.

"This is what you've wanted, Hasum. Get it over with quickly." The Master didn't beg. He seemed resigned to his fate.

"No." Kalan jumped to his feet and blocked the Commander's sword.

Amazement flashed in the eyes of the Commander and the Master. An angel of the Host protecting a demon was unheard of. It wasn't a fair fight. Kalan was weak from being drained of power by the Veil. On the third blow of the Commander's sword, Kalan's broke in two and he jumped back to avoid being sliced. A cut opened in his skin from neck to stomach. Kalan cried out as he folded to the ground.

Beltaine couldn't believe it. She didn't have a weapon to fight with, and she couldn't use the swords. The Commander's weapon was coming down again — this time to end Kalan's life.

"No," she screamed, as she threw her body sideways to put a barrier between Kalan and the sword.

The shock of the blade entering her shoulder made her lose her breath. Gasping, she grasped the sword with her hands, trying to pull it out. Pain exploded from her palms and her chest.

Standing in front of her, the Commander grinned at her. "Finally, you've come to the end of my patience." He shoved the metal deeper into her.

Her legs lost their strength, and if not for the sword, she would have fallen. As her vision faded to black, a sound like a thousand wings filled the air around them. The sword tore from her body and flew several feet away. She knelt beside Kalan and pressed her hand against her wound. The blood made her hand slick.

Shaking her head, she cleared her vision. The Master was crouched next to her. She caught his gaze and raised her eyebrows. He shook his head, letting her know he had no idea what was happening.

A voice like thunder boomed over them. "You dare to touch the one being marked by God and me. The one being you were ordered not to harm."

Azrael appeared. Only it wasn't the creature she'd seen before. Gone was any resemblance to Starrer's son. In his place was a being almost too terrible to look upon.

Transparent skin allowed everyone to see the bones under it. His waist-length hair was done in millions of braids trimmed with ebony beads. Taller than the Commander, he wore his muscles as a set of armor, covered in black leather. A wind blew in gusts as he beat the large, obsidian-colored wings sprouting from his shoulders. Fluttering, the wings showed Azrael's agitation.

"Azrael." The Commander's voice shook.

"Hasum dares to attack another angel and the Master who, at one time, was his brother. The Commander of the Host of Heaven dares to believe he is worthy of being second to the Creator in power."

Azrael stalked to where the angel cowered. The dark creature glared down at him. One feather from Azrael's wings brushed over Kalan. Beltaine gasped as she watched the wound in Kalan's chest heal. The

Master was already on his feet but stayed out of the way.

"Azrael, can't you see why I had to do this? Mortal weaknesses make God vulnerable, and the mercy He showed demons proves He's become soft." The Commander knelt before Azrael.

A shiver of awe raced down Beltaine's spine. She never thought she'd see the day when the Commander would kneel before anyone. What sort of creature was Azrael?

"All I see is a creature who believes himself better than God. Isn't that the fault you have always despised in the Devil? Yet you've become worse than he. He never killed innocents for his own selfish wishes. You would condemn every mortal to death by the fiery weapons of the Host. Compassion doesn't make God weak. It shows His strength and willingness to give each person another chance. You judge too harshly, and that shows your own weakness." Azrael reached a hand toward the Commander.

"Weakness? I have no weakness. My strength made me the Commander. My intelligence brought Hell and Earth to their knees." The angel boasted, even as he shrank from the creature.

"Arrogance is a weakness because you don't understand the consequences of your actions." Azrael gripped the Commander by the nape of the neck, drawing him to his feet.

"Consequences? There can't be consequences when I was only doing what was right. It is my purpose. I've stood beside Him through the rebellion and everything. Where is my reward? That's all I'm asking for, to be rewarded for my service." The Commander struggled against Azrael's hold.

"Your reward? Your reward for bringing us to the brink of annihilation is your own death," Azrael said as he shook the angel like a rag doll.

"But that's not fair. I'm not like mortals or demons. I'm an angel. Where is the mercy for me?" the Commander protested.

"Are you sorry for what you did? Do you want to ask God's forgiveness?" Azrael stared into the blue eyes of the Commander as he asked the questions.

"Forgiveness for what? I did what I thought was right. You're jealous because you didn't think of it first." The Commander pouted like a petulant child.

There was a slight look of surprise on Azrael's face. "You do know who you're talking to, right?"

"I know who you are, but I still think you're jealous of me. You've always been upset because I'm the Commander." He took a swing at Azrael.

Beltaine felt her mouth drop open. She could see that the Commander had lost it. No one in their right mind would antagonize Azrael. Kalan moved closer to her and held a pad of material to her shoulder. She realized he must have conjured it up while she had been caught up in the drama going on before them. She winced as he applied pressure to try to stop the bleeding.

"Jealousy isn't an emotion I have any knowledge of, Hasum, but it is something you've held close to your heart for centuries. It's time for you to embrace your own death." Azrael leaned forward.

The Commander screamed and tried to push the creature away. There was no fighting Azrael as he wrapped his wings around the angel in his hands and placed a kiss on the Commander's lips. A blinding light flashed, causing the trio to cover their eyes.

Chapter Forty-Three

When the light disappeared, they opened their eyes to see Azrael standing in front of them. The sadness in his eyes looked out of place in the otherwise emotionless face. He gestured for Beltaine and Kalan to stand. She leaned on her angel as he helped her to her feet. One pale finger traced a circle over her wound, and she bit her lip to keep from screaming. The pain was worse than when she'd been stabbed. A red, odd M-shaped scar rose where the wound had been.

"You and your angel must finish repairing the Veil. There will be no further interference from anyone." Azrael turned to leave.

"Wait. Who are you?" Beltaine wasn't sure she wanted to hear the answer, but she had to ask.

"I'm the angel of death. The one creature every mortal, demon or angel sees before they die. I am the one creature no one can escape, and the one being they all spend their lifetimes trying to avoid. Do your job." Azrael disappeared.

"He's the creepiest being in Hell," the Master muttered. The demon started to walk away.

"Hold on," Beltaine said. She held out the Devil's book. "Can you make sure the Devil gets this? Also, thanks."

"I'll make sure it gets returned to him. Thanks for what?" The Master took the book.

"For coming to help us."

"I wasn't coming to help you. I came to ensure you didn't fail. I had no interest in meeting Azrael any sooner than I had to. The kiss of death isn't sweet, and if I can avoid it, I will." The Master disappeared as well.

"I should have known he didn't do it out of the goodness of his heart," she muttered.

"He's a demon, love. He doesn't have a heart." Kalan drew her to him and kissed her hard. "I almost died when I saw the Commander pull you away from the Veil. I had to get to you, even if it caused me pain."

"I'm here. We managed to survive, though I seem to have gained another scar. For a creature who isn't supposed to scar, I have an awful lot of them." She kissed him back then pushed him toward the Veil. "Get on the other side, and let's finish this. I want to go home and let you fuck me into the bed."

"Sounds like a plan to me." He touched her cheek and crossed back over.

This time when they touched palms through the barrier, the connection was instant and strong. The rest of the holes in the Veil healed themselves within minutes. She wanted to strengthen the barrier, so she allowed a little more power to seep out before she broke the connection between them. She pulled her hand away then crossed over into the altar room.

Roger threw his arms around her and hugged her tight. "I was so afraid for you, Beltaine. Don't ever do something like that again."

"I didn't really want to do it in the first place, Roger." She kissed his cheek.

Kalan took her into his arms when Roger let her go. She sighed as she laid her head on his chest. She reached out and took Roger's hand. This was home for her. Kalan and Roger would always be where her heart sheltered.

"Well done, my angel." Infinity rose and fell in the voice filling the catacombs.

All of them fell to their knees as God's presence overwhelmed them.

"What sort of reward would you ask of me, Kalan?"

She wondered what he was going to ask for. It wasn't often that God gave out rewards without asking for payment later on.

"I want to stay here with Beltaine," Kalan said, keeping his head bowed and his eyes on their joined hands.

A soft breeze ruffled Kalan's hair. "Are you sure, Kalan? I had planned on you taking over as Commander of my Host."

"Did you know who was to blame for the tearing of the Veil?" she inquired.

"Yes." The simple word didn't answer the questions she really had.

"If you knew the Commander was behind it all, why didn't you stop him?" She knew her voice held a hint of belligerence.

"My dear Beltaine, as with any thing I do, it's about free will. If at any time in this horrible adventure, he had come to me and asked for forgiveness, I would have fixed it all, but he never did." Exasperation echoed in His voice.

"His arrogance makes the Devil seem like a spoiled brat," Beltaine couldn't help but comment.

"Yes." The definite tone told her the discussion was done. "Are you sure, Kalan, that you wish to stay here?"

"Yes, Sir. I've found my true home."

"That's all I want to hear. What about you, Beltaine? Will you welcome Kalan into your heart and life?"

Here was her chance at happiness. Did she have enough trust that it would last? She looked at Kalan. She saw the love shining in his blue eyes. Smiling, she nodded. "Yes, I love him, and I'd welcome him anywhere."

"Love each other is all I ask then." The peaceful feeling He emanated began to fade.

"Wait. Where can we find Father Simon?" Roger interrupted.

"You may find him at Beltaine's apartment." God evaporated from the room.

* * * *

Father Simon looked up at them when they burst through the door to Beltaine's apartment. She knelt in front of the priest. He rested a shaking hand on her head. In his other hand, he held the other copy of the Devil's book.

"Did he hurt you?" She demanded to know.

"No, child. The creature sent to kidnap me was told not to harm me. I think the bishop had something to do with it. The man had a key to my room." Father Simon's voice was weak, but he smiled at her.

"I know he was involved, and I plan on doing something about it, but not right now. I think we all need to rest before we take on the Board." She glanced around her apartment. "How did you get in here though? I didn't give you a key."

"The angel you know as Jasper brought me back here."

"Jasper?" Kalan raced over to the priest. "Is he all right?"

"He told me to let you know he's a little worse for wear, but he'll be fine." Father Simon sighed.

She knew he was tired. It had been a long night for the priest. "You're welcome to stay here for the night. You can have my bed and the rest of us will sleep on the floor."

Father Simon declined. "I want to go back home and sleep in my own bed tonight, Beltaine. You and Kalan need to rest without worrying about guests." He accepted Roger's hand to pull himself to his feet. He hugged her and Kalan before he and Roger walked out.

The door shut, and Beltaine turned to Kalan. Pinning her against the door, he crushed his lips to hers. Their tongues dueled while their hands stripped each other. Clothes flew across the room. She encircled his waist with her legs as he lifted her off the floor. There was no gentle teasing to make sure she was wet enough. He plunged in.

The wave of desire flooded her body and overrode any bit of pain she felt. Her head cracked against the wood of the door as she arched her back, begging silently for him to take her nipples in his mouth.

He obliged her, sucking her nipple and as much of her breast as he could into his mouth. Using teeth and tongue, he tormented her until the breast ached and she was pleading for more.

"Kalan," she whispered.

He braced her against the door and angled her hips. Sliding out, he pushed his fingers between her thighs. Thrusting hard and deep into her pussy, he pinched her clit. With his teeth on her nipple, his fingers tugging her clit, and the feel of his cock head buried in her, Beltaine thought she was going to shatter into a million pieces.

"Let go, love. I'll keep you safe," he murmured in her ear as he continued to ride her.

Her orgasm built from her pussy to her breasts. It spread to the rest of her body from there. Her toes curled and she swore the top of her head was going to explode. She cried out as pleasure raced through her. Her inner muscles contracted around his cock, and she tried to milk his climax from him.

"Not yet," he said, clutching her tight to him as she collapsed into him.

She didn't say anything as he carried her to the bed without pulling out of her. He laid her down and began to piston in and out of her. At first, she didn't have the energy to do much but lie there. Soon the scraping of his cock against her sweet spot managed to excite her. She grasped his ass in her hands and added her own strength to his thrusts. She knew she was leaving bruises on his skin. The sound of their skin slapping together filled the apartment, along with their harsh breathing.

Leaning his head down, Kalan licked the crucifix scar and an unusually strong flash of pleasure ripped through her, causing her orgasm to hit with mind-numbing force. She screamed as her pussy encouraged him to come. His face contorted into a grimace of ecstasy when his climax erupted, and he sent spurts of cum deep into her.

His arms gave out and he sank down on top of her. Beltaine cradled him close within the warmth of her arms and legs. Smoothing her hand down his cooling back, she closed her eyes and smiled. She could get used to having him with her day and night. She sent a little prayer of thanks up to God for the opportunity to have an angel watching over her.

Kalan's breathing deepened and he shifted to his side, bringing her back tight to his chest. She caught a flash of movement out of the corner of her eye. Sitting up, she turned to see Azubah perched on the couch in the living area of the studio apartment. The demon's red eyes held a question.

Nodding, she said, "You're welcome to stay here, Azubah. You helped us out to the best of your ability, and we couldn't have asked more from you. Consider this your place from now on."

The demon smiled and settled down for the night.

Beltaine snuggled up to Kalan again and closed her eyes. For the first time since the whole adventure started, she knew she'd get a great night's sleep.

* * * *

Late that night, Beltaine woke, wrapped in Kalan's arms. The room was ice-cold. Shivering, she tried to wake her angel up, but she didn't get a response.

"He won't wake up, Beltaine."

She glared out into the shadows of her bedroom. A lessening of the blackness drew her eyes to one of the corners. Azrael coalesced in front of her bed.

"What do you want?" She challenged the creature.

"Maybe I've come to bring you death."

She didn't know if he was joking or not. "You wouldn't have healed me just to come and get me later."

"The purpose you were born for has been fulfilled."

"So do it and be done with it. I'm not much for talking." Sadness filled her heart at not having more time with Kalan, but when death came in person to get you, you didn't argue.

"You're very impulsive. Sometimes it's good. Other times, it only brings trouble. I'm not here for you."

"You're not?" She leaned over and put her body between Azrael and Kalan.

Azrael's laugh sounded like ice cracking. "I'm not here for your angel either. Enjoy your time on Earth. Be no one's servant, but should angel, demon or mortal come to ask for help, give it without question. Your presence is the only thing keeping the worlds in balance." He nodded once and faded.

Kalan opened his eyes when she settled back in his embrace. "What's wrong?"

"Nothing. Just a nightmare." She kissed him, trying not to think about what Azrael had told her. She didn't want to be a hero and keep any sort of balance. She wanted to love Kalan and beat up on demons. Yet something told her the world would never be the same, now that the Angel of Death had marked her.

About the Author

I've been writing for most of my life, but was first published in 2004. I believe everyone deserves love in all its forms. I write about women and men who find strength in loving each other. I live in the Midwest with my two cats, and when I'm not writing (which isn't very often) I read and watch movies.

Tiffany Aaron loves to hear from readers. You can find her contact information, website details and author profile page at http://www.totallybound.com.

Totally Bound Publishing